THE **BREAKFAST** CLUB

Betting on
Forever

FELICE STEVENS

Betting on Forever (The Breakfast Club, Book 2)
November 2015, 2021

Copyright (c) 2015 by Felice Stevens

Edited by Keren Reed
Cover Art by Reese Dante
Cover content is for illustrative purposes only. Any person depicted on the cover is a model.

Published 2021.
First Edition published 2015. Second edition 2021.
Published in the United States of America

This is a work of fiction. Any resemblance to persons living or dead is entirely coincidental.

Dedication

Forever and always to my family.

Acknowledgments

I have to start out by thanking my editor Keren Reed, who asked for Zach's story for book two before I'd finished book one. I'm glad you loved him as much as I did. Thank you to Hope Cousin for your help, advice and friendship; you'll never know how much it means to me. Thank you to Jessica de Ruiter for your wonderful eagle eye. To Denise, thank you for your assistance and support. It means the world to me.

And to my readers, especially my Facebook group, Felice's Breakfast Club, it really is all about you. Without your encouragement and love for these characters there would be no stories. You guys are the best!! I love you to the moon and back and look forward to meeting all of you one day.

Chapter One

Hell couldn't be any worse than traveling southbound on the Garden State Parkway in the summer. The only blessing for Zach Cohen was that someone else was behind the wheel. It was nice of the sponsors of the convention to send a driver for him, saving him the hassle of driving himself.

He blinked against the glare of the late afternoon sun streaming in hot and bright through the car windows; the new contacts he got specifically for this weekend still gave him trouble, but after all these years of wearing glasses, he decided to give them a try again. This was going to be a weekend of change for him, and Zach figured he'd remake himself from the outside as well as the inside. The old him wasn't doing so well.

His phone pinged with a text from his best friend, Marcus.

Knock 'em dead. And remember, go crazy and let loose. Atlantic City is like Vegas—what happens there, stays there.

He should be so lucky, Zach thought morosely, staring out the car window at the endless winding ribbon of cars. Mentally he slapped himself, remembering yesterday's conversation at breakfast.

He and his two friends Julian and Marcus and Julian's boyfriend Nick had met in their usual breakfast place in the city, though it was more like brunch by the time they all arrived.

"Zach, are you ready for tomorrow and A.C.?" Marcus signaled the waiter with a circle of fingers to bring the three of them their usual mimosas and a beer for Nick. "Man, I'd love to be going to a convention there in the summer. Nothing but sun, sand, and Speedos."

"Have you depleted all the men in Manhattan that you need to expand to cruising beach tourists in Jersey now, Marcus?" Julian quirked a brow and grinned at both him and Marcus. "Besides, Zach is going there for business, not pleasure."

Zach opened his mouth, but as usual Marcus cut him off. "Pffft. Bullshit. Zach needs to go have some fun and get laid."

"That's your answer to everything, but it doesn't mean it's right for Zach," argued Julian. Nick remained quiet; he'd been with Julian long enough now to understand the dynamics of the different friendships in the group.

"Now that you're in a relationship, you think that's the best thing for everyone, but what if he doesn't want one? What if—"

"Umm, hello. Sitting right here." Zach leaned into the table and waved his hands in between the two battling best friends. "Nice that you both think you need to plan my weekend and my sex life for me, but I don't need your help." Bad enough he had his mother giving him dating advice, the last thing he needed was interference from his friends on that front.

Regret glimmered in Julian's eyes. "Sorry. He"—Julian pointed to Marcus—"gets me riled up. We're in our thirties, not twenty-one, fresh out of college, and looking for hook-up after hook-up."

"Not everyone is made for monogamy and a relationship, Juli. You found yours, and I'm glad for you and Nick, but don't shove it down the rest of our throats like it's the only way to be happy. Some of us are perfectly satisfied the way we are—taking care of number one." Marcus sipped his drink and shrugged. "I like my men the way I like Skittles; in every color of the rainbow. Besides,"—his eyes gleamed, and Zach had a sinking suspicion whatever was going to come out of his friend's mouth would be something outrageous—"if Zach is going to Atlantic City, we should have a bet of some kind."

"I don't gamble," said Julian. He braced his elbows on the table. "The business is getting started, and I won't throw away money on some stupid play of the cards."

"You were more fun before you started acting like an old married lady." From years of experience with Marcus's shenanigans, the look on his face spelled trouble for Zach. "I wasn't talking to you anyway. I meant Zach."

He had to hand it to his friend. No matter it was probably completely outrageous and probably involved sex toys he'd never heard of, against his better judgment Zach couldn't help but be intrigued.

"I'll probably regret this later, but what were you thinking?" asked Zach, and heard Julian's groan of frustration, as well as Nick's laughter.

"Now why are you encouraging him? You should know better."

Marcus grinned at Zach with the devil in his eyes, and it was like they were back in middle school again. Wild, beautiful, and crazy; Zach couldn't remember a time in his life without Marcus by his side. They'd known each other since they were babies and were the brothers neither one ever had.

"Over the years I've learned to humor Marcus, otherwise he'll be after me like a dog with a bone." Zach gestured with his hand. "Come on, spill it. What's going on in that demented little mind of yours?"

"You wound me." Marcus pretended to be offended, but a sly smile touched his lips, and Zach braced himself. "It's simple. You're going to a place known for letting loose and having fun. No one knows you there, since all your work is behind that little screen."

"So what's the bet?" Intrigued, Zach ignored Julian's muttering.

"Meet a guy and get his number, or you owe me a hundred dollars."

Nick snorted. "That's boring, especially for you, Marcus." He thought for a moment; then his eyes sparked with an evil light. "I've got something better."

"Oh God. Look out." Julian put his head in his hands. "When he gets that look in his, eyes you're in trouble."

Zach watched as Nick slung his arm around Julian's neck, pulling him in for a quick hug. "Don't be scared, babe. It's so outrageous probably neither of them will go for it. It's just too funny."

It seemed each of his friends had an opinion on how he should live his life. Eyeing Julian across the table, watching him interact so lovingly with Nick, a pang of longing hit Zach hard. What would it be like to love and be loved like that? But Julian and Nick, separated for so many years, had fought long and hard to get to this place. Zach wasn't the kind of man anyone fought for. He was the one people barely remembered.

"Go on, Nick," Zach prodded. "I'm open to hearing what you have in mind. Like you said, it doesn't mean I have to go for it."

Ignoring Julian's glare, Nick folded his arms, his gaze flickering between Zach and Marcus. "Well, the thing about bets is that they should always be extreme on both sides. So betting that you can't get a guy's phone number is boring because Zach could do that. There's no fun in it. Why not bet instead on Zach picking a guy up and having a fling with him for the weekend."

Julian sputtered. "That's ridiculous."

"Wait a minute, Julian. Let Nick talk." Zach couldn't help it. He wanted to hear more of what Nick had to say.

"At least Zach will have a good time. But here's where the good part comes in." Nick's eyes danced with laughter. "The other half of the bet revolves around whether you succeed or fail. If Zach fails, he has to let us fix him up every weekend for three months. Knowing how much he hates clubbing and dating, it's a pretty good incentive to win."

"You have an evil mind, Nick. I knew I liked you." Marcus grinned and drank his mimosa.

"Hold on hotshot, I'm not finished. If Zach wins and has his sex-filled weekend?" Nick leaned back and clasped his hands behind his head. "You, my man, have to remain celibate for three months."

Julian sat silent for a moment, then whooped with laughter while Marcus spit his drink out, coughing his outrage. "What? Are you fucking kidding me? Three months? I haven't gone without a guy for three *days* since before college." With disgust, he peered into his empty glass and called the waiter over for a refill. "Besides, it's stupid. Everyone knows, Zach would never agree to that. He's too nice and not into flings. He'd lose and then be forced to come to the club, which he hates."

Marcus's words stung. "Don't you think I can do it? Or is it that you don't think anyone will want me?"

"Don't be a schmuck." Marcus's eyes hardened. "Of course you can, but you believe in true love, not hook-ups." Marcus made little quote signs with his fingers and smirked.

"You make love sound like a disease instead of something people all over the world hope for."

"Not everyone. And since when did you become interested in meeting guys and having random sex? That's not who you are." Zach winced at Marcus's harsh voice.

Given that Zach wasn't so sure he knew who he was himself, why Marcus appointed himself knower of all things Zach Cohen was a mystery.

Zach considered Marcus, who was busy wiping his mouth. "Maybe I'll surprise you."

Sulking in his chair, Marcus huffed. "This is payback for when we were kids and I'd always get to the ice cream truck first, isn't it?" He waited for the waiter to set the fresh drinks down. "All these years you waited for the right time and place to get your revenge."

"You're ridiculous."

"*I* am?" Marcus scoffed and gazed at him with speculative eyes. "I've never pretended to be anyone other than who I am. Can you say the same?"

Zach had no answer. What was he supposed to say—that he was tired of being a nobody? But if he stopped, would anyone even notice?

These thoughts and more ran through his mind the next day during the ride to Atlantic City. There were nights he wouldn't have minded a simple hook-up, if only to hold someone close in the dark. He wanted to be kissed by a lover. Not that he hadn't been kissed by various men, but the rapid press of lips and hurried plunge of some man's tongue in his mouth as a prelude to sex hardly passed for what Zach craved. He ached for hard, deep kisses; those smutty, filthy, feel-it-deep-in-your-balls type kisses that would leave you breathless for hours.

He'd never had them, but he knew they existed. However—Zach shifted in his seat as the hotel towers along the Boardwalk came into view—finding someone to trust not only your body with but also your heart had proved elusive for him. The affair with Nathan had made trusting another person with his heart an almost impossible dream.

Hiding away in his basement, talking to men online had become his norm. Zach knew he had a problem. Years of put-downs and humiliation will do that; when you've been told no one would want you, that you're boring and nothing special, eventually you believe it.

And maybe Marcus was right. Not everyone was destined for the happily-ever-after life of love; he'd thought he'd found his soul mate in Nathan, but had been soundly kicked in the teeth by his cruel, parting shot.

"You're just...not there. Sometimes I forget you're even in the room when we're together. I need someone to have fun with, not a goldfish swimming around in a bowl, staring at me."

Hurt beyond belief, Zach had no idea Nathan harbored such resentment toward him.

"Why did you stay with me?" Immediately Zach regretted asking.

"You give good head, and you were always there whenever I wanted to get laid." Nathan had hefted his backpack over his shoulder. *"I'd be an idiot to turn it down."*

There were other, more insidious ways Nathan had hurt him, imprinting themselves like a permanent scar on his heart, but those Zach buried deep, incapable of letting the hurt and humiliation see the light. He'd never told anyone the extent of his shame.

And since then, he'd allowed himself at the most a few dates with a man before moving on, unwilling to risk getting close. By cutting off intimacy, there was little chance of getting hurt again. At least he was the one in charge. Maybe Julian and Nick were the anomaly, and Marcus's single life was the way to live.

The car pulled into the curving drive in front of the Tropicana Hotel on the Boardwalk, and Zach steeled himself to face the crowds. He'd accepted the invitation to the Next Big App conference to award the winner of their app design contest the prize, also agreeing to moderate several panel discussions. Normally he hated these social events; they'd always made him feel awkward and inept, but the promise he made to himself—that this weekend he was going to try and be a different man—bolstered his resolve to push forward and transform himself from computer geek to a more self-confident Zach.

After all the years spent watching Marcus and Julian, Zach had the behavior well memorized. He'd spent his youth in Marcus's domineering shadow, crippled by shyness and inadequacy. It didn't matter to Zach that his mother told him how smart he was, and how proud his father would've been that he'd skipped two grades and would graduate high school at sixteen. Nothing could change the nerdy little kid with glasses; the one who always knew the answer to the hardest math problem, but not how to get picked for teams at gym.

Marcus could only help him so much.

It was time to unveil a new and improved Zach, someone who wouldn't skirt the after-dinner drinks and get-togethers in the bar. It would be safe here; no one knew the real him, and he could easily pretend to be someone else. A man confident and in control. All he needed was the balls to pull it off.

He headed to the check-in desk, crossing the elegant lobby decorated in gilt and crystals, all abuzz with families and couples, some in dinner clothes. Checking his watch, Zach found it was close to six in the evening; the ride from the city had been interminable, and he had a scant half hour before the pre-dinner meet-and-greet. With his printed confirmation in hand, Zach approached the young man behind the desk, who flashed him a practiced, bright smile.

"Good evening, sir. Checking in?"

"Yes. I'm with the conference."

"Excellent." All it took was a few taps on the screen, and Zach was checked in and upgraded to a small suite. A pleasant surprise.

"Do you need help with your luggage?"

Zach eyed his garment bag and small carry-on and gave the clerk a smile. "I'm fine, thanks. These design conferences are great 'cause I never have to dress up."

The young man met Zach's stare, his engaging smile no longer forced, its warmth setting off the amber streaks glowing in his deep brown eyes. He handed Zach the cardkey in its envelope. "Sometimes it's nice to get dressed up, especially when you have someone special to share your time with."

Well, damn. Flustered by the man's flirting, Zach retreated. "Uh, thanks." Averting his eyes, he fumbled with the keycard, finally pocketing it, and hastened to the elevator, wheeling the small carry-on behind him. Within minutes the elevator soared upward, leaving his stomach and nerves down below.

Pressed for time, Zach had no chance to appreciate either the sweeping view of the hotels in the rapidly advancing twilight over the Atlantic Ocean, nor the suite's amenities if he didn't want to be late for the cocktail socializing. It took only a few minutes to change into a sky-blue silk shirt and light khaki pants. One thing about having a fashion designer for a best friend: Zach never needed to worry about his wardrobe. No matter how hard or loud he protested, every season Julian sent him an entire wardrobe of clothing. The silken fabric of the shirt whispered like air, sensuous against his skin.

Maybe Julian was right in the sense that clothes could somehow empower a person. After spending most of his days slouching around in jeans and tee shirts or ratty sweaters, dressing in this silky-smooth shirt bolstered his confidence for the bet. He no longer thought Nick's idea was silly, and instead, Zach approached the evening with detachment and a sense of purpose.

The real Zachary Cohen, who enjoyed spending his nights lying on the sofa with Chinese takeout, watching old movies with his overprotective mother hovering in the background, would be replaced with a coolly confident, self-assured Zach. A Zach who loved the New York City nightlife and belonged at a place like Sparks. From his friendship with Marcus and Julian, Zach could've produced a National Geographic Special on the mating rituals of New York City gay men on the prowl. He sprayed on some cologne, and after only the slightest hesitation, took condoms and a small bottle of lube from his suitcase and put them in the night table drawer.

Satisfied with his overall transformation, Zach slipped the cardkey in his wallet and left the room. The ride in that bullet elevator to the third floor of the hotel where the reception was being held left him a bit queasy, and the carpet, patterned in a garish red, black and gold design made him dizzy. The buzz from the crowd only added to his unease, and Zach, who didn't drink much, had never been happier to see a bar in his life.

"A double vodka on the rocks, please."

"That bad, huh?"

Zach accepted the drink and, turning around, was greeted by a bright smile in an extremely handsome, rugged face. The man's hazel eyes reflected humor, warmth, and by the increasing intensity of his stare, desire.

Zach's breath and heartbeat quickened.

"Not anymore."

Chapter Two

"Heads-up, Sammy."

Reflexively, Sam Stein put up his glove and caught the ball before it knocked him on his head. He grunted and tossed it back over to his friend Henry.

"Sorry."

"Not as sorry as you would've been if you'd gotten hit. You're a thousand miles away." Henry took off his cap and scratched his head. "Wanna take a break?"

"Yeah."

Henry walked over to him, first stopping by the cooler they'd brought filled with drinks to dig two bottles out. Henry handed him a bottle of cold water and cracked the other one open for himself, drinking half in one shot.

The shock of the cold water spilling down his dry throat woke Sam up from his malaise. He'd thought coming out here and playing some ball would be good to take his mind off everything that had happened over the past winter, but he still couldn't concentrate. *Guess it will take more than a day in the park to make up for almost getting someone killed.*

"You're not still thinking of Andy are you?"

He followed Henry over to the cooler which sat in the shade of a huge oak tree. They sat on the bench, the sun-warmed wood feeling smooth beneath his thighs.

"Not really."

Henry shot him a dubious look. "Then you're thinking of your ex-partner. Listen, Sam. What's done is done. He's back at work, and yeah, you made a mistake, but you paid the ultimate price for it with your badge."

"I'm sick of talking about it, and I imagine you are as well, but I can't seem to let it go." He pushed his cap up on his head and stared up at the blue sky. "I thought I'd be a cop forever." He closed his eyes, soaking in the sun's blessed warmth.

"Twenty years is a long time, Sammy. And you were able to retire and get your pension."

That was Henry—always one for looking at the bright side. And Sam guessed he was right. But Sam missed the daily routine; police work was an inherently social atmosphere. It had been the toughest decision he'd ever had to make, but his spectacular fuck-up weighed too heavily on his mind for him to continue his job.

The day he handed in his retirement papers and spoke to his borough commander, it became apparent to Sam there was little love lost between him and the force. Any attempt at sympathy and understanding rang hollow to Sam, and there was no attempt to persuade him to change his mind. The two had never gotten along, and Sam long suspected the man disliked having a gay cop, one who wasn't content to hide in the closet, under his command.

And Sam didn't blame any of his former buddies for their sidestepping, mumbled farewells and overall uncomfortable behavior around him. He deserved to be treated like the pariah he was. His stupid, asinine behavior had almost cost his partner his life. Everyone agreed it was for the best for him to leave. The tears he shed at night after he turned in his badge and gun were for him and him alone to taste.

"And," Henry said, "I know your birthday is coming up, so Heather and I got you an early present."

Sam opened his eyes to the sight of Henry's grinning face. That mischievous smile heralded something devious, and Sam's stomach clenched thinking it would most likely cause him severe embarrassment.

"What the hell did you do?"

"Heather thought you needed a change, so she got you a life coach. Someone who is going to work with you to unlock your chi and all your hidden anger."

He did not fucking say what Sam thought he did. "You did what?" Sam kept his tone mild and quiet. Hell, he even smiled, while taking a swift assessment of the park, determining there were too many people around for him to commit murder and hide the body.

"You've been holed up all winter doing nothing but eating takeout and probably watching porn, and not even good porn—that I would watch with you—but your gay porn stuff." Henry finished the rest of his water and chucked the empty in the recycle bin. "It's time, man, for you to forget about that miserable fuck of an ex-boyfriend and move on."

He wouldn't have to kill Henry, just severely disable him. That would unlock his chi or whatever the hell Henry was talking about. Sam jumped up and pointed in Henry's face. "I don't watch porn, and I sure as hell don't need you signing me up for a fucking life coach." The last part of that sentence was yelled at the top of his lungs. At this point he didn't give a shit who heard him. "Are you fucking crazy? What possessed you to do that?"

Henry remained unperturbed and glared right back at him. "Because you're fucking wasting your life missing a man who never gave a shit about you, to be honest. And it pisses me off because I know you deserve better."

Well, crap. What was he supposed to say to that? He rubbed the back of his neck. He couldn't hit Henry when he did something out of the goodness of his heart. "Well, thanks," he muttered. "But you shouldn't have done it. Now you went and wasted your money because I'm not going to meet him."

"Her." Henry's cheerful smile made Sam's blood run cold. "Your coach is a woman. I figured you'd relate better to a woman than any straight guy. Except for me, of course."

"I *am* going to fucking kill you."

"Now, now, Sammy, come on." Henry nudged his leg. "It's time to rejoin the land of the living. Why sit around moping when you could be out having fun? You should be going to clubs, partying and meeting people. Not sitting around watching old movies and eating day-old Chinese food." Henry tossed the baseball up and down. "I know you think I'm only doing this because I'm married now and I'm not going to have time to spend with you, but Heather loves you, you know that."

"She's great. I still don't know why she married you; I thought she was smarter than that." He caught the ball Henry tossed at him. No matter how annoyed Sam was, he knew what was done was out of love and concern for him. Henry was his oldest friend, more like a brother. He was the one Sam came out to in sleep-away camp when they were fifteen and the one who stood by him when the debacle of his personal life exploded into his professional one. If it wasn't for Henry, he wouldn't even have a job, but thanks to his friend's nagging, he'd gotten his Private Investigator license and now worked for Henry's company whenever he was needed.

Ignoring him, Henry continued. "Heather said this woman will help you figure out what steps to take to make your life run smoother and not make the same mistakes all over again with your next relationship."

"I'm not interested in another relationship. Everyone lies about something: their age, their job…something."

He'd rather poke his eyes out than admit he sometimes still wondered what Andy was doing. The last Sam had heard, Andy had moved to Washington, D.C. Two years together weren't easy to erase in five months, no matter how people tried to make him forget.

"Andy is gone," said Henry bluntly. "He's not coming back, and I guarantee he isn't sitting around thinking about you. You need to get out and meet people, because no one is coming to find you. Maybe try online dating or join those singles lunches or club nights."

Ouch. That hurt. But Henry had a point. Spring was a good time to start thinking of fresh starts and new beginnings. "Fine, but that doesn't mean I have to be a loser and go to singles events. I'm doing fine on my own."

Henry snorted. "Yeah, right. Number one, you don't leave the house except for jobs I give you, or to play ball. Plus, the latest statistics say that one third of all marriages start from some kind of organized activity."

"Did anyone ever tell you that you're very boring, especially when you start quoting statistics?"

Henry stood up and grabbed his mitt. "Nope. Heather thinks I'm a hot geek. Now we have to find someone for your grumpy ass."

"I'm not grumpy." He huffed and fell into step next to

Henry. "You're annoying as shit."

"Well, I have another proposition for you."

"What the hell? Shouldn't you be thinking about your wife and taking care of her needs instead of worrying about mine?"

A smile curved Henry's lips. "Oh, no worries about that, she is taken care of just fine, thank you. I can give you the details if you'd like."

"No." Sam held up his hand, turning his face away. "Please. The last thing I need to think of is you having sex. And you shouldn't be so involved in my sex life."

The smile faded from Henry's face, and he looked uncharacteristically serious. "You don't have one, that's why I *am* involved. Now," he said as they exited the park. "Tomorrow is that big computer software convention in Atlantic City."

"Yeah, so?" Sam tossed the ball up and down. "What about it?"

"Come with me. Heather's out of town on a girlfriends weekend, and I don't want to go by myself. You may pick up some of the computer stuff."

The last thing he wanted was hanging out all weekend at a convention full of computer geeks. They spoke a foreign language as far as Sam was concerned, and he had zero in common with them.

"No way. You couldn't pay me to hang around with those guys. Half the time I can't understand what they're saying, all that talk of coding and data mining and shit."

"You're so with the times, aren't you?" Henry poked him in his side, and he grunted. "Come on, Sammy," pleaded Henry. "I don't want to go alone. All you have to do is come with me; you don't have to talk to anyone. The company will pay for everything."

FELICE STEVENS

Hmm. Hard to turn down a free trip. "You're so desperate. Is this how you got Heather to marry you, by begging and making such a nuisance of yourself she couldn't say no?"

"That and my other talents." Henry smirked and studied the baseball in his hand. "Besides, maybe you'll meet a guy who'll make you beg and plead for him, or end up begging for you."

No way. He wouldn't let himself get that caught up in a relationship again that he'd need another person so badly he'd beg for them. He'd been in love already, and it had sucked the life out of him, forcing him to change who he was to please another person.

Never again, Sam swore. But he owed Henry; he supposed it wouldn't hurt to join him for the weekend. Maybe it would be warm enough to go to the beach. He loved the ocean; one of his dreams was to have a place by the beach and walk along the shore every night. When he was young, he'd pictured having a man by his side to share it all with, but now he guessed he'd have to settle for a dog.

"All right, all right." It cost him nothing conceding to Henry, and seeing his friend's broad smile, Sam felt guilty about his hesitation. "I'll come, but don't make me go to any of those boring-ass panel discussions. I'd probably fall asleep and embarrass you."

They'd reached Henry's car, and Henry deactivated the alarm, opened the door, and tossed his glove and ball into the passenger seat. "You won't regret it, I promise. Who knows, you might have fun."

Fun. What could be fun about sitting around with a bunch of nerds? At least he'll be by the beach.

"And what the fuck is my inner chi?"

Bright laughter filled Henry's eyes. "Damned if I know. I thought you gay guys were supposed to be into all that stuff. You're one big fail, huh?" Henry ducked his punch and slid into the front seat of his car. "I'll pick you up tomorrow at three, okay?"

"Yeah, yeah. See you then." Sam walked down the block whistling to himself.

*   *   *

"Come on Sammy, move it or lose it. We gotta be on the road, or we'll never make it by tonight."

"Chill out, Henry." Sam flung his overnight bag into the back of Henry's Jeep and settled into the seat next to him. He slid his sunglasses on, pulled down his baseball cap, and smirked. "I'm ready; what are you waiting for?"

"Wise-ass," cracked Henry. He started the engine and within minutes they were on the Brooklyn Bridge. "So what're you gonna do this weekend if it isn't warm enough to hang out at the beach? You don't gamble; are you sure you won't come with me to the panel discussions?" Henry expertly maneuvered his way onto the FDR Drive, and they were caught in the stop-and-go traffic of the city on their way to New Jersey.

"I'm not sure. I'll see. Those panel discussions are gonna be so boring I'll go crazy if I have to sit through them."

"Well, you're definitely coming with me to the cocktail party. Free booze, food, and plenty of people to talk to. I bet you could find some hot-shot software developer to teach you some of his special coding." Henry laughed at his own joke.

Great. His life was fast becoming a late-night comedy routine. "You're a regular riot. Hopefully that used up your allotment of cheesy gay jokes for the evening."

"Nah, I got a million of them." Henry shot Sam a glance, and the two of them laughed that easy, comfortable laughter that only comes from knowing someone as well as yourself.

"Listen, you've been too long without a guy. Maybe this

weekend you can have a little fun in the sun, find a guy to—"

"No." That came out a little harsher than he intended. "I know what you're trying to do, but I'm not interested. I'm fine."

"You're not fine, you're scared. It's understandable after you've lived with someone and found out they've cheated on you. But I know you hate being alone despite your auditioning for a job as a hermit."

"I'm not alone, I'm fine."

"You've had a break," said Henry, continuing to argue his point. "You've been alone for months, busy working with me on this business of mine. Now, I've already had to force you to come this weekend, I'm not going to let you sit in your room while I'm at panel discussions."

Henry stopped at a traffic light and looked him up and down. "You're not a bad-looking guy; I'm sure there are a few hot men who might want your grouchy ass."

"I'm not grouchy," said Sam in a huffy tone. "I'm selective." He glared at Henry. "And I don't need your help to find a guy."

For a few miles Henry said nothing, and only the music of some pop-rock station played.

"What is this crap you're listening to?" He pushed the buttons of the radio until the music of Billy Joel filled the car. "There. That's better."

Henry chuckled. "Heather's in control of the music when I drive; I could care less. Back to this weekend—we haven't been out together in years, and now we have the whole weekend ahead of us. I want you to get back into life, man. Stop hiding and enjoy yourself."

They pulled in front of the hotel, and Sam stared out the car window, contemplating his friend's words, as Henry waited for the valet.

The sight of a nice ass leaning into his car caught his eye. Sam had no problem staring at it; round and tight, that beauty was practically in his face. For the first time in months desire hit him hard, heating his blood. The rest of the guy wasn't too bad either—he straightened to his full height, hefting his small suitcase, then slammed the door and walked into the hotel. Sam didn't get a chance to see his face, but he quickly assessed the stranger's attributes from the rear. He didn't seem too tall or broad, but his body looked tight and fit. Dark hair curled at the back of his neck, and Sam could practically feel his fingers sliding through those silky strands while he held the man down and banged into him.

"Hey, Sammy, are you getting out, or are you planning on sitting there all day?"

Henry's loud voice knocked Sam out of his perverted fantasy. His cheeks heated, and he unbuckled his seat belt and gingerly got out, keeping his duffle bag in front of his body. The last thing he needed was for Henry to catch him with a hard-on. Shit. Was it possible Henry was right after all? Maybe he did need to get laid and get it out of his system.

The afternoon summer sun still beat warm against his shoulders, and he pulled his cap off his head to let the air circulate to his scalp. Sam couldn't hear the sounds of ocean though; they were too insulated from the water by the hotel. He needed to take a walk on the beach tonight and clear his head. The mystery man with the great ass was gone, presumably into the crowd of the hotel. He and Henry stepped into the air-conditioned lobby, and he casually scanned the spacious interior while they walked to the registration desk, but there were too many people milling about for him to spot someone he'd only seen for a moment. What was he supposed to do, stop every guy and ask him to turn around so he could ogle his ass?

Maybe he'd find himself someone this weekend, but not if he stayed in his room. Perhaps he should go with Henry and mingle with people, even if he wouldn't understand a thing they said. Sam tapped his friend on the shoulder as he was signing the credit card receipt for the room.

"I'll hang out with you, if you promise not to bug me about dating."

One thing about Henry, he never held a grudge. His face broke out in a wide smile. "Yeah? Excellent."

After check-in, they agreed to meet in the Ambassador Room for the cocktail reception, then separated to change their clothes. He thought longingly of a shower, but knew he didn't have enough time, so he quickly stripped, did a fast wash, then sprayed on a subtle cologne he hadn't used in a while. He put on a black, short-sleeve, button-down linen shirt and a pair of tan slacks and left his room, remembering the Ambassador Room was on the third floor and Henry was meeting him there.

It felt strange going out in the evening without Andy, but for the first time there was no pang of sadness when thinking about his ex. Looking back, Sam supposed he might've been as guilty as Andy in neglecting their relationship, but instead of cheating, he'd immersed himself in his police work.

Traveling down in the elevator, Sam nervously jingled some change in his pocket and hoped Henry wouldn't abandon him for work-related discussions with computer-savvy people immediately upon entering the room. He wouldn't begrudge his friend the chance to network. Henry had left his job on Wall Street to start his own company, specializing in computer forensic investigations, which he took care of, as well as private investigations, which he hired Sam for on an as-needed basis.

Not seeing Henry yet, Sam spied the bar and made a beeline for its darkened interior, weaving in between the groups of people standing around chatting about apps and shit he didn't understand. Damn, he hadn't realized so many people would be attending this convention. Why not, he supposed, when it was Atlantic City and the weather was forecasted to be perfect, early-summer weather.

Sam leaned his hip on the bar, waiting his turn to order a drink. Since high school he'd played the "gay not gay" game whenever he was in a crowd and had time to kill. Scanning the crowd, he picked out several likely men, wondering if he was ready to spend the evening with someone. No one sparked his interest, and he shifted his attention back to the bar to order.

"A double vodka on the rocks, please."

Now that was a drink for a person who'd had a rough day.

"That bad, huh?"

The man stared at the floor, not making eye contact with anyone. His jaw flexed tight, and his shoulders hunched tense. Sam sympathized with him; it was hard being alone at these functions.

When he looked up, Sam was struck by the pure blueness of his eyes. Coupled with the man's dark, curling hair and fair skin, the combination was enticing, and Sam's body stirred for the second time today. He hadn't wanted anyone sexually in months. Until now. He couldn't hold back a smile.

And the Gods were in Sam's favor for once as the man smiled back up into his face, laugh lines crinkling outward from those mesmerizing eyes. There was an intensity that drew Sam closer; he must have been mistaken about the man's uncomfortable vibe. He pictured the two of them naked and sweaty and hoped from the stranger's sudden stillness, the man sensed it as well.

"Not anymore."

Sam breathed out in relief. "I'm Sam. Sam Stein."

"Zach Cohen."

Sam extended his hand and they shook, Sam holding on to Zach's hand for a moment. "Have dinner with me? Later?"

At Zach's hesitation, Sam's stomach dropped. He should've known a guy like him wouldn't be alone.

"I'd love to."

Chapter Three

Two hours later, Zach sat in the hotel's steakhouse waiting for Sam Stein to arrive, nervous anticipation chewing away at his insides. Planning a hook-up in his mind was one thing. Executing it in person was something he didn't think he'd ever consider. Zach stared unseeing at the flickering candle at the center of the table.

Being with someone like Sam Stein would be the first step in throwing off the invisibility cloak he normally wrapped around himself at these events. If he hadn't swallowed his nerves and answered yes, he'd be sitting in his room right now, watching television, wishing he was back home and anonymous in front of his computer.

He'd been to enough conventions over the years to know the night games were always the more interesting of the activities than what took place during the day. Zach drummed his fingers on the tabletop, his heel tapping on the floor with pent-up stress. Maybe Sam wasn't going to show up, and this would all be moot.

What if he couldn't pull it off? Just because he'd watched Marcus for years didn't make Zach comfortable with strangers. Marcus came out of the womb confident and able to charm with a smile.

"Hey, I'm really sorry I'm late."

Zach froze and swallowed hard, his fingers curling into his sweaty palms. *Breathe, relax, and think calm.*

"Hi. You're not. I'm always early. Bad habit."

Sam slid into the chair across from him, his face creased in a smile. "I don't think it's bad. I think it shows you're considerate. I always try and be on time, but sometimes outside forces intervene." He accepted the menu from the waiter. "What are you drinking—still the vodka or do you want wine with dinner?"

"Wine would be nice." Their eyes met over the flickering candle on the table, and Zach smiled. *Oh, how easy it would be to fall for this man.* But falling wasn't part of his plan. One night only, maybe two, but that was it. Hot sex and then a good-bye. Something to prove to himself he could be attractive to another man. Whom he was proving it to, himself or Nathan, negating those last hurtful, hateful words that had never completely faded from his mind, Zach wasn't sure.

"White or red do you think?"

Zach studied Sam's face as he pondered the wine list; his brow furrowed, and he bit his full lower lip. "I'm planning on a nice big steak, what about you?"

"Huh?" Zach tore his mind away from what Sam's mouth would taste like—rich and dark like a Cabernet or slightly sweet like a Riesling. He wondered if he'd get a chance to find out later. "Oh, yeah, steak, definitely."

"Then we'll go with the Cab." Sam handed the leather-backed wine menu back to the waiter, and Zach furiously thought about what to say, figuring work might be a good subject to ease into. After all, they were at a computer convention, so obviously they had that in common.

"So—" Zach began.

"What—" said Sam at the same time.

They laughed a bit self-consciously, and Sam gestured to Zach. "Go ahead; you're the star of the show here. I saw your name on the program for tomorrow night. You're the presenter for the big award, right?"

From the time he was little, Zach had never known how to "sell" himself. He'd always had the inclination to stand on the sidelines and watch everyone else draw acclaim. Even when he'd made his big sale, the one that brought him all his wealth, he remained modest about it, refusing to fall into the lifestyle of easy drugs, casual sex, and instant gratification. He valued himself too much for that world, which prized nothing but fast money and fast living.

He shrugged. "Yeah, I developed a few apps, no big deal, but it's nice to see the young guys, the up-and-coming people in the industry."

At his words, Sam laughed out loud, his eyes dancing with humor. "Young guys. I love it. What are you, thirty?" He reached inside the basket the waiter had placed on the table with the water glasses, and pulled out two crusty breadsticks, taking one and offering the other to Zach.

"Almost," Zach admitted, begrudgingly. He was younger by a few years than Marcus, but had been in the same grade with him at school, having skipped a few grades along the way. Julian was older than them both, having graduated FIT before going back to college to take business classes. None of them ever thought twice about their differences in age though; Julian and Marcus had bonded easily over their sexual escapades and seamlessly fit into the friendship between Zach and Marcus.

"Wow, you're even younger than I thought," said Sam, his smile fading and the light in his eyes dimming a bit. "I'm about forty. You're probably used to being with guys your age or younger."

Yeah, the master of experience over here. Sam should only know, almost all the action I had for the past year was through a computer screen.

Instead of answering, Zach chose to crunch on a breadstick, and watched the waiter approach with the wine and show the bottle to Sam.

Sam sloshed the wine around the glass and tasted it. He nodded his approval. "That's good."

The waiter filled both their glasses with the rich ruby liquid, took their orders for their steaks, and left.

Leaning close, Sam smiled; the candlelight hit his hazel eyes, bringing out the gold and green glints. "I always say it tastes good. What do I know?" He leaned back laughing and rubbed his chin. "As long as it doesn't taste like vinegar I'm good, but I wonder if anyone ever sends back the wine when they do that."

Lost for a moment in Sam's smile, Zach wanted to skip the meal and head right upstairs. Jesus, he sounded like a slut; it wasn't common for him to have such a physical reaction to a man. Over the past few years, as he retreated more into his computer work and app development, Zach retreated more into himself. He told people it was necessary, that he needed the alone time to perfect his work.

And because by nature he was the quiet one, the one who stood at the fringe—there but not there, present but never really accounted for—it was simple for Zach to play the charade without too many questions. His game wasn't meant to be solved by anyone.

This weekend, he had a shot to be the man he wished he could be; the man he might have been before the self-doubt and humiliation Nathan inflicted on him had sunk its barbed-wire grip into him. He could do it at this conference with no ramifications, then withdraw back to the sanctuary of his computer screens and anonymous online presence, where there was no prejudgment, and nothing and no one could touch or hurt him.

"I'm pretty easy…when it comes to wine." He held Sam's gaze and smiled, although from the heat in his face Zach knew with a miserable, sinking feeling, he'd turned red. From childhood he'd blushed as easily as breathing.

Sam quirked a brow and said nothing.

If he was interested, Sam would return it with a little flirting of his own. Zach took a deep swallow of his wine, already exhausted from being "on." There was something to be said for hiding on the sidelines while others took the lead. It had been years since he'd actively flirted, and if he admitted it to himself, he hated it as much now as he did back in college.

Usually more circumspect, Zach drank his wine down, more from nerves than the excellence of the vintage. Their meals came, and Sam surveyed his steak with a gleam in his eye.

"This looks amazing."

Zach had to agree; they'd both ordered the strip with caramelized onions and mushrooms on top and extra-crispy fries. "I'd answer you, but I need to eat these fries." He poured the ketchup, then popped a fry in his mouth, the salty potato taste mixing with the ketchup. "Umm, yeah these are pretty awesome."

Sam gave him a strained look. "You have some ketchup on your lip." He touched the top of his mouth with his finger. "Right there."

Zach went to wipe at it, stopped, and thought about what Marcus would do. Suddenly he didn't give a damn about the bet; he wanted Sam Stein to touch him as a lover. "Why don't you wipe it off for me?"

Did I really say that?

Apparently he did, as Sam's eyes darkened, and he reached across to wipe off the spot of ketchup. Sam's thumb rested a second on Zach's upper lip, then, with a tantalizing slowness that brought an ache to Zach's groin, drew the pad of his thumb down the side of Zach's mouth.

"All clean," Sam murmured, then returned to eating his steak with gusto.

Obviously, a man like Sam Stein, big, virile, and good-looking, his rugged face only adding to his overall appeal, had no trouble finding someone to warm his bed. Determined to keep his newly-discovered courage in the forefront and not let it fade away, Zach attempted small talk as they ate.

"What line of work are you in?"

Sam chewed, then swallowed and took a sip of wine before answering. Zach watched his moves avidly, the pit of his stomach in a tight knot. Damn, even the man's throat was sexy.

"Private investigations. I go undercover a lot. People hire me when they have issues at work and they need someone in the mix to see what's happening."

"I've seen those kind of shows on television." Zach finished his second glass of wine, feeling reckless and wanting a buzz to help settle him for the night he planned. "You pretend to work with the employees while in reality you're looking to see if they're stealing or something, right?"

Sam wiped his mouth with a napkin and tossed it on the table. "Something like that." His plate was pretty much cleaned, while Zach had barely touched his food. He'd been too busy drinking and staring at Sam.

"Not hungry? You barely touched your food." White teeth flashed in Sam's tanned face; the scruff of his evening beard was more pronounced now than it had been at the cocktail hour. Zach wanted to feel it scrape against his cheek, abdomen, and thighs.

Wow.

"Not really." Zach held Sam's gaze.

"Let's get out of here then. I have something I've been dying to do since I came here tonight." Sam signaled the waiter while Zach's nerves skyrocketed and his heart pounded. Was he really going to go through with this?

"Oh yeah?" he choked, wondering where he found the voice to speak. Zach fumbled for his wallet to pull out his credit card. "What's that?"

"Put your wallet away. Dinner's on me."

"Don't be ridiculous," Zach protested. "I can't let you pay for me."

Sam ignored him and signed the check, slid the pen into the leather case with the receipt, closed it, then handed it to the waiter. "It's fine, don't worry about it."

"But—"

"Hey." Sam's quiet tone focused Zach's attention back on Sam's handsome face. "How about you buy breakfast for the two of us, then?"

Funny how Sam seemed uncertain about Zach's response. Determined to still keep up his façade of unruffled cool, Zach's heart nevertheless stuttered a few times before he found his voice. "Sure. I hope you have a big appetite in the morning."

They left the restaurant, Sam slightly behind him, his hand resting on Zach's hip. It may have been a light touch, but it left an indelible mark on Zach. As they walked through the casino, Sam spoke softly. "I'm planning on working one up tonight." It took all Zach's strength not to stumble; the warm, spicy scent of Sam's aftershave coupled with the rich wine of his breath created a heady concoction that set Zach's long-neglected libido into overdrive. He barely paid attention to where they were going, until the cool night air hit his face, and Zach shook himself out of his daydream.

"Where are we going?" He blinked and peered out into the darkness. His contacts itched; this was the longest he'd worn them in months, and he desperately wanted to take them out already. The yawning black surface of the ocean lay in front of them, its waves rolling up against the shore with a hushing sound. There was a certain insignificance, standing at the edge of the sea; the endless horizon and the water's inky black depths coupled with its force remained a mystery to those on land.

He'd been derided as being "not there" by Nathan, and Zach could almost understand now what he'd meant. He'd always thought of himself as an inconsequential drop in those infinite waters, creating a momentary ripple that spread out until all remained calm once again and he was forgotten. Only, as the saying goes, still waters run deep; no matter how close he and his friends were, there were parts he held back, tight to his heart.

"I always wanted to take a walk along the beach at night." Sam stopped by the steps leading down to the sand and shoreline. "Want to come with me?"

He extended his hand and without hesitation Zach took it, their palms sliding, fingers naturally lacing together. There was neither the desire nor inclination to speak as they advanced to the edge where the tide rushed in and pulled back.

Zach let go of Sam's hand, took off his shoes and rolled up his pant legs. Sam did the same; then once again they held hands, still silent, and walked along the coastline, letting the cold water lap at their ankles and toes. A few other people had the same idea as them; Zach spotted several couples entwined on the sand, but he barely paid them any attention. How could he, when every nerve ending in his body was zeroed in on the touch of his fingers with Sam's?

Always the romantic, Zach held firm to the belief it was possible to find that true love and happy ending, though life made it more elusive for some than others. It wasn't the Lifetime movies Marcus teased him about watching that he could point to for proof—he knew the real thing when he saw it happening before his eyes. Julian and Nick reunited after all these years, finally able to show the world how much they loved each other, was like a fantasy turned to life, and he was thrilled for his friends.

Not to say he didn't have his own fantasies—he may not be the wildest guy, but he wasn't dead yet either. This right here was at the top of his list: to walk along a moonlit beach with a handsome man and be kissed. Zach had the moonlight, the beach, and the handsome man. Now he needed that kiss.

Sam stopped and stared out to sea, his strong profile unreadable in the black of the night sky. Zach could smell the salty tang and fishy scent wafting up from the tumble of rocks jutting out from the coast, the spray of the waves pounding up hard against them. He imagined the tiny crabs and other sea dwellers scuttling about, blindly searching for a hiding place, a safe harbor to seek shelter in.

Zach identified with those little creatures—hiding, shy, afraid of exposure for fear of hurt and capture. But where had it gotten him? Nowhere. And though he knew his friends loved him and would never abandon him, Zach didn't want to be that friend, the third wheel, the one everyone felt sorry for because he was alone. He wanted to make his mark, not with his work but with his heart. For without love, was the journey even worth it?

A day of firsts and a night of chance. Zach was taking control, figuring out who he could be without his friends—

his crutches—by his side. Wasn't that what he came here to find? He'd sworn not to succumb to his cautious nature, not to let shyness and uncertainty defeat his goal. Zach would have the night he planned, and it would be with Sam Stein.

"Beautiful, isn't it?" Sam murmured. "I've always been in awe of the power of the sea."

"One of my favorite memories is of my father taking me to the beach in the summer," said Zach thoughtfully. "We'd play in the waves and eat our sandwiches and grapes; then I'd bury him in the sand until only his head showed." He huffed out a self-conscious laugh. "I haven't thought of those times in years."

His father had died suddenly when Zach was eleven, leaving his mother broken and incapable of dealing with her solitude and widowhood. Overnight he'd become the man of the house without ever having the chance to grow up or mourn the loss of his father. He sighed and kicked a line in the sand.

Sam turned away from his study of the ocean and placed a hand on Zach's shoulder. "I hope I didn't bring up unpleasant thoughts for you."

"No, you didn't. I like thinking of him; it makes his memory more alive. I should do it more often in fact."

To Zach's surprise, Sam pulled him close, resting an arm across his shoulders. "How about you think of me right now instead, and how much I want to kiss you?"

His heart beating madly, Zach pressed his lips to Sam's and sank into his arms, heedless to the water pooling around their feet, soaking the hem of his pants.

Chapter Four

Zach's mouth tasted warm and darkly rich from both the wine and the steak. The softness of Zach's lips, the lush and tranquil shushing sound of the waves, all coalesced, providing unexpected, yet perfect pleasure. Then Zach's tongue slid inside his mouth, robbing Sam of his breath and ability to think straight at all.

When he decided to join Henry this weekend, Sam had no expectation he'd find anyone to pique his interest. He'd figured it would be a boring conference filled with computer people spouting off gibberish. Finding Zach by accident at the bar was pure luck on his part.

Standing here now, kissing Zach, his body humming with need, skin hot despite the coolness of the night air, for the first time in months, Sam wanted someone. Deeply, viscerally, so much so that he hoped they could make it back upstairs before he lost control.

"My room or yours?" He spoke against the corner of Zach's mouth, the silk of Zach's shirt sliding up underneath his hands, so Sam could touch the warm, smooth skin of his back.

"Let's do mine," whispered Zach.

Did he imagine a hesitation? He must be wrong, Sam thought, feeling the press of Zach's unmistakable erection against his thigh.

They walked none too slowly, and Sam had to commend the both of them for not sprinting full speed into the hotel. He managed to keep his cool through the elevator ride and even when Zach fumbled the card out of his wallet.

When the door shut behind him, Sam grabbed Zach, slamming their bodies together. "I'm so fucking hard for you I don't have time to be sweet and pretty."

"Let's go to the bedroom." Zach pulled him through a dark room to the back of the small suite, where a king-size bed, already turned down for the evening, awaited them.

Through narrowed eyes, Sam watched Zach undress, his heart skipping a beat at the sight of Zach's body when he was finally naked. Though he gave a slight appearance while dressed, Zach's body was beautiful, with lean sinewy muscle under his long limbs. His chest had a nice covering of dark hair, and his cock, thick and long, stood up flushed and gleaming at the tip.

"Your turn." Zach pointed at him. "It works much better if both of us are naked." He grinned. "At least for me."

"Wise-ass," growled Sam, but pulled off his clothes until he too stood naked. For a moment he was unsure about his body. Zach was younger and more fit; his body didn't bear the scars of knife attacks Sam's had, nor did it show the inevitable creep of age. Suddenly self-conscious, Sam turned away, only to have Zach, naked, hot, and smooth-skinned, press flush up against his back. Sam's cock jerked against his stomach.

"Don't." Zach's lips were buried in his hair. "I want to see you."

"I'm nothing special," said Sam, laughing a bit to hide his discomfort. He hadn't experienced this awkwardness with a lover before, but Zach wasn't an ordinary hook-up, though for the life of him Sam couldn't say why.

They tumbled down on the bed together, legs tangling, arms reaching for one another. Zach's lean thighs straddled Sam's hips, his face still hidden in the ambient darkness. This was the time when Sam usually made haste with the preliminaries, wanting to get down to the raw basics of why he and the man were in bed together. Give him minimal prep and hard, hot fucking. Anything to achieve the all enveloping post-orgasmic bliss, obliterating everything in its path. Physical satisfaction rather than emotional was his desired end.

But at the touch of Zach's hand on his face, Sam tensed. He wanted to tell him, "Stop; that's not how I want it to work for me." Instead, Sam leaned into Zach's hand and grabbed the nape of his neck, pulling him down for a deep, searching kiss. Their tongues twisted together and their breaths merged; Zach's cock rested hard against Sam's thigh, and Sam groaned into Zach's mouth.

"Where's your stuff? Tell me you brought."

Breathing heavily, his mouth slightly open and gleaming wet, Zach nodded and scrambled to the opposite side of the bed, retrieving his supplies from the drawer of the night table.

"C'mre." Sam held out his arm, and Zach slid in next to him, their bodies molding together. He began kissing Zach, trailing a hot, wet path of kisses from Zach's smooth brow, down his bristled cheek and tightly clenched jawline, stopping only to whisper in Zach's ear. "Relax." He continued to press kisses down the side of Zach's neck.

Zach swallowed, his throat moving against Sam's lips. "I am. Don't stop."

Not a fucking chance. Sam grinned to himself and gazed down at the man now spread out beneath him, his body perfect in the lavender dimness of the room. He dipped his head again and with their eyes locked, Sam braced his hands on either side of Zach's body and kissed down his chest and flat stomach until he reached Zach's cock. Before he took it in his mouth, Sam licked around its rigid length, enjoying Zach's groans and pants.

"Jesus, stop torturing me already."

Sam gave him only a brief smile before tracing the head of Zach's cock with his tongue. Zach's harsh breath and quickened pelvic thrusts all spurred Sam on, and he engulfed Zach's cock in his mouth, sliding down fully until he reached its base. He increased the pressure of both his lips and tongue, sucking hard, until with a harsh cry, Zach came, streaming hot and heavy down Sam's throat. Sam swallowed and pulled the last bit of pleasure from Zach.

After he withdrew, Sam leaned his face against Zach's thigh, breathing in his warm scent, sensing the ripples across his skin. Several moments passed before Sam kissed Zach's thigh and sat up.

Zach lay still, but his eyes were wide open, and a small smile curved his lips.

"Feel good?" Sam couldn't help but ask, shocked at the nervous flutter in his chest. He was almost forty years old for Christ's sake and had been having sex since he was sixteen; all of a sudden this was different in a way he didn't understand.

"If you have to ask, I guess I wasn't loud enough, huh?" Zach rolled over on his stomach, giving Sam the first look at his ass. "But now it's about making you feel good." Peering over his shoulder through the tumble of dark waves of his hair, Zach flashed a smile. "Once you're inside me, I promise to let you know how good I feel."

Desire pooled in Sam's groin, and his cock twitched; the sight of all that naked flesh in front of him short-circuited his brain cells. Zach's body gleamed like cool marble in the dim light of the bedroom, but he was warm to his touch. And Sam touched Zach all over, smoothing his hands over the round globes of Zach's ass, sweeping up Zach's back to his shoulders. Sam followed the touch of his hands with his lips, pressing kisses along each vertebra of Zach's spine, licking the cords of Zach's neck until Zach writhed beneath him, spreading his legs wider and tilting his ass in the air.

"Now. Come *on*."

Sam grinned, pleased by Zach's insistent need, and slid his fingers in the crease of Zach's ass playing up and down, while Zach vibrated beneath his touch. Yeah, it fed his ego a bit, no lie. Having this young guy out of his mind, wanting Sam so desperately, was a huge turn-on.

With one hand, Sam reached for the bottle of lube and snapped it open, dribbling it over his fingers and Zach's opening. Zach shifted his legs wider and braced his knees on the bed.

"Now; do it now. I've been waiting all evening."

For a moment Sam faltered. He hadn't misheard, nor was he imagining Zach's naked, lithe body and perfect ass under his hands. He ripped open the condom wrapper and rolled it down his shaft, then pushed the head of his sheathed cock into Zach, sinking deep inside.

Zach groaned, a dark, powerful sound, sending a surge of lust through Sam's blood. He wasn't going to last to make it pretty and nice for Zach; he wanted him too much. Zach's ass clutched his cock tight, drawing him in deeper; Sam held tight to Zach's hips and thrust inside him three, four, five times before his orgasm pounded through him, shattering him into a thousand pieces, leaving him gasping for air.

The intensity of his orgasm robbed him of the capacity to think straight. Sam collapsed, flattening Zach to the bed, his cock still buried in Zach's ass, balls-deep. It had been months since he'd last gotten laid and even then, the sex hadn't been as off the charts as this. He nuzzled against the curve of Zach's neck, wondering if he had it in him to go again later tonight, and if Zach would ask him to stay.

"Please get off me." Beneath him, Zach's body stiffened and shook. Alarmed, Sam slipped out of Zach's body, then rolled to his side.

"Are you all right?" He reached out with a tentative hand to touch the smooth expanse of Zach's back, but when Sam's hand came in contact with his skin, Zach flinched and pulled away. "I didn't mean—"

"It's okay." Though Zach's voice was muffled, Sam didn't detect any anger. Zach rolled over to face him, and even in the dim moonlight, Sam could see anxiety creasing Zach's face in the furrowed brow and pinched skin around his mouth. "I, I don't like being held down. I'm sorry."

Sam stripped off the condom and tossed it in the trash, then returned to the bed and lay down next to Zach.

"You have nothing to be sorry about." He traced the jut of Zach's cheekbone with his finger. "I didn't think to ask how you like it. Things happened so fast, and you kind of blew me away."

A small smile teased Zach's lips. "Yeah?"

Somewhat unsteady and uncertain, Sam brushed his lips against Zach's. "Yeah."

Zach bit his lip and looked surprisingly nervous after his wild abandon in bed. "Sam?"

"Hmm?"

"You're staying, right?"

Relief coursed through him, yet he kept his tone nonchalant, as if that alone would make what had occurred between them commonplace and rote. "Sure, if you want."

Zach gave him an endearing, sleepy smile. "I want." Those hypnotic blue eyes fluttered shut. "Let's try and get some sleep."

Ignoring the skip-beat of his heart, Sam stretched out beside Zach, listening to the even cadence of his breathing. He wondered what the hell had happened tonight; why he wanted to stay, to spend the night with a complete stranger when in the past he couldn't wait to get dressed and hightail it away from the few men he'd slept with.

Unable to process all this deep thought after such heart-seizing sex, Sam turned on his side and fell asleep.

*   *   *

It took Sam a moment or two upon waking to recall his surroundings; it was disconcerting to wake up in an unfamiliar bed and recognize nothing. Not only was Sam not at home, he wasn't even in his own hotel room. The solid warmth of a body pressed up behind him reminded him, and recollection of the prior evening flooded through him; his blood pooled in his groin.

"Good morning."

He rolled over and faced Zach who, though sleep-disheveled, scruffy, and only half awake, was still the best thing Sam had woken up to in a long time. Maybe they had time for a quickie.

"Morning."

Blinking, Zach rubbed his eyes and flopped back on the pillow. "I hate being up this early, but I have a breakfast meeting with the company giving the award tonight and panel discussions I have to attend all day." He yawned and scrubbed his face with his hands. "I don't get a break until tonight after the awards dinner."

Well, there went the idea of morning sex. But Sam understood. This was Zach's way of brushing him off: a "thanks for last night and see ya around" but more subtle. What else did he expect from sex with a stranger? Sam took the hint and slid out of bed, in search of his clothes.

"Yeah, I have to get going too."

Zach sat up and brushed the hair out of his eyes, a puzzled look on his face. "Oh. I was kind of hoping we could at least get room service together. Maybe make plans for getting together later tonight after all the ceremonies and nonsense are finished?"

Surprised, Sam stopped buttoning his shirt; Zach's sweet, slightly anxious smile seemed to be in earnest. "Ahh, yeah, I'd love some coffee. And we can play the rest by ear, how's that?"

Something dark flickered through Zach's eyes; more likely it was a trick of the light streaming in off the ocean, now shimmering blue-gray in the early morning fog. If Zach was anything like Sam, he was feeling extremely awkward. Everything looks different in the light of early morning.

"Sure, play it by ear, see how the night goes." He gave Sam a funny half smile and got out of bed. "I'll call for room service, then shower, how's that?"

"Sounds good." Sam had no idea of the mechanics of the morning after. He followed Zach's lead, as he was obviously more experienced in the ways of the world of casual sex. He'd hoped to get the chance to spend more time with Zach later on, but didn't count on it, knowing how in demand and popular a guy like Zach must be, given his status as a presenter and app developer in his own right. Sam didn't want to sound too needy or desperate.

Zach emerged from the bathroom freshly shaven, with his hair curling about his head in wet waves. He'd dressed casually and wore a pair of dark glasses that strangely fired Sam's blood. Sam stared at him for a moment, wishing they could go another round in bed together, but he understood it was time for them to move on from the night.

Sam gathered his boxers and pants from where he'd flung them last night and went into the bathroom to take a piss and wash his face, wondering if Zach felt as uncomfortable as he did, waking up with a stranger. The sex had been amazing, but it did nothing to chase away the awkwardness of making small talk.

The coffee and croissants Zach had ordered were waiting when Sam reentered the room. The rich aroma of the fresh brew wafted toward him, teasing his brain, and he couldn't wait for the first taste. He poured himself some from the thermal carafe and held it up to Zach, who was reading something on his tablet.

"Yeah, give me one second." Zach finished typing and then sprang up from the bed to claim his cup. "Thanks." He sipped the coffee, closed his eyes, and moaned. "Nothing like that first cup."

Sam had to agree. He attempted a mask of indifference, where sleeping with a man meant nothing more than a sudden, hot rush of pleasure, a physical need for release, all the while hiding his enjoyment in being a couple again and waking up next to someone in the morning. Until now, he hadn't realized how lonely he'd been since Andy had moved out. But, like his relationship with Andy, this right here with Zach wasn't real either.

They made idle talk over their coffee, and Sam wondered if Zach normally went to conventions and picked up random men. He'd hate to think that, remembering how sweet Zach's kisses tasted last night by the water.

"Uh, I hate to rush, but I have to prepare for my meetings today." Zach's apologetic smile didn't make Sam feel any better about leaving.

"Sure," he said, affecting a nonchalant tone. "I'll catch you later, hopefully." He bent and gave Zach's cheek a perfunctory kiss, then drained his coffee and left.

It wasn't until he returned to his room to change and shower that the inevitability of his solitude crept up on him. With a thump, Sam sat heavily on the bed and stared at the walls of his room. Last night, when they stood by the edge of the ocean and Zach spoke of his father, the vulnerability in his eyes had surprised Sam.

He needed to refocus and remember he wasn't here to find a soul mate; that was crap dreamed up by Hollywood and the romance books his mother read when he was a child. All he had to do was find a way back to living his life and tone down his regrets. Try to find some normalcy out of the madness. Sometimes he thought it might be easier finding Narnia.

He took out his phone and called Henry.

"Good morning, Sleeping Beauty."

"What?" Henry croaked. "It's fucking seven thirty in the morning. What do you expect?" A huge yawning sound filled Sam's ear. "Where did you go after the cocktail hour last night? I thought we would meet up."

"Uh…I found something better to do."

"Oh yeah?" Henry instantly sounded more awake. "Details, brother. I need details."

"I don't kiss and tell. You'll have to trust me."

"Breakfast in an hour," said Henry. "I need some information, some proof; at least a name and pictures of you together. I'm not asking for a blow-by-blow of your night." He started cackling, and Sam swore.

"Asshole. You're pretty proud of yourself with that one, aren't you?" Sam took out his clothes for the day and collected his razor and shaving cream.

"You have to admit it was a good one." Henry chuckled. "Blow by blow."

Sam couldn't help but smile at his friend's crude joke. "Jesus, you're pathetic. Are you looking for pointers or something? Let me get ready and I'll see you in an hour."

He ended the call and got into the shower. He'd have loved to have taken a shower with Zach, but the man didn't ask, and Sam wouldn't push himself to ask either. Besides, he thought as he soaped himself up, it wasn't as though one amazing fuck made a relationship.

Sam hoped he could keep his heart as hard as his dick the next time he saw Zach.

Chapter Five

Sitting in his second meeting of the morning, Zach's mind began to wander. There was only so much interest he could muster toward a discussion of the hybridization of apps for android, windows, or iOS.

Jesus, people, it's not world peace here, it's an app.

He drummed his fingers on the table, and his leg jiggled a dance out of boredom, imagining Sam upstairs, enjoying a lazy morning in bed. Zach resented sitting here, when he could be upstairs with Sam, kissing and touching him. Making love to him. Desire burned hot through his bloodstream.

"Zach, what do you think of the way they've integrated their native user interface? This company has worked for years to make their coding available for all platforms."

Startled out of his sexual fantasy, Zach guiltily realized

he should pay attention; after all, they were putting him up for the weekend.

"Uh, yeah, it's great." Could they tell how much he didn't care? But he needed to at least attempt to make the effort and show some enthusiasm. His dirty dreams could wait until later. "I wanted an app that would pull from all the different social media sites of the user. By integrating their Yelp reviews, Facebook page likes, posts on Tumblr, and other web footprints, I thought it was a unique way to pair people up for a dating site."

That was his spiel, the one he'd used when he sold the site to a software company for an insane amount of money. And it had proved to be a winner, as people flocked to the website to sign up for the monthly service. He was glad for his foresight to include stock options in his sales contract and had gifted Julian and Marcus some stock in the company as well. Zach hadn't forgotten how his friends staunchly supported him, even though they freely admitted they had no idea what he did.

"It's brilliant, Zach, just brilliant," gushed Cicely Long, the director of development for Rocket Launch software. "In the first year alone we've had over twenty thousand subscribers, with hundreds signing on every day."

"Good. I'm glad," said Zach. He wondered how he could create a dating site for others to find love, when he was so woefully inadequate in his own personal life. The night with Sam Stein had been a wonderful distraction, but Zach knew it was a one-off, designed to give him dreams to last a very long time. This morning when Zach threw out the dinner invitation, he'd hoped Sam would've wanted to spend another night together. Instead he'd vacillated and failed to pick up Zach's hint, giving at best a noncommittal answer.

Even when he tried to be a player, Zach was a failure. Always had been. He was too awkward, too certain people wouldn't like him. This was why he didn't normally bother.

The meeting broke up, and he saw by his watch it was lunchtime, but he had to call his mother first. She'd be anxious to talk to him, and he didn't want her to worry unnecessarily. Finding himself a secluded spot in the lobby, he sat in a comfortable chair and pulled out his phone.

"Sweetheart, how are you? How is the conference?"

His mother's familiar, voluble tone filled his ear. "I'm fine, everything's good."

"I was worried when I didn't hear from you last night. Usually you call me when you check in, to let me know everything is okay."

The slightly condemning tone sent that familiar stab of guilt through Zach. No matter how hard he tried, he ended up disappointing someone. Considering her fears, he tried hard not to worry her and let her know where he was.

"Sorry, Mom. I got caught up in something that lasted a bit longer than I thought, and it became too late."

"That's all right. As long as you're okay. Anyone nice there that you like?"

Another thing for him to feel guilty about. Cheryl Cohen never gave up the hope that he would meet a nice girl and settle down. "A grandchild would be so lovely" was her usual refrain.

But, Zach justified to himself, there had never been a right time to tell his mother he was gay. She had been as thrilled as anyone when Julian and Nick got together, but after commenting to him how disappointed Nick's parents must be that he would never have his own children, Zach shut down any thoughts of confessing his own sexuality to her. She'd had enough pain and loss in her life; why tell her she'd lost the only chance for a grandchild by having Zach as her son?

"I'm here for business, not to find a date." He heard a smothered chuckle and darted a sideways look, catching the eye of the man sitting a few feet away on the sofa. Zach's face burned when he realized the good-looking man had overheard his conversation, and he hastily looked down, away, anywhere but at the laughing stranger.

"There's no reason you can't combine both. You're young; you should be having fun and be able to enjoy yourself."

Yet Zach knew if he began seeing someone and spent time away from home, his mother would become nervous and fearful by herself. "I'm fine. How are you doing, that's really why I called. Everything okay at the house?" Over the years he'd tried not to go to too many conferences and leave his mother, knowing how she hated being alone, but she'd been better lately, and he absolutely had to go to this one.

"I'm all right. Marcus stopped by for a visit. He really is a darling."

"He's a good friend, and he loves you. I'm glad he came to see you." Zach checked his watch and saw that he had ten minutes to go before a panel discussion began that he was supposed to be moderating. "I gotta go. Love you."

"Love you too, sweetheart. Call me later."

"I will," he promised and hung up. There was nothing he wanted to do less than moderate a panel discussion right now; he'd love to be able to sit in this comfortable chair, hidden behind the palm trees, and people-watch. Or go to the beach, listen to the waves, and recreate the magic from last night with Sam. Unfortunately duty called, and with a deep sigh he stood and walked toward the lobby.

"Family obligations, huh?" The man from the sofa fell into step next to him. "Those can be a drag."

Surprised by the man's blatant admission to eavesdropping on his conversation, Zach politely nodded and shrugged. "Uh, yeah. But it's my mom, so I'm okay with it."

The man slanted a look at him from beneath raised brows. "Not many guys will admit to that."

Zach shrugged again but didn't answer. He didn't need to justify his relationship with his mother to a stranger or anyone. Sure, she was a bit overbearing and intense, and Zach had rebelled like many teenagers, but that was before he understood how his father's precipitous death affected her, creating a deep-rooted sense of fear of loss and anxiety. He'd made sure to take some psych classes in college, so he understood her behavior was a result of her love for him, not a need to control; if she clung a bit too tight and worried a little too much, he never complained. It was a small burden, and he counted himself lucky to have a parent who cared. Realistically, he knew he should break away, exert his independence, but with him always home and not involved in any relationship there'd been no need.

"You're here with the convention, right?" The man wouldn't leave his side and continued to follow Zach as he made his way through the lobby to one of the smaller ballrooms where the panel discussion was being held.

"Uh, yes. Are you?" The man wasn't gay; he wasn't trying to pick him up, at least Zach didn't get that vibe from him, so he wondered what he wanted.

"Yes." The man extracted a card from his wallet. "Henry Walker. I'm the owner of Eyes on You, a computer forensics investigations firm."

Zach pocketed his card. "Nice to meet you. I'm Zach Cohen."

"I know."

Zach looked startled until the man laughed and pointed at the placard set up on an easel in front of the entrance to the room. On it were pictures of the four panelists and himself as the moderator. He winced at his picture; it was a year old and showed him with his glasses, sitting in front of a computer, the screen advertising the dating website he'd created.

"You're famous. I admire your work, and I've followed

your success the past few years."

The heat rose to Zach's face. "Hardly famous. Well, nice to meet you." He walked inside to the front of the room and sat at the end of the long table where a placard with his name had been placed. Henry followed him and sat in the front row, studying the brochure they handed to everyone who walked in the room. Zach hated that his social media information was put out there; his brief bio as well as his Facebook page, Twitter, and other footprints, but he knew it couldn't be helped. Besides, anyone with a little knowledge could find those things out. His phone buzzed with a text from Julian.

Having fun? How's the conference?

At that moment, Sam Stein strolled into the room, and Zach forgot about the text, his mother, and what day of the week it was. Strong, tough, and with a sharp, watchful look in his eyes, Sam Stein in person was better than any fantasy Zach could've ever dreamed up. It was hard to believe he'd woken up this morning, naked in bed with this man, but the soreness of his ass and the ache of underutilized muscles brought a slight smile to his face. The memory of Sam slamming into him last night, breath hot and heavy on his neck, large hands gripping his hips, had Zach fighting for self-control. Damn. He could hardly moderate a panel with a hard-on.

To his shock, Sam took the seat next to Henry Walker. Zach recalled Sam saying he was a private investigator and wondered if the two men worked together. Were they lovers? Maybe Zach had been wrong before about Henry, but then to his relief, he saw the shine of a gold wedding band on Henry's finger. God, he was like a kid with his first crush, but nothing could have stopped the steady pounding of his heart.

His phone buzzed with another text, and he was certain it was from either Julian again or Marcus. If he didn't answer, Zach knew the next thing would be a call. With those two, it was like having a collective of mother hens constantly pecking at him. Normally he handled their overprotectiveness with humor and tolerance, but right now he needed some space.

Moderating a panel discussion. Talk later.

It didn't take five seconds before he got a response.

Too bad. We thought maybe you got lucky.

Zach once again eyed Sam who was talking to his friend.

Maybe he would after all.

Chapter Six

Despite not understanding what the hell he'd sat through and listened to for the past hour, Sam knew enough to be impressed with the panelists and especially Zach as the moderator. For all his youthful appearance and modesty, Zach kept the discussion flowing on topic and was able to answer questions on the fly from the audience if one of the panelists came up blank.

Henry folded up his program and stuck it in his pocket. "This guy Zach Cohen is crazy-smart, even if he is a bit nerdy."

Sam bristled. "What do you mean, nerdy? He has a brain, a freaking brilliant one. What's your problem with that?"

"Is that the guy you were with last night?" Henry's eyes widened in shock at Sam's nod. "Well, damn. Don't bite my head off, big guy. I wasn't saying it in a mean way." He cocked his head and quirked a smile. "You like him, huh?"

Sam shrugged and kept his voice as noncommittal as possible. "We had a good time, nothing else."

Henry shot him an amused look, but Sam refused to say anything further. The crowd in front thinned, and from the corner of his eye Sam watched Zach chat with one of the panelists as they stood together. He wondered why a man like Zach, brilliant, good-looking, and well respected, had to resort to a hook-up with a stranger.

Then he caught Zach's eyes watching him—that damn blue-eyed stare that attracted him in the first place—and breathing became difficult. Sam couldn't let Henry see how affected he was by a simple look from a man he barely knew, and instead of giving Zach an encouraging smile, Sam forced himself to look away.

"Are you done?" His voice came out more clipped and short than usual, and Henry studied him from under a furrowed brow.

"What's wrong? You got an angry look on your face all of a sudden." He glanced over at the front of the room to where Sam knew Zach remained, checking his phone. "I thought maybe you'd want to talk to him."

"Nothing's wrong." His jaw flexed. "And if I wanted to talk to him, I would. Can we leave?"

"Uh, yeah, sure."

Without giving Zach another look, Sam followed Henry out of the conference room. They took the escalator down to the main floor and walked out to the boardwalk. The sun hit Sam on his back, surprisingly warm for early June. He stood at the railing, looking out at the ocean.

"What's wrong, Sammy? Talk to me." Henry leaned on the iron of the boardwalk rails, facing the hotel.

It took him a few minutes to marshal his thoughts before

he spoke. "Do you ever feel like you missed out? Like somehow life passed you by, but you didn't know it because you had no idea there was anything else?"

"I'm not sure what you mean."

No surprise. Sam wasn't sure even he understood what he was trying to say. But being with Zach last night made him think about what he missed by staying with a man who, in the end, hadn't been worth his time or love.

"I think I wasted so much time trying to make a doomed relationship work that I forgot sometimes it's better to cut your losses and run. Maybe I missed out on meeting the right person because I was too busy trying to mold the wrong one into something he could never be."

The sounds of the boardwalk intensified as lunchtime crowds spilled out from the hotels and casinos. Everyone wanted to be outside on this beautiful day. Seagulls swooped overhead, their raucous cries piercing in the afternoon sun. The aroma of grease and sugar, the sharp salt tang of the ocean, and that indescribable beachy smell; Sam loved it all.

Squinting into the sun, Henry regarded him with a thoughtful expression. "Is this because of the night you spent with Zach Cohen? I wouldn't make any life-changing decisions based on that."

"I have no intention of doing that," said Sam gruffly, understanding Henry's wish for him not to get hurt by a stranger he barely knew. "I'm speaking in generalities. If I start dating again—"

"You mean when," interrupted Henry.

"*If.*" Sam glared at Henry. "If I start dating again, I plan on being with a man I won't have to change or change for, who wants the same things I want. I don't plan on making the same mistake twice."

"How can you know that for certain? No one really ever knows everything about a person, especially in the honeymoon phase. You know what I'm talking about. That 'getting to know you' phase where everyone puts on their best face to make sure they don't screw up what looks like the start of a great relationship." Henry shrugged and turned to face the water. "It takes time to find out about people."

"Look, take the guy I was with last night, Zach. Casual sex is probably common for him. He's young, good-looking, and smart, and probably goes to these conventions all the time. I don't want someone who's a serial hook-up artist."

"He seems like a regular guy, not a player."

"Who knows? But I'm not deceiving myself. Yeah, we had a great night, and I hope to see him again tonight, but I know how these things go."

A hint of a grin touched Henry's lips. "Yeah, Mr. Experience? Tell me how they go."

"Oh, fuck you," said Sam with a laugh, but he turned serious as he faced the water once again. Several boats bobbed out in the distance, and the water sparkled where rays of sunlight touched down. "You know what I mean. I'd be crazy not to want to spend time with the guy. I'm not betting it's gonna last forever though; I've got my eyes wide open. It's a weekend fling, and that's all."

He nudged Henry's shoulder with his own. "Let's get something to eat. You made me sit through that boring shit, the least you can do is buy me a hot dog or a funnel cake."

Henry shot him an incredulous look. "Are you crazy? Who eats that shit?"

"I do. Come on." In companionable silence they strolled down the boardwalk, dodging the pedicabs and hoards of sticky-fingered and ice-cream-smeared children.

"Let's stop here. I want some fudge." Sam stopped in front of Steel's, the famous boardwalk fudge store. The sugary chocolate scent filled his head, and his stomach growled.

"Hungry?" Henry murmured. "Guess you worked up an

appetite last night."

"Shut up." Ignoring his friend, Sam strode inside and came face-to-face with Zach, who had a bag in one hand and a hunk of fudge in the other. A crumb of chocolate fudge hung off his upper lip, and Sam wondered what Zach would do if he leaned over and licked it off his mouth.

"Oh, hey."

Zach seemed flustered at seeing him in the light of day. Maybe he didn't want anyone to know they'd been together, but he needn't have worried. It wasn't as if Sam was going to grab him in front of everyone, but it was still nice to be recognized.

"Hi."

"Good?" Sam indicated the piece of fudge, enjoying this less confident side of Zach; it made him seem more human than the data-spouting, computer-whiz kid he watched earlier.

"What? The fudge? Yeah."

From the size of the bag the man either had an enormous sweet tooth, or he was buying some to take home.

"I was going to buy some myself. Maybe eat it as a midnight snack." He winked and smiled to himself, watching the red stain of a blush creep up Zach's neck. "What kind did you get?"

"Um, plain chocolate, chocolate peanut butter, and rocky road." Zach indicated the piece in his hand. "I took a slice to go since I was hungry." He thought for a moment, then offered it to Sam. "Want a bite?"

Without any hesitation, Sam leaned over and bit off a piece of the fudge from the chunk Zach offered. There was something almost intimate and sensual about his action; Sam glanced up and found Zach staring at him, his gaze dark and unreadable. Sam licked his lips and grinned.

"Thanks, that's delicious. I love chocolate. My favorite

thing is the chocolate cannoli at Caruso's pastry shop around the corner from me."

"Yeah, I love chocolate too; it's my favorite." Zach hefted the shopping bag. "Well, um, see you around." He passed by Henry and exited the store, leaving Sam standing there, watching him leave, feeling strangely bereft.

"You look like someone kicked your puppy, Sammy-boy. If you want to have lunch with the guy, go after him. I've got work to do, and I'm sure you'll have more fun with him than with me."

What did he want? With Zach retreating farther down the boardwalk, away from him, Sam knew he'd better make up his mind soon, or lose Zach in the throngs of people. Still he held back.

Henry, of course, understood without Sam needing to say a word. "You're not marrying the guy. It's only lunch. We'll sit together during the awards ceremony, as I'm sure Zach'll be up on the dais since he's a presenter. Go on and have a little fun for once."

Throwing a grateful smile to his friend over his shoulder, Sam sprinted out of the store and down the boardwalk after Zach. Maybe he was silly to feel so lighthearted; after all, it wasn't as though he and Zach were in a relationship. But for so long he hadn't had anything in his life to look forward to that even this little taste of fun made him happier than he had been in months. Sam caught up with Zach and fell into step behind him.

"Hey." He placed his hand on Zach's shoulder, and to Sam's surprise Zach recoiled and pulled away from his hand. "Um, I forgot to tell you something."

"Oh, hi, sorry. What are you doing here?" Zach peered over his shoulder. "Where's your friend?"

"He had some work to do."

Zach faced him, a confused look in his eyes. "What did

you forget to tell me?"

Fortuitously, that piece of fudge still clung to Zac's upper lip, providing Sam with the cheesiest excuse ever to snag a kiss. Sam grabbed him by the shoulders and pressed his lips to Zach's, sliding his tongue over Zach's lips to lick that errant piece of fudge from his top lip. At first Zach stood stiff, but at Sam's insistent pressure, his mouth softened, and soon they were kissing, oblivious to the whistles and catcalls of the crowd on the boardwalk, passing by them.

He had never been a demonstrative man, preferring to keep his sex life under wraps for the most part. But Zach's mouth tasted sweet on Sam's tongue, and all thoughts of lunch faded from Sam's mind, replaced by a different kind of hunger. The libido from when he was twenty-five reappeared, and he could've kept kissing Zach forever.

What was it about this unassuming man that brought out the desire that frankly Sam thought was gone for good? None of the men he'd been with since his breakup had made him feel this way. Right now he couldn't care less, as Zach dropped his bag of fudge at their feet and slid his arms around Sam's waist, opening his mouth and leaning into the kiss.

Without any idea how much time had passed, Sam broke away from the kiss, resting his lips on Zach's forehead. The beat of Zach's heart pounded frantically.

"What was that about?" Zach murmured against Sam's chest, yet he made no move to pull away.

"I couldn't have you embarrass yourself by walking around with chocolate on your mouth; you're the star of the show tonight." Sam picked up Zach's bag of fudge and handed it back to him, but kept his other arm around Zach's shoulders. "Consider what I've done for your image as a public service of a kind."

"So very kind of you," said Zach drily, but when Sam caught his eye, Zach's smile seemed genuine.

"Think nothing of it."

They began the walk back to the hotel in silence. "Are you ready for tonight's ceremony?" He thought it was a pretty neutral conversation, but Zach's shoulders tensed underneath his arm.

"Not really. I hate these things."

That was a surprise. Sam figured Zach would be used to these events and receiving the accolades from his peers. "Why?"

Zach shrugged but didn't answer.

Deciding it was time to change the subject, Sam steered the conversation to something more pleasant—the after the ceremony activity.

"So do they have you tied up after the dinner or are you free?"

They'd reached the part of the boardwalk where their hotel was located, but as neither of them made any effort to go indoors, Sam motioned to one of the empty benches. "Want to sit for a while?"

Zach chose the closest bench and sat without answering, placing the bag with the fudge next to him. Sam sat beside him and stretched his legs.

"I was thinking maybe we could get together afterward." When Zach failed to acknowledge him, Sam's grin faded. "Unless you already have plans."

"No. I have no plans. But don't you?" Zach watched the Frisbee players on the beach. "You came with a friend; don't you want to spend time with him?"

Not if Sam had Zach waiting for him and they could end up like they did last night. The thought of being inside Zach again sent the blood straight to his dick. "Henry has work to do, and he's married. He's not into the party scene."

"And you are?"

Not wanting to seem too old, Sam gave a self-conscious laugh. "Isn't everyone you meet these days?"

A surprisingly thoughtful look crossed Zach's face. "I wonder if that's true, or it's because people are so lonely these days they pretend. We have everything at our fingertips; our phones and computers have made it possible for us to isolate ourselves, or only show people what we want."

This was a pretty heavy conversation, one Sam hadn't anticipated, but Zach was right. "And sometimes you can live with a person, see them everyday, and not really know who they are; you don't have to hide behind a screen. You think you know them, but they never were the person they claimed to be." *Shit*. He hadn't meant to say that out loud.

The searching look Zach gave him didn't encourage Sam to open up any further. This was not the way he anticipated spending his day; he was here to have fun and let loose.

"How about we make plans for after the dinner? We can meet and have drinks, maybe go to the casino." He nudged Zach's shoulder. "And whatever else we can think of."

When Zach didn't answer right away Sam grew a bit nervous, thinking he came on too strong, or maybe Zach wasn't interested anymore.

"Hey, it's all right. I understand you not wanting to tie yourself down for the evening."

"No, not at all. I'd love to get together." Zach stared out at the ocean, which was calm now. The gray-blue surface shimmered in the afternoon sunlight, and far out in the distance, Sam watched the sailboats gliding on the sparkling water. Maybe he'd get a house and a boat.

"You know what I'd really love to do?"

Hopefully what Zach was about to suggest involved a bed and getting naked and sweaty. "No, but go ahead and tell me."

"I'd like to come back to the beach and walk along the

water. Like we did last night." That endearing blush crept up Zach's neck again. "It's one of the things I've always wanted to do, and since I'm leaving tomorrow, I want to do it again." He hesitated. "With you. Is that okay?"

Emotions long held at bay rushed up to choke Sam, thwarting his ability to speak for a moment. So much conflict ran through him; from the start he'd intended to keep things light and easy between him and Zach. After all, this was a convention, and people got together without any expectation of forming an attachment. No strings. The two of them had nothing in common and would never have to see each other once the weekend was over.

But there was something so vulnerable about Zach, something Sam couldn't put his finger on yet that drew him closer instead of pushing him away. What if there was something more, something that ran between them, burning brighter than mere mutual sexual attraction? Was Sam ready to take a chance and explore it? Was Zach? Underneath Zach's youthful appearance and big blue eyes was a man who, Sam sensed, had climbed over roadblocks in life and suffered from them.

Somehow Zach had insinuated himself under Sam's skin to the point where Sam thought about him in a different setting than the glitz and flash of the casino. Who was the real Zach Cohen? Was he a computer wonk, endlessly spouting details about apps and development software and stuff that made Sam's head spin? Or was he a player, one of those whiz kids Sam would see on the news, who'd gotten too much, too soon, and used his money and fame to get what he wanted. Was it all an act to get Sam into bed?

Sam hated doubting himself; he'd always been so strong in his beliefs about life. But being cheated on, losing the job he loved, and having to start over at thirty-nine had left him wobbly and uncertain. As a cop, he'd prided himself on his instincts both in figuring out who committed a crime and the motives behind the person's behavior. Too bad he'd paid more attention to his job than he did his own crumbling personal life, so now he floundered, suspicious, and second-guessing everyone he met.

Feeling more like a kid than a grown-ass man, Sam slipped his arm around Zach's shoulders. "I'd like that too."

Chapter Seven

"And the winner of the Next Big App award is Paul Smith, for his innovative design of It's My Party, an app that allows people to collect data from multiple party-planning sources along with calendars, event planning websites, and everything anyone would need to make their special occasion run seamlessly."

Applause rang out through the crowded ballroom, and after Zach handed the plaque to the nervous young man, he casually scanned the tables, trying to find Sam. He found him, along with his friend, at a table in the back. All the tables in the front and center were purchased by the big-name software developers and the other major sponsors of the event, so Zach wasn't surprised to find the little guys conscripted to the tables with poorer visibility.

This was Zach's second year attending this particular conference which had become something of a big deal in the industry. The crowd was bigger, and with more well-established companies attending not only as presenters but as sponsors, he'd had to devote more time to the events than he'd expected. In past years, attending events like these, Zach had tried to make himself as invisible as possible, and after any awards ceremony, he'd sneaked out to hide in his hotel room, except for meals.

Tonight was different. His blood quickened at the thought of spending more time with Sam; for the first time in forever he wanted a man to touch him. To hold him close. The tenderness Sam had shown him last night could almost erase the humiliation he'd endured during the time he and Nathan had spent together. In fact, Zach had surprised himself with the eagerness of his response.

They'd agreed to meet at the hotel bar in the lobby half an hour after the ceremony ended. That would give Zach enough time to get out of the stifling constraints of his tuxedo and into something more casual for beach walking. That thought and whatever else might occur afterward spurred Zach on to press a few more hands, wish the winner a smiling congratulations, and head back to his room.

It was only after he'd stripped out of his clothes that Zach thought to check his cell phone messages. The happy anticipation over the night ahead with Sam drained from his body at the sound of his mother's nervous and tearful voice.

"I'm so sorry to bother you, Zach. I know it's your big night, but I had no one else; all the boys went away for the weekend, and I'm so alone. I think someone tried to break in, but I'm not sure; I heard breaking glass and strange sounds. I know I'll never get to sleep tonight; my heart is beating so fast."

The phone beeped off, and Zach was left not knowing whether to laugh or cry. He knew it was too good to be true that the evening he had planned and hoped for would go off without a hitch. But he couldn't get angry at his mom; she was all alone, and he was all she had. He'd shouldered that responsibility from the day his father died, promising himself never to let her down and always take care of her.

With a heaviness stemming from the knowledge his night was about to go up in flames, Zach called home.

"Hi, Mom. What's the matter?"

"Oh, you shouldn't have called. I'm fine really; my heart settled down. I saw someone in the backyard, but when I turned on the porch light, they ran away. I looked around to see if there was a broken window, but I couldn't find one." Her laughter belied her shaky voice. "When are you coming home, in the morning?"

Zach looked at his watch, making a swift calculation. If he left now, he could be home hopefully by midnight. "Nah, I was thinking of coming home tonight."

"I ruined your evening, didn't I? I didn't mean to, I'm sorry."

"No, no," he soothed, not wanting her to disintegrate into tears. "It's boring here, and there's nothing to do. The dinner is over, so I can be home before you even realize I was gone."

"Oh, sweetheart, I always know when you aren't around. I know I'm a burden to you, and I don't mean to be. I can't help it. Even after all these years,"—her voice dropped to a whisper—"I still miss your father." She laughed again, but there was little humor behind it. "Maybe I am crazy."

Zach's heart broke for her, and he understood her fear. The pain of solitude was like a snarling pack of wolves snapping at your heels, waiting to devour you if you let down your guard.

Lucky for him, he had his friends, and when it got too bad, they were always there to meet for breakfast; he could get lost in their absorbing lives, and for those few hours at least, Zach's equilibrium centered, and he could move forward. His mother had nothing; it was only recently she'd begun to volunteer at the senior center, and when he tried to push her to involve herself with other charities she'd balked, claiming it was too fast. One baby step at a time.

"You're not crazy, Mom, you're sad. I miss him too. But your sadness is overwhelming you and making it impossible to live your life."

"Don't be silly," she said, her voice snapping with anger. "I'm perfectly capable of living my life. I had a momentary lapse, and now I'm fine. I don't know why you called if you're only going to yell at me."

Sadly, Zach understood why she lashed out at him; she was embarrassed and ashamed. "I'm not yelling at you. I'm going to come home, and that's it."

"But, but don't you have people you want to see and plans?"

For one brief second he remembered the frantic kisses from last night, when he and Sam were so desperate for each other they'd barely made it to his bed. Disappointed as he was, Zach owed his mother so much more than to put her off for a second night of sex with a stranger, no matter how amazing that sex would be.

"Nah. Like I said, it's full of boring people. I can pack and be on my way home within half an hour. Try and relax, make sure all the doors and windows are locked, and I'll call you when I'm close to home, okay?" He hoped the forced cheeriness of his voice would fool her.

"Oh, I know I'm being selfish, but I'm glad you're coming home. I feel better when you're close. Not that something couldn't happen to you here in New York, but still…"

"It's fine. I'll see you soon. I love you, Mom."

He ended the call and, on autopilot, moved through his room, swiftly packing the few belongings he brought with him. Since the company sponsoring the convention was paying for him, Zach didn't need to worry about the bill. At the last moment before shutting the lights, he remembered the condoms and lube in the night table drawer. With a sigh of what could have been, he retrieved them and tossed them into his bag. Zach shut the lights and left the room.

At the front desk, he handed his cardkey to the young woman. "Could I leave a message for someone?" Zach had realized he didn't even know Sam's telephone or room number. "His name is Sam Stein, and he's registered here, but I don't know the room."

"I can't give out a guest's room number, but I can put you through, and you can leave him a phone message, or I can give you paper and an envelope, and you can leave him a note; so if he inquires at the front desk, we'll give it to him."

Zach thought for a moment. "Can I do both?"

"Certainly." She checked her computer, punched in some numbers and handed him the phone.

Wishing he had more privacy, Zach spoke as neutrally as possible, unable to show how disappointed he really was. "Hey, Sam. It's Zach. I, uh, had an emergency at home I had to take care of, so I ended up leaving tonight. Sorry I messed up our plans." He hesitated for a second, unsure what else to say. "Um, well, ah…have a great rest of the weekend. Bye." Zach stumbled over his words, realizing with a sinking feeling he'd probably never see Sam Stein again.

The desk clerk gave him a sympathetic smile and handed him a pad with hotel stationary, a pen, and an envelope. "Here you are, Mr. Cohen. When you finish, give it to me, and I'll make sure your friend receives it."

Zach gave her a grateful smile. "Thanks."

What to say, Zach wondered, sitting down in one of the hotel chairs. He couldn't say he had to run home to take care of his mother; he didn't owe Sam or anyone else an explanation for why he did what he did. There wasn't much else then. He didn't even leave his phone number; just a short and to the point message that didn't expand much on the voice mail he left, with one exception.

Had to leave. I was really looking forward to our walk. I guess it's just one of those things I'll have to keep wishing for.

He folded the paper up, slipped it into the crisp envelope, and sealed it shut. The desk clerk took it from him and pointed toward the main entrance. "Your car is waiting out front, Mr. Cohen. I'm sorry you had to cut your stay short, and I hope you'll return soon."

With his mind still filled with images of what might have been tonight, Zach thanked her with a half smile and left, crossing the lobby at a swift pace, as if now that he'd decided to leave, he couldn't wait to get away.

The entire ride home was spent staring out the window into the darkness of the road rushing past. For the first time in years, perhaps forever, Zach resented his mother, resented the life he'd built for himself where everything he did was for the most part to please other people. He was always the good one, the one who could be counted on never to say no when asked for a favor, to be there no matter the inconvenience to himself personally, because of what a nice guy he was.

Marcus wasn't kidding when he said nice guys finish last, that most guys liked a bastard. Zach had been finishing last all his life and was tired of it—tired of being last on the list for love, last on living his life. There was no one he could blame for his choices but himself. He'd painted himself into the proverbial corner by being so nauseatingly agreeable.

But remembering how his mother had stood with him and supported him through everything, Zach bit down on his resentment; from when he was little and couldn't understand why no one but Marcus would play with him to when he got older and spent most of his weekends alone at home, helping her with the food shopping and whatever else she needed. She told everyone what a perfect son he was: so helpful and uncomplaining.

How could he ever turn his back on her, even if it all became a bit too much for him to bear?

Despite the uncomfortable ride and the thoughts rolling around in his head, Zach must've dozed off at some point because he woke up as the car glided to a stop in front of his house. He scrambled out of the car, reaching back in to grab his overnight bag and unhook his garment bag from where it hung in the back.

"Thanks," said Zach, peering into the front window at the driver hidden behind tinted glass.

"You're welcome, sir." The driver tipped his hat, and the car pulled away from the curb, leaving Zach standing outside his house. The front porch light glinted off the two windows, and Zach could see the inner glow of light from the back of the house, indicating his mother was most likely still awake and in the kitchen waiting for his return.

Though his body still ached pleasantly, as much as Zach hated admitting it, he knew within days, the recollection of Sam's taste and touch would fade. He wondered how people like Marcus did it; jumped from man to man without any care or feeling. How did a person learn to disassociate the heart from the head?

He thought it would be easy to come home and forget about the encounter with Sam; after all, it was only one night, and they barely knew one another. What Zach didn't count on was that in leaving Sam, he might have left a little piece of himself behind.

There was no time for him to dwell on this, Zach thought, trudging up the steep front steps of his house. It was what he'd planned on all along, a fun weekend and then back to life as he knew it. And he had no intention of telling the guys; let them think he'd missed out on his opportunity to let loose and have fun. It was more than likely what they expected from him anyway. Without incriminating pictures or some other proof, Zach had no doubt neither Marcus nor Julian would believe that he'd slept with a man he'd just met.

Zach had trouble understanding it himself, but it didn't matter. He'd have that memory to hug tight when his loneliness got too much to bear in the coming months. He opened the front door and headed to the back of the house and the kitchen, where, as he'd suspected, his mother sat with her ubiquitous cup of coffee, an anxious expression on her face.

"Oh Zach, I'm sorry. I'm such a terrible mother." The regret in her voice was real; she couldn't help her fear. It was there, a live force consuming her every day movement, until one day, Zach feared, she may decide it wasn't worth the pain. He faced her tearful gaze. "I ruined your weekend with my stupidity, didn't I?"

Ignoring her self-pitying remarks, he bent to kiss her cheek. "Mom, you shouldn't be up," said Zach, chiding her gently. He dropped his bag on the floor and draped the garment bag over the empty chair; his father's chair. "And it's not a big deal. I didn't have any plans. Really." He forced a smile, knowing it would appease her.

And he was correct, watching her anxious look replaced by her smile. It hurt Zach to think his homecoming was the only reason she would be able to rest easy tonight. He sat across from her at the kitchen table, noting the pronounced lines on her face. Lines that grew deeper with each passing year. He'd never forgotten when the police showed up at their house to tell them his father had been struck and killed by a hit-and-run driver; overnight his mother aged, the light and laughter disappearing from her eyes.

"It's not that late, only a little after twelve thirty. I was watching television." She indicated the small TV sitting on the wrought-iron baker's rack. "They have some very interesting shows on late at night; teen pregnancies, joke playing, and naked dating." Her brow furrowed. "Who thinks up this stuff? Naked dating?" She shook her head in disbelief. "I don't get your generation at all."

They shared a laugh, and she gave him a cup of hot coffee. Zach didn't worry about it keeping him awake; there was little sleep left in him. Most likely he'd be up thinking about Sam, regretting what might have been, what could have been, and what would never come to pass.

Chapter Eight

"Nervous?"

Sam fidgeted with his cutlery. "Why would you say that?" The dinner and ceremony seemed interminable, and all Sam could think of was the night to come, walking on the beach with Zach, and what would come afterward.

Tonight he'd let down his usual guard, and Henry, perhaps sensing that weakness, swooped down on him like a hawk to a field mouse.

Henry smirked. "Oh, maybe because you haven't stopped staring at Zach Cohen on the stage, and your leg is bouncing around like an out of control spring."

Shit. That was the problem with having a best friend who not only knew him almost—if not better—than he knew himself, but was an investigator in his own right. Henry may work on computers, but he had that enviable ability to hone in and pick out the one weakness or flaw and, if he chose, exploit it. That, and being married to a woman like Heather, who was the smartest person Sam had ever met, despite—as he liked to tease her—marrying Henry.

"I have an itch." Sam forced his leg to remain still and reached for a roll from the bread basket.

"Itch my ass. Admit it. You like the guy. I don't blame you; I already told you I think he's brilliant. One of *Forbes Magazine*'s Up and Coming, a millionaire before the age of thirty. Come on." Henry's eyes narrowed with a seriousness Sam hadn't seen since he broke up with Andy. "The guy has it all, and you like what you see."

Unwilling to engage in conversation any further, Sam chose to butter his roll instead of speaking, but from under lowered lashes his gaze remained focused on Zach, even when other members of their table arrived. He managed to give them all a perfunctory greeting, while keeping an eye on Zach up on the stage. From his body language, Sam sensed Zach wasn't thrilled to be there, but the audience couldn't tell from his carefully neutral, pleasant expression. It was an expression Sam sensed Zach had perfected and used much of the time.

It pleased Sam, perhaps almost in an inordinately ridiculous way, that he alone in the entire room of industry professionals knew how Zach Cohen tasted, knew the weight of his body and the feel of muscles sliding under Zach's smooth skin. Only he had heard Zach—the cool, unruffled, and reserved man up on the stage—moan Sam's name as he came apart in Sam's arms. Zach wore his glasses tonight, and Sam wanted to push him up against the wall and, with Zach wearing only those glasses, fuck him until he screamed Sam's name again.

Cheeks burning, Sam gulped down his ice water only to catch the knowing eye of Henry, whom he studiously chose to ignore for the remainder of the dinner, deciding to talk to the other men and women sitting at their table. He had thought he'd be bored, but Sam found himself drawn into conversations of computer security, so when the actual dinner and ceremony came to a close, he was pleasantly surprised and wide awake, in spite of it being close to ten o'clock.

Now for the fun part of the evening. He exchanged cards with the other people at the table who'd already stood up to leave. It seemed everyone had places to go and after-dinner plans. Sam glanced up at the stage, hoping to catch Zach's eye, but it was empty; only the row of unoccupied chairs remained. Zach must've returned to his room to change out of his tux, and Sam had every intention of doing the same. When they walked on the beach later, he didn't want to wear anything restricting his body.

"Well," he said, standing up and addressing Henry, who remained seated, answering a text on his phone. "I'm going back to my room to change."

Without missing a beat from tapping on his phone, Henry grinned. "And to meet Wonder Boy?"

"Shut up." Sam kicked Henry's foot. "I'll see you tomorrow."

"But not too early and not for breakfast, right?" Henry's grin grew wider.

This time Sam joined him in a smile. "Got that right."

The room had emptied out until only a handful of people remained. Earlier that afternoon, when he and Zach had returned from the beach, they'd arranged to meet downstairs in the lobby bar after the dinner was over. Thinking of the night to come, Sam hurried back to his room, stripped and jumped into the shower, relaxing under the heated spray. He rolled his shoulders, the tenseness in his muscles melting away.

Not fifteen minutes later, Sam stood in front of the

bureau, buttoning up his shirt. Although his hair still curled in damp waves around his neck, he had no desire to waste time and blow-dry it, not when he had Zach waiting for him downstairs. It was stupid how neither one of them had thought to exchange phone numbers, but it was easy for Sam to forget; despite working for a computer forensics firm, he was hardly the tech-savvy type. In fact—he smiled to himself, sliding his phone into his pocket—if it was up to Henry, Sam would've had a smartphone years ago, instead of doggedly remaining with his old flip phone.

"All right, let's do this," he muttered to himself, closing the door behind him. The elevator took no time, and he traversed the lobby with eager steps, surprisingly excited about the night to come. Sam surveyed the bar area, but failed to spot Zach. He settled into a chair at a small round table, and a smiling, barely dressed cocktail waitress, sleek black hair twisted in a knot, immediately appeared at his side.

"What can I get for you, sir?" Her keen brown eyes assessed him with an interested look, and her white smile brightened considerably.

Wrong team, Sam wanted to say, but refrained.

"I'll have a Heineken."

"Bottle or on tap?"

"Bottle, please."

She sashayed away, but he barely registered her leave-taking, he was so caught up in keeping his eyes opened for Zach. The glass and beer bottle appeared in front of him, and he absently thanked the waitress while checking his watch. Zach was only fifteen minutes late, but Sam thought if he wanted to see him, he'd have made an effort to come on time. Sam remembered last night he was a little late to their dinner, and eased up on his growing impatience.

Half an hour later, the beer finished and his patience long gone, Sam paid for the drink, and leaving the disappointed waitress a nice tip, left the bar. At a loss as to why Zach would stand him up after the afternoon they'd shared, Sam stood in the lobby, momentarily at a loss, before heading toward the front desk.

Several people milled about in front of him, and it took another fifteen minutes before he reached the desk clerk.

"May I help you, sir?"

Finally. "I'm trying to find a guest. Zach Cohen?" His nervous fingers played a tap dance on top of the smooth granite surface of the check-in desk.

"I was supposed to meet him down here almost an hour ago, but he hasn't shown. He was a presenter with the conference tonight. Could you ring his room for me?"

A knowing light sparked in her eyes. "Oh, yes. Are you Mr. Stein?" She held an envelope in her hand, and Sam could see his name printed across the top. An uneasy feeling flooded through him.

"Uh, yeah, I am."

"Here. Mr. Cohen left this for you before he checked out." She extended her hand and presented him with the envelope that signaled the end of his evening plans.

"Thanks." With a grim smile he took it and shoved it in his pocket. No need to rip it open here in the lobby to read some lame-ass excuse. It was exactly what he'd suspected from the beginning. It was a Saturday night, and a guy like Zach Cohen wasn't going to waste it with a washed-up ex-cop like Sam. In between the time they'd parted ways on the boardwalk and the dinner, Zach had probably received a better invitation from his friends to return to the city and party and couldn't wait to leave.

He returned back to the lobby bar, and the same waitress, mindful most likely of the nice tip he'd already left once, hustled over to serve him again.

"You're back," she said, laying a napkin down and a small

bowl of salted peanuts. "Can I get you another Heineken?"

"Keep 'em coming until I tell you to stop."

Her brown eyes widened, but she said nothing, leaving him with a nod, only to return swiftly with a bottle and a glass.

"Bad news?" She poured it for him, and he watched the froth reach the top of the frosted glass, then settle down.

"Why do you say that?" He took a sip and welcomed the blessed slide of the cold liquid through his body.

"The look on your face. Like something or someone disappointed you."

"No," he said, and took another swallow of his beer. "No disappointment."

She walked away, promising to keep an eye on him and bring him another one when he finished.

"Can't be disappointed when you expect nothing," he muttered to himself. The envelope crackled in his pocket. "What the hell." Sam ripped open the seal and pulled out the sheet of paper, scanning the few lines. Nothing he read made him feel any better, no *I'm sorry* or any explanation.

If this was what awaited him in the dating world, he hadn't missed anything by staying at home, and it reconfirmed what he already knew: he wasn't cut out for the party lifestyle. Maybe Henry signing him up for that life coach wasn't so wrong, though he'd be damned if he'd tell him so. So much had changed in his life, from the breakup and his retirement to figuring out what the next step in his life might be; it couldn't hurt to get a fresh perspective.

The third beer went down easier than the first two, and at that point Sam knew it was time to leave before he couldn't get up from the chair of his own accord. It would not be a pretty sight to have someone come and haul him out of the bar. Weaving slightly as he stood, Sam tossed several bills on the table, and with as much dignity as he could muster in his drunk-ass state, slowly made his way to the elevator and into his room where he hit the bed, fully clothed.

All afternoon, and throughout dinner this evening, he'd planned on having Zach with him in this bed. Last night's encounter had so far exceeded his expectations, Sam hadn't known what to think. Everything about Zach excited Sam; his soft mouth with its plush, warm lips and hot, eager tongue, his slim hips and round, perfect ass, and those killer blue eyes framed by long, curling black lashes that pierced right through the calm, unruffled life Sam had created for himself, sending him spinning out of control.

Over the span of his prior relationship, Sam's sex drive had lessened in intensity and ardor. And whatever desire there had been between him and Andy, if Sam admitted to himself, had burned out long before their breakup; they'd been holding on to the thread of a relationship that had unraveled, without either one of them expressing the desire or having the capacity to sew it back together and make it whole again. He'd been living a farce, Sam now understood. People believed being a policeman meant Sam was a tough bad-ass, incapable of emotion, interested only in the physical. But for Sam the physical part of their relationship was only half the equation.

Making love with Zach, opening himself up to another man, had revived the deeply buried hunger within Sam for a personal connection; for something more than sex. Now, to have lost it when it had been there at his fingertips, giving him an elusive taste of passion that disappeared as rapidly as a virgin's smile, had him wondering if it had all been in his mind. Lying in his bed, drunk, body aching with want for a man who no longer existed for him, Sam fell asleep.

* * *

It was never a good sign to wake up with a pounding head and a furry mouth. The damn bright sun pouring in through the half-drawn blinds had Sam almost whimpering, his fingers clawing at the sheets to pull them over his head, shielding his eyes. Damn, when was the last time three beers had brought him to his knees? Probably when said three beers were consumed within a one-hour time period. He hadn't bothered with the rubbery chicken dinner they'd served at the awards banquet, counting on some after-dinner snacking from room service that had never materialized.

"Fuck my life." Several minutes passed before he found the strength to lift his head from the damp pillow. Gingerly, he rolled on his back, grateful his still-attached head traveled along with the rest of his body. The blinking red light on the phone next to the bed caught his eye.

It was safe to move, Sam decided, then grabbed the phone and pressed the button to retrieve his message. He wedged the receiver in between the pillow and his head and listened to his message.

"*Hey, Sam. It's Zach. I, uh, had an emergency at home I had to take care of, so I ended up leaving tonight. Sorry I messed up our plans. Um, well, ah…have a great rest of the weekend. Bye.*".

Coupled with that note which told him virtually nothing, Sam decided to forget about Zach Cohen. If he wanted to, Sam knew he could find out more about the man in a matter of minutes; between his investigative skills and Henry's—if he chose to ask for his help—the two of them could find out what the guy had for breakfast last Tuesday if they wanted to.

There was no point to it though. Zach had proven to Sam what he'd already feared: that Sam was a one-night stand, and Zach never had the intention to continue on after the weekend. Sam tossed the phone on the bed, pushed himself up to a sitting position with minimal carnage to his remaining living brain cells, and went to the bathroom to try and make himself feel somewhat human again.

Standing under the shower until it ran cold gave him some perspective. Why did he have any expectation other than sex and a good time? That was why he came here this weekend, after all. He turned off the water, dried himself off, brushed his teeth, and shaved. Getting dressed to go home took nothing more than pulling on shorts and a tee shirt and jamming his baseball cap on top of his head.

It took only seconds to throw the few belongings he brought in his overnight bag and leave a tip for the maid. The phone rang, and though he knew it had to be Henry, for a moment he wished it were Zach calling to talk to him and apologize. Angry with himself for dwelling on a man who proved to be less than what he'd seemed to be, Sam grabbed the phone and answered a bit harsher than he probably should've.

"Yeah?"

"Good morning to you, too, sunshine." Henry's cheerful voice grated on Sam's nerves. "Sounds like someone didn't get something stroked last night."

"When are we leaving?" Dull pain throbbed behind Sam's eyes. Drinking to excess had never been something he overindulged in, and Sam had forgotten the utter misery of a raging hangover. He slipped on his sunglasses, welcoming the darkness. "I'm ready whenever you are."

"I'm ready. Meet you downstairs in five minutes, okay?"

"Yeah." Sam replaced the phone in the cradle and glanced around the room briefly before picking up his bag and leaving. On the ride down the elevator, he steeled himself to field questions from Henry, but to his surprise, his friend merely gave him a quick nod hello when they checked out, and nothing more.

It wasn't until they were on the highway and Sam was fiddling with the radio looking for some decent music that Henry spoke.

"I've given you your space so far, you know, because you're so damn touchy all the time, but are you going to tell me what happened last night?"

Sam's finger hovered over the button on the dashboard for a second before he jabbed it, and Britney Spears came on. Henry quirked a brow but said nothing.

"There's nothing to tell. The guy went back to New York and left me a note saying he was sorry. End of story."

"And you're going to let it end; you won't try and contact him when you get back to the city?" A car cut them off, and Henry swerved and swore. "Fucking asshole."

"Are you talking to me or them?" Sam wasn't so sure of the answer.

"Both of you." Henry changed lanes, settled to a reasonable 70 mph, and Sam braced himself for the onslaught of questions. Sneaky bastard that he was, Henry waited until Sam was a captive audience before attacking him.

"If the guy wanted, he would've left me his number. It's no big deal; why are you blowing out of proportion what was only a weekend hook-up? Nothing more, nothing less."

Henry grunted. "Bullshit. I've known you almost your whole life and haven't seen you that caught up in a guy in years."

"Not true."

"Liar. And I'm going to prove it."

The struggle to keep quiet was real. Several miles flashed by on the parkway with only Britney singing "Hit Me Baby One More Time," before Sam gave in.

"All right. Prove it." Sam shot Henry, who had a shit-eating grin on his face, a dirty look. "I'm gonna regret this, aren't I?"

"Nah," said Henry cheerfully. "Once I saw how much you liked him, I did a little research—"

"Snooping," corrected Sam.

Henry remained quiet. "Okay, sorry. Go ahead," prodded Sam.

"My research brought up a story in a small indie computer magazine that did a profile on Zach Cohen when he sold his app and began to really make a name for himself. It talked about not only his rise in the industry but also about his personal life. How one of his best friends owns a club in Tribeca called Sparks, and they, along with the fashion designer Julian Cornell, their other friend, meet for breakfast every week or so to keep in touch and stay close. Nice, huh?"

"Yeah, so? We meet and play ball on the weekends. Same thing."

Henry sped up to pass a slow-moving SUV, glaring at the driver through the window. "Well, I was telling you this because they gave the name of the restaurants they go to. One's in downtown Brooklyn near you, and the other's in SoHo. Maybe you want to check it out."

"You're suggesting I stalk the guy to find him? That's fucked up, even for you." Still…there was a quality about Zach, sweet but with an edge of steel, that appealed to Sam. A past of hidden heartbreaks Zach was quick to hide, revealed in the moments of quiet vulnerability they'd shared on the beach the other night and sitting together the next afternoon. But Sam had glimpsed it, albeit for a brief moment. It was enough, however, to make Zach unforgettable.

Sam stared out the window, watching as the landscape changed from rural to suburban, then back to the ugly grittiness of the warehouses, steel and cement buildings along the Turnpike. The traffic built as they approached New York City. Henry's incessant tapping on the steering wheel and frustrated sighs proved too much for Sam to ignore.

"What already? You've been dying to talk for the past hour."

They sailed through the EZ Pass lane and entered the Holland Tunnel before Henry chose to speak.

"I only want to see you happy again."

And damn if that didn't hit Sam harder than anything Henry could have said to him right then. He struggled for composure, unwilling to give into the emotions battering him from the inside. Always an expert at hiding his own feelings, it was the reason Sam thought he recognized a kindred soul in Zach.

Henry pulled up in front of Sam's house and killed the engine. "I'm sorry it didn't work out the way you wanted it to this weekend, but you shouldn't let it keep you in the house and hiding away from people. Just because it didn't work with Zach, doesn't mean—"

"Henry?"

"Yeah?"

"Shut up and give me the info."

Chapter Nine

Since his appearance last month at the awards ceremony, Zach had been inundated with requests from the media for interviews and from technology companies for help in development. He'd spoken to some of the lesser known publications, in an effort to help out the small, independent tech magazines and websites trying to make it, and had recently agreed to do beta-testing for some software companies. If all it took was a healthy bank account to be content, he'd be the most satisfied man in the world.

Instead, Zach was lonely beyond belief.

Even more so than before, he kept to the house, hiding from his friends, ignoring their attempts to lure him out. When he wasn't working, Zach spent his time staring at his screen, seeing nothing but the image of Sam. With the passage of days and then weeks, even that had blurred around his memory's edges, erasing the aching of want, leaving him with nothing but the sting of his own cowardice.

"Yep, you are one stupid coward."

The door at the top of the stairs opened, and light spilled into the room.

"Zach, sweetheart, isn't it a little early for you to be on the computer already? You spent the whole night down here as well." His mother, dressed in one of her usual, colorful outfits, held on tight to the banister, the steep steps forcing her to move slowly. He watched as her small frame came into view.

"I'm coming up, Mom." He logged off the different message boards he'd been reading and saved his notes on the app he was beta-testing. "I had to finish something first."

She'd reached the bottom of the steps, and her gaze swept the room, lighting on the corner where Zach sat with his two computer screens in front of him, various laptops open on the long table behind him. "I don't understand what you do down here, but I guess that's to be expected. But please, come up and have some coffee at least, and see the light of day." She smiled at him. "If I didn't know any better I'd swear you were a vampire."

He shared a laugh with her, stood and stretched the kinks out of his back. "And coffee sounds great. I always need some, even when I'm meeting the guys for breakfast."

He followed her upstairs, into their small but comfortable kitchen. Funny how his father had been dead for more than half of Zach's life, yet his mother still set three placemats at the old wooden kitchen table, as if any minute Robert Cohen would come walking in through the front door and ask what was for dinner. As if the past eighteen years had simply been a bad dream they'd finally woken up from to find his smiling face with them once again.

He curved his hands around the warmth of the mug and sipped the cinnamon flavored coffee. "This is great, thanks." He drank more down and smiled when she automatically refilled his cup and sat across from him. "What're your plans for today? Are you going over to the senior center?" Since he'd returned from Atlantic City it appeared she'd made a greater effort to gather strength around her, to try to push aside the demons on her shoulders and become more independent.

Of course, he'd barely left the house, but Zach didn't dwell on that depressing thought.

"Yes. I'm reading to them and then running the book fair this afternoon. I may stay and help with the dinner service. I'm glad you're meeting the boys for breakfast today. You haven't seen them for a while. I hope you have something fun planned for the rest of the day and not coop yourself up in that basement." She kissed and patted his cheek, then stood, gazing at him with sad affection. "It's beautiful outside. Enjoy yourself."

Zach couldn't help but smile. No matter how old he and his friends were, his mother always called them her boys. Last night, both Julian and Marcus had texted and called him, threatening him with bodily harm and severe personal embarrassment—that from Marcus—if he didn't come to breakfast today.

"Yes, I am. I'll give them your love."

"Please do." She rinsed out her cup at the sink. "And tell Julian thank you for the tickets to the fashion show. I can't wait to go."

"I will." He kissed her cheek and hurried up the stairs to get ready. Within three quarters of an hour he was showered, shaved, and dressed. Pocketing his keys and wallet, he found his mother back at the kitchen table, planting seeds in little flowerpots.

"I thought it would be nice to grow fresh herbs." Her

hands were dirt-covered, but her smile was bright, and he breathed easier, knowing he could leave, and she'd be happy today.

"Great idea. I'll see you later."

Children played hopscotch and sold lemonade on the streets, and the pizza places had their takeout windows open, displaying ices for sale. It all spelled summer in the city: Zach's favorite time of year. The days remained long and heated, and there was always a thought of something new happening when you least expected it. Perhaps it was the bright sun, the birds winging their way in the leafy trees as he walked past, or the obvious joy on people's faces that warmth and light had settled in to stay for a few months.

Zach walked into the restaurant in Brooklyn Heights where he and his friends normally met. It was a nice walk from his house in Carroll Gardens, but he was ready for something cold to drink; the sun had already done a number on him, and he could feel a slight burn on his cheeks.

"Zach, we thought you'd forgotten about us." Marcus patted the chair next to him. "I was all prepared to send my surprise to your house to bring you over. Come sit. I ordered you a coffee, but nothing else to drink." He sipped his mimosa and waved over the waiter who hovered in the background with the menu in hand.

"George, bring me another, and what do you want?"

"I'm not that late, am I? Hi, Julian, Nick.

"Nah, he's being annoying as usual." Julian had a mimosa in one hand while the other was toying with Nick's fingers. Zach suspected it was an unconscious act; the two men constantly touched when they were near.

"I had two of my hottest waiters ready to go to your house and carry you here if you didn't show." Marcus's grin broadened. "You would've been grateful, trust me."

Zach rolled his eyes. "And I'm sure you know that from

personal experience. Sometimes, Marcus, I don't know whether to worry about you or be jealous of you."

"You know you love me. Now, where the hell have you been? Since you came back from Atlantic City we've barely seen you, and I believe we had a bet."

Zach thanked the waiter for his drink and ordered Belgian waffles with a side of fruit. "I've been busy."

Julian raised a brow. "Too busy to call or even text? We invited you out last weekend to Sparks, but as usual you blew us off."

Wincing from Julian's tempered rebuke, Zach shrugged. "You know it's not my scene."

"Yeah, but it was Nick's birthday, so I thought you'd be okay with coming to hang out."

Damn. "Sorry, Nick, and happy belated birthday." He caught Nick's eye and smiled. "I hope you had a good night."

"Well, when you didn't answer our text, we decided to postpone the festivities. It wouldn't be right to have a celebration without all of us there." Nick winked at him. "So now you're gonna have to come." He leaned back and crossed his powerful arms. "I won't take no for an answer."

"Nick, you've been promising me for forever to introduce me to some hot firemen." Marcus quirked a brow. "I mean, what's the point of having a friend who's uniform if he can't send some of the goodies your way?"

Julian snorted. "I would think you had enough to handle with all the pretty boys in your club."

"I can never have enough, baby. There are so many men yet to try in this city, there aren't enough days in the week and hours in those days." Marcus refilled his coffee from the thermal carafe. Zach watched Marcus as he took a sip without meeting anyone's eyes.

"Besides, this isn't about me today, we're here for Zach."

"What is this—an intervention?" Though Zach laughed, no one else joined in with him. "I'm fine, he's the one you need to worry about," he said, pointing at Marcus.

"Leave me and my sex life alone." Marcus turned the conversation back on him. "I'll tell you what needs to happen. Zach, you need to get out of that house. I love Cheryl; you know that, we all do." There was regret in Marcus's voice but also determination. He'd always vociferously argued against Zach living at home, insisting to anyone who'd listen that Zach should get his own apartment. "But no matter how much we love your mother, she's killing your chance at fun and a normal sex life."

"It isn't always about me and my personal life. She's my mother, and I'm all she has." He toyed with his cutlery and waited when the waiter put down his steaming, fragrant plate of waffles, syrup, and fruit. "I can't abandon her. It doesn't bother me when she butts into my life. I'm used to it."

"That's the problem, don't you see?" Though Julian spoke quietly and kindly, his face was shadowed with sadness. "You don't even care anymore. It's like you've given up on everything."

"And I'm sure she wants you to have fun and be happy, not sit at home all alone every night doing whatever the hell it is that you do all by yourself." Marcus stabbed at his eggs benedict. "Why do you think you're abandoning her?"

Zach's appetite fled, replaced by an uneasy sinking feeling in his stomach. "Can we stop talking about this now, please?" He doused his waffles in syrup, cut them into small bites and began eating without tasting a thing.

"No, as a matter of fact, we can't. All these years we've let you do your thing and hide away, blowing us off on weekends or at parties. It's gotten worse since you came back from A.C. You've barely talked to us about what happened there. Instead, you've hidden away even more. Are you ashamed of us?" Marcus held his gaze.

Horrified, Zach's fork fell from his hand to clatter upon the dishes. "Don't be insane. And yeah, I lost the bet in Atlantic City, but I didn't want to tell you guys and have you teasing me about failing to score."

"We'd never tease you. You know that, right?" Julian braced his elbows on the table, his green eyes dark with concern as he searched Zach's face. "I, for one, can't stand seeing you alone all the time, knowing you'd be happy with someone to love who loves you back."

The air in the room closed in, choking him. Sam's face rose before him, as clear and vibrant as when they made love that night, and Zach flushed hot and cold, from his sweating scalp to his toes which wouldn't stop clenching inside his sneakers. What a mess he was. "I know. And nothing happened in Atlantic City. I'm okay. You all need to let it go."

They ate their meal in relative silence, Marcus shooting him disapproving looks from under his dark brows, while Julian and Nick spoke quietly amongst themselves. Zach ignored him; there was never a point in engaging Marcus in a discussion since the man always thought he was right when it came to telling Zach how to live his life. Now that Julian had settled down into a life of domestic bliss, Marcus had no one to have fun with any longer, and Zach had a sinking suspicion he hadn't heard the end of Marcus's lectures and complaining.

Julian and Nick were deep in a discussion of their summer vacation plans, which involved renting a house by the beach and sailing. No longer hungry, Zach toyed with the idea himself of buying a house by the ocean—he and his mother could spend summers there, away from the oppressive humidity of the city. Wishful thinking, since she probably wouldn't want to leave the familiar comfort of her house. Still, Zach remembered that night, walking along the water with Sam, and how it had been one of the most romantic times of his life. Desire pulsed deep in his groin, and he hardened, remembering Sam's strong, sure hands and gentle kisses.

To Zach's surprise, Marcus moved his chair close to him, sliding an arm around his shoulders. Zach flinched; Marcus's touch felt wrong, out of place for the first time. Maybe because he'd been thinking about Sam and wished it was him and not Marcus. He thought he'd covered up his discomfort quickly, but not before Marcus pulled back to study his face. "What's wrong?"

"Nothing. I'm fine." Zach drank his coffee and forced a smile. "See?"

"I'm sorry if I pushed before. You know I meant it with the best of intentions, right?" Marcus's gaze anxiously searched his. "You're not like me; you want that happily-ever-after bullshit like those damn movies you watch. More than that, you're the one who deserves someone to love. For once you need to think about yourself and to hell with anyone else."

Touched, Zach planted an impulsive kiss on Marcus's cheek. "You deserve that too, for whatever reason you won't admit. But I love you, and you'll always be my best friend."

To Zach's surprise, Marcus didn't laugh or make a joke. "I love you too, which is why I worry about what you're doing with your life, why you hide away in that basement, never coming out with us or meeting anyone."

"I, I don't…" His weak protest failed to derail Marcus, who, now that he'd begun to speak, couldn't stop.

"You do," Marcus whispered, his lips close to Zach's ear so his voice barely carried. "You do, and I don't know why."

That old humiliation reared up, squeezing Zach's throat until it hurt to swallow. Nathan's demeaning treatment lived like a parasite inside Zach, feeding off his insecurities. Every night he told himself to be a man, to get over it. Neither Julian nor Marcus would ever allow another man to hurt them, and

Zach wished for even half of their confidence.

But Zach wasn't like his friends; his limitations stared him in the face, mocking him with the impossibility of changing who he was. He could be on the cover of every magazine in this country, and it wouldn't change a damn thing. In his mirror stared back the same nerdy, geeky Zach with the glasses slipping down his nose, the boy everyone laughed at when he couldn't kick the ball far enough, and who didn't curse or get drunk. The man who stood on the outside looking in, too shy to push himself on anyone. The last thing he needed was pitying smiles and attempts to persuade him what a wonderful guy he was.

Poised to answer, the smile faded from his lips and the words died in his throat when across the restaurant he met the eyes of an unsmiling Sam Stein.

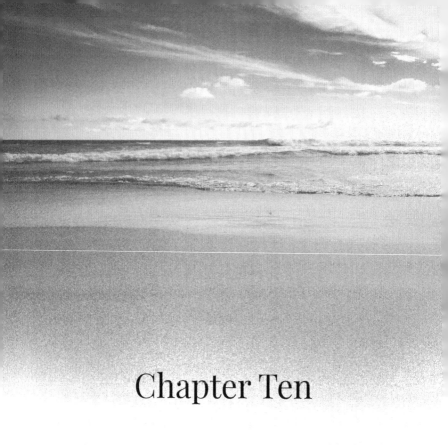

Chapter Ten

Summer had descended on the city; the elusive promise of the sun dragged people from their self-imposed exile out to soak up the warmth they'd only dreamed about in February and March. The sky stretched before him endlessly blue, and the leaves barely rustled with the tiny breath of fresh wind rolling off the water. Only the madly chirping birds playing tag in the bushes and the children running through the sprinklers in the park with delighted screams were having fun. The rest of the living plodded along, dreaming of air-conditioning and a large iced coffee. Extra ice.

It'd been a long time since Sam had someone to share the hot days and sultry nights with. He didn't think he'd miss it, but there was something to be said about holding hands and walking down the street with a lover. The last time he'd held anyone's hand had been over a month ago, in Atlantic City, when he and Zach walked along the beach that one night they were together.

On his way to meet Henry, Sam couldn't help but think, as he had done so many times since then, that it was only one night. How was it possible Sam couldn't put that memory and Zach out of his mind? He'd spent nights with other guys before, playing the dating dance—why had that night, that whole weekend, stuck in his mind?

The buzzing in his pocket startled him for a moment until he remembered his new phone. Stupid technology.

"What?"

"Damn, you're grouchy."

Despite himself, Henry's cheerful voice made Sam smile.

"And you're annoying."

"Guilty on all charges. Otherwise, your ass would be planted on the sofa, surrounded by old Chinese food containers. We might not find you for days."

"I'm walking, what is it?" Sam switched the phone to his other ear to dig out money to buy the newspaper.

"You can't walk and talk at the same time? I had more faith in you, Sammy."

"You're a comedian. A word of advice? Don't give up the day job." He smirked to himself.

Ignoring his witty comeback, Henry continued. "Listen. I did a little research, which required numerous hours reading Page Six of the *Post* and hours on social media, but I think I found him."

"Hours on social media. You love that shit, don't lie." Sam hesitated. "Found who?"

"Mr. Zachary Cohen, your weekend fling, the guy you've been moping about for a month."

"I have not been moping."

"Liar," said Henry cheerfully. "Besides, I'm not here to debate that point. Meet me at the Cadman Park Restaurant. If I'm right, your guy will be meeting his friends for breakfast."

A bit disturbed at how his heart sped up at that news, Sam refused to give in so easily. "I don't know. I was planning—"

"Nothing," said Henry, so blunt and to the point Sam winced. "You have nothing planned, which is why I am telling you to meet me because if you don't, I'm going to go over to Zach Cohen if he is there and tell him how much you've missed him and want to see him again."

"You really are a bastard, aren't you?"

"Yup. Be there in half an hour."

Sam heard a voice in the background and presumed it was Henry's wife. "Tell Heather I may have to kill you, so she should make sure the life insurance policy is paid up in full."

"Heather says she wants the first dance at your wedding, but I told her no. I get it." For a moment Henry was silent, though Sam knew he hadn't hung up. "I'll see you in a little while, right?"

"Yeah."

Half an hour later, he entered the restaurant and spotted Henry in a side booth, nursing a cup of coffee.

"Hey." He slid in the seat opposite his friend. Years of police work had blessed him with the ability to rapidly scan an area for suspects, and Sam immediately saw Zach wasn't in the restaurant.

Sam ordered pancakes and eggs, figuring if nothing else happened, he might as well have something to eat. "Why did you insist on me coming here?"

"You see those guys over there in the back?" Henry tipped his head to the side, and Sam glanced over his shoulder.

Two men sat together, one blond, one dark-haired and obviously a couple from their intimate touches and looks.

The other man, his back to Sam, gestured with his hands, in the throes of some story. His voice rose above the chatter of the other diners.

"Yeah, so?" The new phone he'd shoved in his jeans pocket poked him in his thigh, and Sam placed it on the table, between him and Henry, eyeing it like it was about to come alive and attack him.

"Those men are Zach Cohen's best friends." Henry accepted his toasted corn muffin from the waiter and unwrapped the little pat of butter. "It's my opinion," he continued, while spreading the butter on his muffin and watching it melt, "Zach will be joining them soon."

"Fucking hell." Sam fell against the back of the booth. "Why are you pushing this?"

Henry glared at him. "Because you're acting like an asshole by refusing to admit what I see, even if you won't. That you fell for the guy, and you're afraid of getting hurt again. And there's nothing wrong with being afraid. But to sit the rest of your life with the covers over your head? Jesus Christ, Sammy. What kind of life is that?"

Saved by the waiter bringing his food, Sam doused his pancakes with syrup and dug into his short stack. Henry opened his mouth, but Sam cut him off. "I'm not interested in a player. I had one of those already, remember?" Chewing on his food gave Sam time to marshal his thoughts. "Disappearing on me without any explanation or way to get in touch again was a player-asshole move." He swallowed. "I'm not afraid. I'm not interested."

Henry cocked a brow. "Do you really think that about him, because if you ask me—"

"I didn't, but you're gonna tell me anyway."

"You think you're better off staying at home, doing nothing and jerking off in the shower?"

"You're disgusting." Sam sipped his cooling coffee.

Thank fuck the waiter was there to pour him more to put an end to this conversation. He'd studiously ignored the corner where Zach's three friends sat.

"I speak the truth. You haven't gotten any in months, now you meet a guy you seem to hit it off with. Are you gonna pull the trigger and try and see if there's something between you two, or make do with dirty fantasies in the shower? I always thought that was a waste of a hard-on if there was someone willing to take care of my needs, you know?"

"Sometimes there's more to it than sex; you're married, you should know that." How the hell did he get dragged into a personal Dr. Phil show at eleven in the morning?

"You've already taken care of the sex part and seem to hit it off there."

Sam's eyes narrowed. "That's never been an issue. Sex is easy to come by. Trust, not so much."

"Heather says   "

"I love your wife, but she has no idea about my life, or what I'm looking for or want."

"Do you?"

Refusing to rise and take Henry's bait, Sam scowled, then jumped when his phone pinged and vibrated. "Jesus, does it have to sound like it's coming every time I get email?" With some trepidation, Sam picked the phone up and held it in the palm of his hand, staring at the screen.

"You're such a technology maven."

"Every time I get a message, the phone has a damn orgasm."

"Even your phone has a better time than you."

The waiter cleared their plates, and he asked for the check, tucking his phone back in his pocket without checking the message. It was probably from the life coach he'd actually seen a few times. She'd sent him exercises to do and lists of books to read. None of which he'd bothered with. Instead, he spent his time wandering his neighborhood, looking at all the happy couples, wondering how they knew the secret of keeping a relationship alive.

Though he wouldn't dare admit it to Henry, he'd even looked—not registered for but looked—at a few dating websites, reading profiles that all sounded the same.

I like exotic vacations, going out to dinner, and long walks on the beach at night.

His mind wandered back to the night with Zach on the beach—the soft warmth of his mouth and the hot clench of his ass. Damn, he wished he'd never met Zach Cohen.

I need to move on, Sam thought grimly. Though forgetting Zach was proving harder than Sam had imagined.

He scrubbed his face with his hands, blinking hard when to his shock, there he was in the flesh. Son of a bitch, Henry was right; Zach Cohen had shown up for breakfast with his friends. A very good friend from the protective way the man held him around his shoulders and the kiss Zach placed on the man's cheek. Anger warred with disappointment in Sam's chest, squeezing his heart.

"Fuck, that's him, huh?"

"Yeah." It was the only word he could spit out; his jaw muscles ached from grinding his teeth together. Even from across the restaurant Sam could see the deep connection between Zach and the other man. The kiss Zach gave him on the cheek was more than simple affection. It didn't matter— Sam had no desire to see any more; it was like a train wreck occurring before your eyes. You didn't want to see the crash, but you couldn't help but watch.

"Are you gonna go over there and say something?"

He never had the chance to answer Henry because at that moment, Zach met his eyes, and the shock on his face told Sam he'd never expected to see Sam again.

Anger surged inside him. Why the hell should he be the one to feel awkward—he wasn't the one who cheated on his boyfriend, then ran away into the night from the overwhelming guilt. Funny how Sam would've laid bets that Zach wasn't that type, but he supposed after being cheated on for years, his vision of what made a real relationship might be somewhat skewed.

"Yeah." Surprising himself, Sam rose out of his seat. "I think I'll go over and say hi to the happy couple."

"Sam." Henry's uncharacteristically somber tone drew Sam's attention.

"What?" He rocked on his heels, anxious to confront Zach. From the corner of his eye Sam could see Zach hadn't stopped staring at him, even though the boyfriend's arm remained around his shoulders.

"Don't make a scene. He doesn't owe you anything, and it's up to him to tell his story not you."

It wasn't anger so much as embarrassment. He'd opened himself up and once again to the wrong man. The thoughts played around in his head like an out of sync carousel as he walked toward Zach's table. Alarm flared in those blue eyes, and for a moment Sam felt sorry for Zach, and remembered his odd reactions when Sam held him down in bed and grabbed him by the shoulder on the boardwalk.

Was Zach being abused by this guy? Warning signals blared in Sam's head, and the anger drained from him, replaced by a heightened awareness.

"Zach, hi. Remember me, Sam Stein?"

Unbelievably, Zach's brow furrowed as if in deep thought. Was he really going to play that game with Sam?

"Um, yeah. At the convention last month, right? Sorry." Behind those black glasses Sam found so sexy, Zach blinked those big blue eyes of his. "Things were so hectic, and I have a terrible memory for faces."

Especially since you were face down in the bed while I shoved my cock inside you, huh? Remember that?

By some miracle Sam held his temper and his thoughts. "Yeah, the convention. I thought it was you, but I know what you mean. Sometimes I get it wrong and think I know a person when all along I was mistaken and they were never that person at all." He and Zach held each other's gazes and a faint blush streaked Zach's cheeks.

Good. Sweat a little.

The sound of multiple throats clearing caught his attention. Sam focused first on the two men sitting together. The blond man gave him an easy smile. "I'm Julian Cornell, and this is my partner, Nick Fletcher."

Sam gave them a brief smile. "Sam Stein, nice to meet you."

"Are you a computer geek too, like Zach here?" This was from the handsome man who still had his fucking arm around Zach. His sleek black hair gleamed in the sunlight, and his sculpted cheekbones and lips were all in perfect proportion to his face. Sam found himself the subject of scrutiny from the man's hard, violet-gray eyes and held that cool assessing gaze with his own. It wasn't in his nature to be intimidated, but damn if this guy didn't raise the hairs on the back of Sam's neck.

"No, I was a police officer. Now I'm retired and work as a private investigator. My friend Henry, who I'm sitting with, runs a computer forensics investigations firm."

"I'm Marcus Feldman, by the way, nice to meet you." Sam automatically took the hand Marcus extended, and they stood there, gauging one another, each one deciding if the other was good enough. Sam didn't appreciate Marcus's easy familiarity with Zach, but had no right to voice an opinion.

"Same here."

"So you and Zach met last month?" Marcus nudged

Zach. "You never mentioned anything to us. You said the conference was boring as usual." Once again, there was that assessing look from Marcus. "Sam here looks anything but boring."

And whereas Marcus couldn't stop studying him, Zach, his face red, kept his eyes averted and steadfastly refused to look at Sam, focusing instead on his half-eaten plate of waffles and the fascinating pattern of the table cloth. "He and I talked for a while; you know how it goes." Zach spoke so softly Sam almost missed what he said. "I didn't think he'd remember me."

Marcus's eyes narrowed, and Sam could almost see his mind working. "I see. No big deal." He tapped his fingers against the tabletop and, as if reaching some internal decision, dug into his pocket and pulled out a slim leather billfold. "Here, Sam." Marcus held out a card he'd extracted from his wallet.

Sam took the plain black plastic card. It simply said SPARKS in bold white letters, and when he flipped it over there was a strip running across the back and nothing else.

"Uh, thanks? But what…" He flipped the card between his fingers.

"That's my club. I'm the owner. The card is a pass. Anytime you want to come, show it to the bouncer at the door and you get in; your friends too. No cover, no waiting."

"Um, thanks." Another lie from Zach Cohen. The irrefutable proof the man was a partier was right here in Sam's hand. When your damn boyfriend owns a club, you spend your time with him there. He stuck the card in his back pocket. "Well, nice to meet you all. Thanks for the card, Marcus."

"Come tonight. Do you have plans?"

To Sam's utter surprise, Henry appeared by his side and answered for him. "No, he doesn't, and he'll be there."

Betting on Forever

He didn't know who he wanted to punch first.

Chapter Eleven

"I know you're both angry with me."

The pounding music might have been muffled by the closed door separating Marcus's office from the rest of Sparks, but the deep bass beat still managed to shake the floor beneath their feet. It was late in the evening, around eleven thirty, a time Zach would normally be watching television at home, or playing around on the computer. Instead, he found himself dressed in an outfit supplied by Julian, defending his cowardice to his two best friends who sat scowling across the room at him.

"This isn't fucking ninth grade; we aren't mad at you." Marcus threw his pen on the desk, his face tight with anger. Little ever managed to wipe the perpetual humor off Marcus's face; over the years Zach had been privy to those occasional blow-ups, and when it happened, it could turn very ugly, very fast.

"I can't speak for Juli, but what I'm pissed about is that you met someone in A.C. when you told us you didn't. So you lied. You told us it was no big deal, which I know is a bigger fucking lie by the way Sam reacted to seeing you. Why? Why are you lying about this? And what else haven't you told us, your best friends. You know, the ones who'd do anything for you?"

Too much, Zach wanted to say. *Everything.* How was it possible to be friends with people almost your whole life yet hide the most important part of you? Secrets, lies, and shame had been part of his makeup for so long Zach hardly knew truth from fiction. The ugly truth remained raw even after all these years, so vivid and alive he burned, remembering every hurtful word hurled at him, every painful touch on his body. Zach feared his friends' reaction if he ever told them, so he remained silent. Better that way than to listen to their roars of outrage.

"It didn't go anywhere. Remember, it was supposed to be a fling. That was the bet."

"Fuck the goddamn bet." The angrier Marcus got, the more vicious his swearing became. "You meet a fucking guy for the first time in forever, and you share nothing about it; you even fucking lie to us. What kind of bullshit is that?"

"Why didn't you say anything, Zach? You know we, or at least Nick and I, want you to meet someone. If Sam is that guy—"

"Will you both get off my back for once? This is the reason why. Because you don't let up." The spindle he'd wound all his grievances on had been kept so tightly wrapped all these years it allowed for no slack, but over the past few months it had begun to unravel, and tonight Zach's normal, patient attitude unraveled along with it. "I'm not your project to take care of; my life isn't a reality show you get to watch and vote on every week." Years of holding back the anger had built up, and now the curtain had finally ripped, allowing his hurt and shame to pour through. "I don't need your help, I never asked for it, and I want all of you to stay out of my life. What I do, I do for a reason, and I don't owe either of you or anyone else an explanation. Understand?"

The room spun, and he felt sick to his stomach, yet freer than he had in years.

Marcus stared at him, mouth open, eyes wide with shock, but Julian sat back in his chair, a small smile teasing the corner of his lips. "How long have you been wanting to say that to us?"

Breathing hard, Zach flopped back in his chair. "I don't know," he admitted. "Probably forever. I'm sorry—"

"Don't apologize," said Marcus. "Don't ever apologize for how you feel, especially to us. It's why we've been friends for so long. Right?"

And in all the years they had been friends, Zach couldn't recall Marcus so heartfelt and serious. The thing he appreciated most about his friends was their honesty. Still, that tiny niggle of doubt regarding Nathan got buried back down deep. He didn't trust himself to tell his story, and his dishonesty ate away at his heart.

"Yeah. So back off now, please, with this Sam thing, okay? It never meant anything, that's why I didn't tell either of you."

Julian stood and stretched. "I'll do what you asked, but you're only fooling yourself. If you like the man, you certainly know how to find him. I have to get home; Nick isn't feeling well, and I promised to bring him some chicken soup."

"Shit, you really have turned into the Happy Homemaker, haven't you?" Marcus stood and came out from around his desk. "Next thing you'll be telling me is you're gonna get married and have kids."

For once, Julian didn't smile or rise to the bait.

"One day, Marcus, I'd like to find out what happened to make you such a cynic about life. And," Julian added, smiling again, "I'd like to see you fall in love. When that happens, I won't say 'I told you so,' I'll say, 'Now you understand.'"

"Get out of here and go home to your boyfriend." With an affectionate shove, Marcus pushed Julian toward the door. "Zach and I are gonna have some fun tonight. After all," he grinned, and Zach knew he was in trouble, "if I'm not mistaken, he lost the bet and has to hang out here with me."

The phone rang, and Marcus answered it as Zach said his good-byes to Julian. A glint fired Marcus's eyes to dark violet when Zach faced him, after closing the door behind Julian.

"Ready to go out there and party?"

There was no forestalling Marcus once he was determined, and Zach had no strength left to fight. The good thing was Zach knew he'd only need to spend an hour or so at the club before Marcus would become distracted by a pretty face and forget about Zach, leaving him free to go home to his empty bed and thoughts of Sam. Lately, all he could do was think about the man and wonder what might have happened if he'd had the courage to stay.

From when he was a teenager, Zach hadn't had much experience with sex beyond a few hesitant kisses or touches, and Nathan had been the first man he'd had sex with. Coldness swept over him. This was not the time or place to think about Nathan and their time together. That relationship had been toxic; pure poison. It had taken him too long to see how he'd been used and deserved better. He'd only had a few flings after that, but it wasn't until Sam and their weekend together that he discovered the difference between having sex and making love.

Since that weekend, Zach had woken up every morning

with an aching hard-on, thinking about the one night they'd spent together. He'd taken more showers and jerked off more in this past month than he had since first discovering gay porn on the internet as a teenager.

With Sam, there'd been no problem with his sex drive; even now, he wanted to be back in that hotel room wrapped in Sam's strong arms. Zach still couldn't understand why a man like Sam would want him; except for a healthy bank account, he had little to offer anyone, once they got to know him.

"Yeah, let's get this over with."

Marcus opened the door, the waves of pounding music flowing over them. "If you have that attitude, it will be a disaster." He danced around Zach, swaying his hips. "Let the music move you and make you forget everything. Lose yourself in it. Drown in it." Marcus continued to move, bumping his chest, rubbing up close while they made their way to the front of the club.

"Is that what you do? Use this to forget everything?"

Instead of answering, Marcus grabbed his hand and pulled him onto the dance floor where he proceeded to undulate and flex his hips in an almost obscene manner. His arms twined around Zach's neck, and his lips brushed up against Zach's ear.

"Don't look now, but your guy is here, and from the way he's staring at me, he's one step away from coming on the dance floor and dragging you off like a Neanderthal." Marcus danced away from Zach, who suddenly couldn't move.

Blinking madly, his heartbeat racing faster than the beat of the music, Zach stared up at Marcus. "What?" He swallowed hard. "I couldn't hear you."

"Don't lie. You're all freaked out, like a deer caught in the headlights."

Zach remained mute; there was no answering Marcus back. Most likely he was correct.

"Do you want him? Fucking admit it already, Zach. Say it for once." Marcus's harsh voice breathed hot in his ear.

"Yes," Zach whispered back, desperate for the first time in his life with his own needs and desire. "I want him."

Marcus's face lit up. He grabbed Zach close and kissed him. "Well fucking hallelujah. Finally. Let's make sure you get him, then."

Strobe lights streaked, lighting up the dancers on the floor in garish colors, and Zach had a hard time tracking Marcus's swaying body in front of him. He'd always been an awkward dancer, missing out on the rhythm of the music and shuffling around in a tight circle. Aiming a glance over his shoulder, Zach no longer saw Sam glowering by the edge of the dance floor where he'd been standing only moments before.

"This isn't helping," Zach yelled over the music. "I don't see him anymore. Maybe he left."

Marcus took Zach by the hand and dragged him past the bar and down to the front of the club. Sam was nowhere to be seen, and Zach's confidence faded. "See, you were wrong. He wasn't interested."

"Bullshit. I've never been wrong; I know when someone's interested." Marcus looked around from side to side. "Ah." His face lit up. "There's our mystery man. Sam!" He waved, and Zach's heartbeat ratcheted up. "Sam, over here."

With a barely-there tilt of the head, Sam acknowledged them approaching. The tight-lipped grin on his rugged face failed to settle Zach's racing nerves.

"Where were you going?" asked Marcus. "Zach was looking for you."

"Oh yeah?" The disbelief in Sam's voice was not to be mistaken. "Why?"

"To…to talk to you. I didn't really get to speak to you this morning."

When Sam said nothing, Zach talked faster. "It was good to see you again. I'm glad you took Marcus up on his invitation and came tonight."

"Yeah, Sam," said Marcus, his ever-present smile broadening. "Come on back and have a drink with us."

Ignoring Marcus, Sam honed in on Zach's face. "Funny, it didn't seem as though you were glad to see me. You acted as though we barely knew each other. Is that because you didn't want Marcus to find out that we'd met and slept together?"

Before Zach could answer, Marcus grabbed him by the shoulder and spun him around. "You two hooked up? You didn't tell us that. You said you barely met." Marcus dug both his hands in Zach's shoulders, and Zach winced.

"Hey, stop. That hurts."

The next thing Zach knew, Marcus was on the ground with Sam standing over him, flexing his fingers. "Don't you lay a fucking hand on him. I've met guys like you; smooth bastards, always putting people down who you think are weaker than you." Zach stood rooted to the floor, still in shock that Sam had hit Marcus.

"Did he hurt you?" Sam stepped closer to Zach, eyes soft and voice gentling, its warmth touching Zach.

This could not have been any more bizarre to Zach; Sam defending Zach against Marcus? "I—I'm fine. Why did you hit him?" Old loyalties sent him kneeling by Marcus's side.

"Are you all right?" He touched Marcus's shoulder, hoping his friend's famous temper would be held in check.

To his shock, Marcus pressed his fingertips against his jaw and laughed weakly. "What is it about me that first Julian's boyfriend and now yours feels the need to punch me?" He stood, though remained careful to stay out of Sam's striking distance. "I'm a nice guy, why doesn't anyone see that?"

Ignoring Marcus, Sam faced Zach. "You're actually concerned about him? He's got you so fucked up in the head you're worried if I hurt him, rather than the fact that he put his hands on you?"

"What the fuck is he talking about?" The muffled curse from Marcus behind him had Zach acting the peacemaker.

"Stop, both of you." Zach stood in the middle between the two men, his heart thumping like mad. "Sam, I don't know what you're talking about. Marcus has never hurt me. Ever. He's my best friend." How had Sam come so close to the truth?

Sam's eyes narrowed, his grim face set in stone. "Is that what you call it? My best friend doesn't kiss and hump me on the dance floor."

Zach attempted to explain. "We've known each other all our lives; Marcus is like my brother. I could never be interested in someone like him."

"Hey, wait a minute," protested Marcus. "There's nothing wrong with me. What do you mean, 'someone like me'?"

Zach quirked a brow. "Answering that question might take all night. May I continue my explanation to Sam?"

With a broad sweep of his hand, Marcus gestured to Zach. "By all means. First explain to Sam we aren't dating, and that I'd never touch you."

The doubtful expression on Sam's face was worrisome. He'd already broken Sam's trust by leaving and then pretending not to remember him. He had to make him believe.

"He's telling the truth. Marcus would never think of hurting me. I don't know why you thought what you did, but there's nothing between us but a long-standing friendship. We're total opposites, but that's why we click. Please," Zach entreated, fearing if he let Sam go now, it might be the last time he'd see him. Knowing, now that he'd seen Sam again, how impossible that would be for him to take. "I'm sorry I blew you off earlier, but," he swallowed, his mouth dry and tasteless, "I'm glad you came by tonight, and I—I'd like you to stay."

For someone as shy and unused to personal drama as Zach, these confessions of the heart both unnerved him and made him want to throw up. It was entirely possible that Sam would blow him off and walk away. So when Sam, after studying him and Marcus, cracked a smile and extended a hand, Zach both inwardly cheered and almost passed out from the stress.

"I'm sorry, Marcus. I feel like a jerk decking you, but after Zach and I met the first night and everything went great, he just up and disappeared. I thought he had a boyfriend and discovered a guilty conscience."

One thing Zach loved about Marcus was that he never held a grudge, at least when it came to things friends-related. There was no hesitation in accepting Sam's apology and brushing it off. He even slung an arm around Sam, leading him toward his office.

"No worries. Come on back and we can get better acquainted." He deftly steered Sam over to the nearest bar, ordering two beers from the gorgeous bartender. The men Marcus hired to tend bar and wait tables were among the best-looking men Zach had ever seen. Marcus took their impossibly good looks for granted, barely noticing the flourish with which the young man presented the bottles and frosted glasses, probably in the hopes of impressing the boss.

"Tell me more about yourself than what I already know. For Zach here to be interested in someone, I know you must be special."

"What is this, an interview? Don't you have some place to be, someone to molest?" Now that Marcus had convinced Sam to stay, Zach wanted to talk to him alone and hopefully recapture some of that magic from Atlantic City. For the first time in his life, he wanted Marcus to go away.

"It's okay, Zach. I don't mind." Sam's smile reassured

him. "I was a police officer and retired from the force last year after putting in my twenty years."

"Did you have trouble being gay on the police force? We know from Julian's boyfriend Nick, who's a fireman, how hard it is for LGBT people in uniform to get respect from their peers."

Sam drank his beer and stared at the bottle in his hand. "It's happening, but much slower than we'd like to see. My captain never hassled me, but I don't think he was too thrilled with having a gay cop under his command, either."

Sensing the shift in the mood, Marcus guided Sam back to the more mundane "getting to know you" questions. "Where do you live, here in the city or in one of the boroughs?"

"I live in Brooklyn, in Carroll Gardens."

Providence, something that rarely smiled on Zach, now shone its bright light directly on him.

"So do I." He spoke for the first time since they had returned to the inside of the club. "All my life. But nearer to Red Hook than Cobble Hill."

"Yeah, me as well. It was the only place we could afford."

"We?" Marcus quirked a brow. "You have a roommate?"

"No. I lived with someone, but we broke up over six months ago."

Of course; a man like Sam wouldn't have been single all his life. He wasn't like Zach, afraid to challenge the place life assigned him as a child. He'd have had boyfriends, probably many. Normal people have relationships; they don't hide in their basements.

"That's tough. Well, good thing Zach here took our little bet. Otherwise you two might never have met."

"Bet?" Sam glanced over at Zach, confusion written on his face. "What bet?"

"Nothing. Marcus is making up stories as usual." Zach

pulled on Sam's arm. "Why don't we find a table in the back and sit down? We can get reacquainted."

"I'm not a liar; why the hell are you saying that?" Marcus stood in Zach's path, barring his way. "You didn't forget the bet; I know you. You meet a guy and hook up, and I have to be celibate for six months." His mouth curved up in an evil grin. "You lied to us and said you didn't meet anyone, so as far as I'm concerned, you've forfeited the bet, and I'm off the hook. Don't you agree with me, Sam?"

Eyes spitting fire, Sam slammed his bottle back on the bar. "A bet? It was all a setup for a bet?" The overhead lights flashed across his furious white face. "You let me fuck you, so why stay any longer?" His gaze raked a stunned Marcus. "It was all a game to both of you, huh? You can go to hell and take him with you." Sam jerked a thumb at Zach who wanted to fall through the floor. "I've already been screwed once in my life by someone I thought I knew. I don't need a stranger to do it again."

Then Sam disappeared, swallowed up into the writhing mass of dancers as he cut through the club to the front exit.

"That wasn't what happened," Zach whispered to Sam's retreating back. "It wasn't like that at all." Without taking time to think about it, Zach took off after Sam as if the hounds of hell were nipping at his heels.

Chapter Twelve

"A bet. A fucking bet." Ignoring the odd glances from the people he passed, Sam exited the club and began striding down the street, oblivious to his direction. "I'm such a fucking idiot." He continued to argue with himself while waiting for the light to change at the street corner.

I should've known something was off. And here I was worried about him being abused, when all along he was playing me for the fool.

"Sam." Red-faced and breathing heavily, Zach hurried up beside him. "Let me explain." Sweat beaded down his face from the humid evening air, and the silky dark curls plastered wetly against his head.

Doubt, shame, desire, and fear. All those damn emotions played within Sam, and he hated it, hated himself for hesitating even a second, for wanting to talk to Zach, yet not trusting the man to tell the truth.

"Please." Zach touched his arm, and Sam stiffened and drew away. "Come back to the club with me and if after I explain, you still don't care, then you can leave and forget we ever met."

Zach's blue eyes met his, and damn it if Sam didn't want him again; and that made him even angrier. But this time the anger was directed at himself. The bedrock of his relationship with Andy had been built upon lies and cheating. The last thing he'd ever do would be to allow himself to get swayed again, no matter how pretty Zach's blue eyes were or how hot and sweet his kisses tasted. He wouldn't get fooled again.

"Sorry, but I'm not interested. Been there, done that. You have fun playing around with people's emotions. It's what you guys do."

The stricken look on Zach's face almost changed his mind, but Sam held firm, knowing he would end up the loser in the end.

"Go back to your friend and enjoy. I'm going home."

Luck was with him tonight for once. The moment he held out his hand, a cab pulled up. Without another word, he jumped in and gave the driver his address. Despite what he'd said about not being interested, Sam couldn't help but turn around as they drove down the block.

Why did he feel like the bad guy watching a forlorn Zach recede in the distance?

*   *   *

The next morning Sam awoke with a fresh outlook, deciding to put Zach, his friends, and the entire damn Atlantic City episode behind him. Perhaps he'd begin dating again, perhaps not. One thing Sam knew for certain: before he opened his heart to a man again, he'd first make sure to check him out; there'd be no more pickups at the bar or allowing Henry to bully him into a quick decision. Nor would he allow himself to be blinded by lust. Never again would appearances sway him, no matter how soft and yielding the man's mouth might be under his own.

He hadn't been a police officer for nothing. Standing in the shower, soaping himself up, Sam vowed the next time he took a lover, there'd be no surprises. He liked his life neat and orderly and hated surprises.

Now that he'd settled his dating life, Sam was hungry. Nothing went better with fresh coffee on a Sunday morning than pastries from his favorite neighborhood bakery, so he pocketed his keys and slipped his phone in his pocket. There were several texts from Henry which he chose to ignore, not wishing to rehash last night so early in the morning without fortification.

But the God of surprises failed to take Sam's needs into consideration when he walked into Caruso's bakery and found Zach Cohen sitting at one of the small round tables, a cup of cappuccino and the crumbly remains of some pastry in front of him.

Hopeful eyes met his across the store, but Sam steeled himself to remain firm in his decision and ignore Zach, heading directly to the glass-topped counter featuring every kind of Italian delicacy imaginable. Leaving his own miserable personal life aside, Sam's happiness could definitely be measured in cannoli cream and fruit tarts, and no one knew how to make him happier than Mrs. Caruso.

"Ahh, Sammy, there's my favorite guy," she gushed. Seventy-five years old and perpetually in black since her husband's death five years earlier, Teresa Caruso had run this neighborhood institution for over forty years. Her twinkling black eyes, sharper than any late-night comedian's, flickered over to Zach, then back to Sam. "I think you have an admirer.

He came in about an hour ago asking if I knew you." As if they were buddies confiding secrets over a beer, Mrs. Caruso leaned over the countertop to whisper, rather loudly to his dismay, "He's a cutie, Sammy. Go sit and I'll bring you over your espresso and some treats."

He opened his mouth, but Cupid, who this morning had taken the form of a white- haired Italian grandmother in orthopedic shoes, shooed him off, refusing to listen to his protests.

"Go, go. Don't worry. You know I love all you boys; I never kiss and tell." She winked at him, and in spite of himself, Sam laughed and shook his finger at her.

"Mrs. Caruso, you're a bad one."

"Go on and sit down. Make that sad man smile."

With an inward sigh, Sam walked over to Zach, who gazed up at him, the solemn expression still etched on his face.

"Do I need to put out a stalker report? Because I remember last night telling you I didn't want to see you again." It might've come out a bit harsher than he intended, watching Zach's face pale in the early morning sunlight.

He didn't mean to be a bastard, but Sam didn't trust himself around Zach. The glimpse of that wedge of skin below Zach's throat, which Sam knew from personal experience tasted of salt and heat and felt soft to the touch of his tongue, defeated his intention to remain cold and impersonal. How could he hold back, when his body hardened and his cock ached at the very sight of this man?

"I remembered you mentioned this place when we were on the boardwalk, so yeah, I guess you can call me a stalker if you want." Zach spoke to the table as if he couldn't bear the sight of Sam's face. "But I wanted to give it one last shot, to see if you'd listen to the entire truth. Then, if you want to tell me to go to hell, at least I'll know you have all the facts."

Sitting down across from Zach at the tiny table, Sam's brain told him he was being an asshole, while his body cheered him on. He'd never been a man who thought with his dick, but the rapidly growing hardness between his legs was proving him wrong.

Mrs. Caruso placed a small cup of espresso and a plate with miniature cannoli and fruit tarts filled with pastry cream in front of him. The sweetness of the sugar mixed with the strong scent of the espresso, and Sam couldn't help but relax his grim expression to a smile of thanks for her.

"This looks amazing as usual. Thank you, Mrs. Caruso."

"My pleasure. Eat up. I brought enough for you and the boyfriend." Another wink from those gleaming black eyes; then she patted Zach on his shoulder.

"You know you're much cuter than that one Sammy wasted his time with before." With that pronouncement she returned to her place behind the counter, listening to her *Top 40* hits on the radio, and sipping her own coffee.

Sam bit into a fruit tart, enjoying the explosion of sweetness on his tongue. He sipped the espresso, staring out the windows which overlooked Luquer Street. He'd be damned if he'd be the one to start the conversation.

"I know you're mad, and you have every right to be. But you have me all wrong; I'm the furthest thing from a partier imaginable. I hate those places; Marcus forces me to go to them."

Sam swallowed another sip of espresso and eyed the rest of his tart before meeting Zach's anxious gaze. "Yeah. That's why you had a bet with him about meeting and screwing a guy that weekend, and lucky me," he said, laughing harshly, "I was your victim of choice. But here's the thing." Sam placed the tiny espresso cup on the table and stood up. "No one fucks me and plays me for a fool. I had enough of that shit already. So thanks for the explanation, but you know what? I really don't give a damn."

He took a ten-dollar bill out of his wallet and handed it to Mrs. Caruso who frowned at him but pressed her lips tight when he shook his head at her. "I'll see you during the week." The door bells tinkled over his head, and he walked out onto the street and headed back to his apartment.

"Sam, wait."

It was déjà vu from last night; Zach running after him, asking him to wait. Only this time he was a block from home and didn't need to wait for a cab. His long, purposeful strides made it harder for Zach to catch up, but halfway down the block, Sam saw from a side-eyed glance Zach fall into step next to him, breathing hard. Slowing down slightly, Sam remained silent, knowing Zach only had to catch his breath before he began to speak.

"There never really was any bet, at least not on my side. My friends were joking around, I think more to incentivize me to meet someone, but also play a joke on Marcus. If you knew anything about me, you'd know I'm the last person to play with someone's emotions."

"I don't know you at all."

"Then let me remedy that." Zach placed a hand on Sam's arm. "I'm so far out of my comfort zone here. I've never gone after a man; I'm not that type."

That caused Sam to stop in his tracks in the middle of the sidewalk. "Yeah? So why me? I'm nothing special. Why pick on me?"

Damn if Zach wasn't blushing bright red, and damn himself if Sam didn't find that a huge turn-on.

"I—I can't explain it. There's something about you that makes me feel safe,"—Zach licked his lips, and Sam couldn't help but be drawn to Zach's mouth, remembering its taste— "yet crazy reckless at the same time." He whispered so the passing parade of young mothers with strollers wouldn't overhear. "Chasing after a guy, following him—I can't believe I'm doing this. But I haven't been able to get that night out of my mind. Maybe it makes me a loser for telling you this, but I'm not a player."

Zach raised his eyes to meet Sam's, and Sam knew the other man spoke from his heart. "It's funny that I'm a man who's made millions creating a dating app, yet I'm the least likely man to have someone else want him." He shuffled his feet and kept his eyes averted. "But you did and we hit it off so well. I'm very sorry I ran out on you that night. It was wrong, no matter why."

"So you didn't go to Marcus's club?" Inching closer to Zach, Sam could see the sweat prickling Zach's brow and sense his vibrating tension. "Why did you run off?"

Six dogs strung together on their leashes pushed past them on the sidewalk, their cold noses bumping against Sam's ankles. This was not a conversation for the public street, he guessed. Eyeing Zach, noting how his eyes darted side-to-side and his face remained tinged with pink in the aftermath of his furious blush, Sam let his instincts take over and decided to give Zach one last chance.

"Want to come back to my place where we can talk with more privacy?"

"Yeah?" The tentative smile of hope on Zach's face sealed Sam's belief that Zach was now telling him the truth and relief flooded through him.

"Yeah, follow me." Sam led the way down the block past the brownstones and neatly kept brick townhouses with beautiful gardens in the front, to the small one-bedroom apartment he rented. He'd always wanted a house, but on a cop's salary he could never afford the prices the homes were fetching now. Twenty years ago yes, but he wasn't thinking about planning for his future back then.

"Come on in." He entered, tossed his keys in the bowl by

the door and headed into the kitchen. "Want some coffee? I didn't have a chance to finish mine at Caruso's. As a matter of fact, I missed out on my cannoli."

To his delight, Zach held up a white paper bag he hadn't noticed before.

"Is that—?"

With a shy grin but a sparkle in his eyes Zach nodded to his unasked question and that prickly awareness of desire swept through Sam once again.

"I had her throw them in a bag before I ran after you; no way could I leave these babies behind." Zach handed him the bag, and their fingers brushed; his grin faded, and he pulled away from Sam, a disconcerted look remaining on his handsome face.

"Um, well here you go." And he retreated to the living room to sit on the sofa, staring off at nothing.

This was not the same man he met last month, Sam decided, as he filled his coffee pot. The self-confidence Zach carried with him during the conference had fled, leaving behind someone hesitant, not the cool, self-assured man he'd seemed then.

Sam was reminded of the time he and Zach had sat along the boardwalk, talking about people's expectations of others, and how he too had pretended to be somewhat of a player, thinking to fit in with the lifestyle he presumed Zach lived. At that point, Sam's only interest had been in getting Zach naked once again. Maybe he wasn't so different from the man he accused Zach of being. All these thoughts flitted through his mind while he rummaged through his cabinets for mugs and a plate.

Zach hadn't moved from his place on the sofa when Sam returned to the living room. If possible, he looked more uncomfortable than he had before.

"Here." Sam handed him a cup with one hand and pointed

to the plate with the other. "Have another one, 'cause if you don't, I'll end up eating them all."

There were half a dozen cannoli and three fruit tarts on the plate. Zach gave him a pointed stare, and Sam huffed.

"Don't judge. I have a sweet tooth. There are worse things in life."

Zach said nothing; however, a brief smile crossed his lips as he raised his mug of coffee. He drank a few gulps, then, obviously coming to a decision, placed his cup on the coffee table and took a deep breath.

"Look, I'm a fail at personal relationships; that's why I stick with computers. I was already going to Atlantic City for the conference, and the guys joked around and said I should find someone to hook up with. Somehow it turned into a bet involving Marcus not having sex, because if you know Marcus, everything with him revolves around him having sex."

"So he's the player."

Finally deciding to take a pastry, Zach was halfway through crunching a fruit tart and took the time to swallow before answering.

"Yeah. I love the guy, but he is no one's boyfriend, and never will be. But,"—Zach licked his lips, sweeping them clean of cream—"he's also the best friend I've ever had and would never hurt me."

Interesting. Sam sipped his coffee and said nothing.

"I never agreed to their bet, but had already decided to be someone different for the weekend. Who would it hurt? I'd be with people who didn't know the real me. I could be a totally new Zach. Someone who wasn't afraid to take risks; someone willing to have fun and be daring." He looked down at his lap. "Someone people would notice."

None of this made sense to Sam. "But why? You're a young, incredibly rich, good-looking guy. Why do you think you need to pretend? Any guy would be lucky to be with you."

The compliment didn't bring a smile of thanks or even a blush of self-awareness. Zach's expression grew gloomier, and he stood, then walked to the windows.

"Perceptions rarely mirror truths. What you see isn't how I see it, and it isn't how most people have seen me all my life. I've never been confident about anything, except my abilities in school. And when you're ten and never picked for sports or thirteen and never invited to any parties, a pattern is set for the adult you'll be. The one on the sidelines; always there but never seen. When you're an invisible kid, you tend to grow up to be an invisible adult."

How wrong he'd been about Zach from the beginning. And knowing how sweet and kind a soul he was, Sam hurt for the young boy Zach had been and the sad and lonely man who stood before him.

"Is that how you see yourself—invisible?" Sam followed him to the window and placed a hand on his shoulder but made no other move.

"It's how I've always been. Marcus always tried to include me, but—"

"You know what?" Sam slid his arm around Zach, turning him so that they faced each other. "You think too much about Marcus." Sam took Zach's glasses off and placed them carefully on the table. "You talk too much about him too. Want to know what I see?"

Zach blinked and nodded.

"I see a guy who's kind, smart, and tenacious. A man who isn't afraid to search out what he wants and go after it." Sam leaned down and brushed Zach's lips with his own, smiling at the sigh of pleasure from Zach. He pulled off his tee shirt and unbuttoned Zach's shirt so their bare chests pressed against each other. Sam pushed Zach's shirt off his shoulders so it fell to the floor, then slid his hand up Zach's back, as warm and soft as he remembered. His fingers splayed out against skin, muscles, and bones, and he held Zach close. It was as if his hands were made to touch Zach. The feel of his skin was everything right and perfect.

"Don't ever pretend with me; there's no reason to. I'm not interested in someone who hangs out at the clubs and parties all night." He buried his lips in Zach's hair, his hands smoothing down the curvature of Zach's spine until he dipped his fingers to gently touch below the waistband of Zach's jeans.

Zach groaned, his harsh breath hot against Sam's shoulder. His breathing grew more erratic when Sam continued to play along the top of the waistband of Zach's jeans, dipping a finger down to flirt with the crease of his ass, while rubbing their denim-covered erections against each other.

Sam framed Zach's face between his hands and kissed his lips softly at first, then with increasing urgency, plunging his tongue deep inside Zach's mouth. It was as hot and sweet as Sam remembered, but now there was more; a renewal of hope that there was more to come. More than simply sex.

Zach curled his hand around Sam's neck, and their kisses grew more passionate and desperate. Sam forgot his best intentions of taking things slow, of learning more about Zach before jumping back into bed. They disappeared once Zach's soft lips, moving warm against his own, parted, and his tongue slid inside Sam's mouth, twisting, tangling, searching for Sam's.

His hands trembling a bit, Sam popped the button tab on Zach's shorts and drew them down, along with Zach's boxers. With his hands braced on Sam's shoulders, Zach stepped out of his flip-flops, then kicked off his clothes, the dark, hungry expression in his eyes never faltering. Sam's breath quickened at the sight of Zach's well-hung cock, flushed red before him; more perfect than he remembered in his dreams.

Any resolve Sam clung to vanished under the wave of desire crashing over him, enflaming every nerve ending under his skin. Sam slid down to his knees and holding on to Zach's hips, took Zach's cock in his mouth and sucked it down.

The first sharp taste of Zach burst hot against his tongue. "Oh God," moaned Zach, widening his stance and clutching the windowsill behind him. "Sam, God, please."

With one hand Sam held on to the base of Zach's cock and sucked at the crown, swirling his tongue first around the edges, then flicking at the tiny slit. Zach shivered and shook under Sam's relentless stroking, licking, and sucking up and down the shaft, then back around to the head. His free hand gently caressed Zach's thighs, then reached down to Zach's balls, hefting first one and then the other. Sam's finger glided back along the delicate skin of the perineum, and at that touch, Zach arched and cried out, shooting his hot, creamy essence into Sam's mouth. He swallowed it all down, one hand resting lightly on Zach's hip, the other holding the base of Zach's cock until it softened and wetly slipped from his lips.

Their gasping breaths mingled with the twittering of the birds through the open windows, creating an oddly sensual melody. Sam ran his hands up Zach's naked legs, relishing the crisp, wiry hair and tight muscles, before cupping his ass. He pressed his lips to the slant where hip bone met thigh and breathed deeply of Zach's rich, masculine scent. At Zach's sigh of pleasure, Sam glanced up, his own breath catching in his throat.

The picture of sated happiness, Zach's head rested against the window; his heavy-lidded eyes and dreamy half-smile twisted Sam's heart into a knot of uncertainty. He shouldn't have succumbed so easily to physical pleasure; he'd never been a man ruled by his dick instead of his head, yet one smile from Zach or brush of his fingers and Sam's brain short-circuited and fried his common sense.

"Sam?"

Zach's tentative, questioning voice pulled Sam out of his introspection.

"Yeah?" He blinked Zach back into focus, his voice a bit harsher than it should be, considering he'd had his mouth on the man's cock a minute ago. "What is it?" His tone a bit softer now, Sam stood up and stepped back from Zach, who must've felt the shift in his mood, judging by the slightly dismayed expression in his half-dazed eyes.

"Uhh, I'm going to put my clothes on first if you don't mind." There went that enticing blush again. Sam watched Zach's cheeks heat pink as he slipped on his boxers and shorts. "I talk better when I'm not half-naked." Zach slid his glasses on but didn't look at Sam.

Was it possible Zach truly was as shy as he seemed? Sam found it—and Zach as a whole—rather endearing. His head hurt from all the thinking about Zach's constant shifts in behavior. All he wanted was the truth. It shouldn't be so hard.

A light breeze ruffled Zach's hair and touched Sam's cheeks with surprising coolness. Perhaps a summer storm was on its way; it would be a welcome cool-down from the humidity of the last two days. Somehow though, Sam didn't think Zach wanted to talk about the weather. Curious, he waited for Zach to speak.

"Can we sit down?" Without waiting for an answer, Zach crossed the room and settled on the sofa. Careful not to get too close, Sam chose the club chair across from him, wishing like hell they didn't have to go through this stage of mistrust. He wanted it to be like it had been back in Atlantic City: the easy interaction, the potential of what might be—the storm of passion pulsing higher between them.

Now that they sat facing one another Zach had grown mute, and Sam's frustration escalated. He'd always been as straightforward in his personal life as he'd been as a cop; he'd never understood the point of skirting an issue.

"Well?" He raised a brow and folded his arms. "Are we going to talk, or is this it?"

Chapter Thirteen

Though it was years later, the experience he carried from Nathan remained a tangible presence, clinging to him like a hard-to-peel eggshell, flaking off bit by bit to expose a ragged surface and an unhealthy core. It hadn't occurred to Zach that his victimization was something he could shed like unwanted weight—that he could rise up against his aggressor and strike back. Zach had never been the type to assert himself and go against the crowd.

In the past, whenever Zach toyed with the idea of opening up to Julian and Marcus about Nathan and the abuse, he recoiled. Those two men, so strong and self-confident, could never understand Zach's fall down the rabbit hole of shame. It had been too many years of keeping secrets and lies, the humiliation rooting him in the past with no impetus to break free, to take back his life, turn himself around, and eradicate the memories of what made him the person he was today.

Instead, he took the coward's way out, as he defined it, content to remain behind the scenes. Lonely, but forever grateful for his friends and even his mother for never pressing him for explanations. Zach immersed himself in his work and shut down his heart and libido, content to live vicariously through Marcus's and Julian's love affairs, though he'd never stopped dreaming of finding someone to love and share his life with. Marcus's relentless teasing never bothered him. After all, what he said was true. Zach was and always would be a romantic at heart. He believed in happy endings.

It had happened for Julian, after all.

In meeting Sam, Zach's bland, colorless world had been upset: spun upside down off its monotonous axis and invigorated with color, light, and sound. For once, someone wanted him—just Zach. Sam didn't seem to want to change him or mold him into someone else. There'd yet to be any criticisms or put-downs; Zach didn't have to pretend he was someone else, nor did Sam seem to want him to be anyone other than who he was.

But would Sam still want him once Zach confessed why he'd left? It was one thing to be shy and geeky. It was another thing for him to admit what he'd gone through with Nathan.

And then there was the issue of Zach still living at home. He straightened up and knew, though it might lose him Sam, he refused to lie about the close relationship he had with his mother. Long ago he'd made his decision to watch over her and that wasn't about to change for any man.

"I think the best place for me to start is to tell you the reason why I left that night in such a hurry."

Sam quirked a brow. "Uh, yeah. That is the reason we're talking. Otherwise I'd have you laid out naked on my bed."

Zach found it hard to breathe at the visual, but after a

brief hesitation he regained his composure and began again.

"I had every intention of spending the night with you; I looked forward to it, especially our walk along the beach. But then I got a call and I had to rush back to the city. I didn't have time to find you and explain."

"Yeah," said Sam, settling back in his chair. "I thought you cheated on your boyfriend and ran back to him when you got cold feet or he found out." Sam huffed out a laugh. "Remember I even thought Marcus was the boyfriend."

Though Sam's laugh rang out full and genuine, Zach sensed there was still an underlying current there to warrant more reassurance on that front.

"Marcus never has been and never will be a man I am interested in as anything more than a friend. I love him, but not in that way."

Zach watched as relief brought out those delightful smile-crinkles to fan out from the corners of Sam's eyes. "I have to admit meeting him now, I couldn't imagine you two together. He's an obvious flirt and not the type I'd ever imagine wanting a steady relationship."

"You have such excellent insight, considering you've only spoken to him for a few minutes."

"I was a cop for twenty years," groused Sam. "If I couldn't pick up on people's behavior, I never would've lasted."

"How come you retired? You're so young still."

The question was an innocent one, Zach thought, until a brief flash of pain replaced the laughter in Sam's eyes, turning them cold and dark, and the teasing grin resting on his lips faded away.

"Are you deflecting the conversation away from you over to me so you won't have to answer any questions?" Sam shifted in his chair and frowned. "This is about you and what happened, not my work history."

Sam might be the intuitive one, but it didn't take an expert to note the shift in the air had nothing to do with the cool breeze blowing in through the windows, portending rain. Zach wasn't the only one with a backstory in his life, and he wondered if it had to do with the man Sam had loved, but no longer lived with.

That conversation would be tabled for a future discussion. This afternoon it was Zach's turn to bare his soul.

After Nathan, he'd decided that he might be a pushover in many ways, but no one would ever tell him how to live his life again. If Sam left because Zach cared for his mother, if it made him less of a man in Sam's eyes, then Sam wasn't the man Zach thought he was and would want. And if Sam was going to freak out because Zach still lived at home with his mother, better that he do it now, and Zach could, not without some regret of course, walk away.

"I did receive a call, yes, but not from another man. From my mother."

"Um, okay. Your mother called and you had to go because…?"

Zach's jaw ached from gritting his teeth. He wanted nothing more than to be done with the conversation and get back to the part where Sam talked about being naked in his bed. "She thought someone might be breaking in, so she became frightened, had a panic attack, and called, asking if I could come home."

Disbelief clouded Sam's face. "You ran back one hundred fifty miles on a Saturday night because your mother called you? There wasn't anyone else she could call?" He huffed out a laugh. "I mean, it's not like you're there all the time. What does she do, make you stop over and do a house check every night?"

Defiantly, he glared at Sam. "I live there. With her."

"You live at home—with your mother?" Curiosity tinged

Sam's voice, but not contempt as Zach had feared. "At your age?"

Unable to sit still any longer, Zach sprang up from the sofa and walked into the kitchen to get a glass of water. Drinking it down, a myriad of emotions passed through him: his father's death, his mother's subsequent neediness—had he made a mistake by not getting her the help she needed? Only a child when it happened, he'd barely been equipped to take care of his own grief. Top that sundae of life's disasters with the internal struggle from his prepubescent hormones pointing him in the direction of other boys and not girls…no wonder he was a mess.

Thank God Marcus, who'd already figured out his sexuality and acted upon it, had been there to help navigate the way for him, otherwise Zach would've been lost.

A large, warm presence brushed up behind him. Sam had followed him.

"If you don't want to talk any further about it, I won't push you."

Grow a pair, Zach argued with himself. Time to sort the junk floating in his head before making decisions on his future.

"No. I want to. Yeah, I live at home with my mom. When my father died I made a promise to myself to always take care of her. She swore it would be okay for me to room with my friends at school, and I did and tried to make it home as often as I could. Since we were in the city, it wasn't a big deal." He pushed a hand through his hair. "But after I graduated things got worse." To his mortification, his throat swelled, making it hard for him to talk.

"Worse how?"

Without Zach even realizing it, Sam had led him to the sofa, but this time sat next to him, close enough to envelop Zach in his heat.

"She wanted to know where I was all the time and what I was doing; if I was in a safe place with friends. It had been years since my father had died, yet she continued to talk to him over the dinner table and late at night in her bedroom."

Sam's hand came down on his. "Sounds like she needed help."

"I know, but I was only twenty—I graduated college early—and she said she was fine; refused to talk to a therapist." He stared down blindly at his hand, now covered by Sam's. "All she needed was me there to make her feel safe. That's what she told me. How could I say no to her?"

Sam gave his hand a reassuring squeeze. "You don't have to say no. There are ways to say things and get her the help she needs, and you the privacy you need as well."

Could he, even after all these years, or would she look at it like a betrayal? The problem was, with Sam touching him, he couldn't think at all.

"Getting back to the Atlantic City story, that's what happened that night. She thought she heard people trying to break into the house and got all panicky, so I came home to make her feel better. Of course, by the time I made it back to Brooklyn it was almost two hours later."

"So crisis averted."

Zach nodded. "And as usual she felt guilty and foolish." Frustration grew within him, fearing what Sam must be thinking. "Kind of like I feel right now. I know you probably think I'm coddling her and immature for not cutting the apron strings. But,"—he gazed up into Sam's serious eyes—"she's my mom."

"I think your mother is lucky to have you, and you in turn might be surprised at how much she might be able to handle."

Surprising himself, Zach moved closer to Sam. "I don't want to talk about my mother anymore." Greedy to taste Sam again, Zach slid his hand around Sam's broad neck and pulled him close, whispering against his mouth, "I'd rather not talk at all."

Sam opened his mouth under Zach's and stole Zach's breath away. Without any hesitation, Zach met Sam's plunging tongue with his own, and they kissed, tongues sliding, twisting, and tangling. Zach's hand crept up Sam's neck to bury itself in his thick wavy hair.

They stayed that way, the heat and need rising between them until Sam broke away first, his mouth red and swollen. Zach enjoyed seeing it, knowing he'd done that to this man.

"Let's move this to the bedroom, shall we?" Sam hauled him up and pushed Zach in front of him, yet kept his bulk flush with Zach's back, so Zach could feel every inch of Sam's cock, pressing thick and firm against his ass.

Zach stumbled and Sam held him tighter. "I could pick you up and fling you over my shoulder, but I reserve that for when I have to resort to chase and capture to get what I want." At the touch of Sam's tongue in his ear Zach shivered violently. "I'm thinking I won't have resistance to getting you naked and under me."

Unable to speak, Zach simply shook his head. He pulled off his clothes, surprised his fingers were steady enough to undo buttons and snaps, never taking his eyes off Sam who'd stripped down in seconds flat, leaving his clothes in a heap next to the king-size bed.

Sam advanced on him and pushed him down, so Zach sat, coming face-to-face with Sam's cock. It was beautiful, and needing no invitation, Zach leaned forward and slid it into his mouth.

"Fuuuck," said Sam, his groan catching at the end. One hand ran through Zach's hair, the other stroked his jaw with a light touch. It was a sweetly tender moment for Zach, who'd never known much affection from a lover. He nuzzled into Sam's skin, inhaling him, wanting to remember the scent and sound of this forever.

Zach licked and suckled Sam's cock, holding it in one hand, cupping the heavy sac in the other, loving the tiny sounds of satisfaction spilling from Sam's lips. Increasing his speed, Zach swirled around the thick head, lightly scraping his teeth along the ridge running down the shaft.

"Uhhh." Sam pulled out of his mouth with an audible *plop*. "I want inside you; I don't want to come in your mouth."

The ache of want throbbed deep inside Zach; all the years of thwarted passion suddenly inflamed him; he could've cried out from the hunger to have Sam inside him again. He moved to the center of the bed and sat, a bit unsure of what Sam wanted.

"Lie down, baby, and spread your legs. I'm gonna get what we need."

He complied, giving himself a few strokes while he waited. It felt so good, imagining it was Sam's hands on him, that he couldn't stop, and he closed his eyes, continuing to jack himself off. The mattress dipped, and Zach opened his eyes to see Sam sitting there, watching him with those dark, hungry eyes.

"Don't stop, baby, keep touching yourself. Nice and slow."

Zach held Sam's gaze and kept sliding his hand up and down his straining cock, rolling his thumb over the leaking head and smearing the escaping fluid down his shaft. His other hand sneaked down and rolled his balls and tugged them, reaching farther back to brush up against his hole. Zach shuddered with the electricity sizzling through him as the sensitive nerves awakened at his touch.

"Keep going, don't stop," growled Sam, skimming his hands up Zach's hips, the roughness of his touch adding to the already crazy sensations zinging through Zach.

"Please," begged Zach, shamelessly arching up to create

skin-to-skin contact between them. He rubbed against Sam's stomach, their cocks bumping and sliding, the wetness providing some friction but not enough—nowhere near enough—for him. "Sam, please touch me."

"You do it." Sam knelt over him. "Pretend your hand is mine when you squeeze the head of your cock. Go ahead do it."

And Zach, unable to tear his eyes away from Sam, complied, a needy moan escaping his lips.

"Up and down now. Jack yourself but think of me, my hand touching you. My fingers inside you, sliding in your ass, all the time your balls ache and you want to come so badly you hurt inside."

Uncaring how he looked anymore, Zach dug his heels into the bed and thrust into his hand, thinking of Sam's hand doing it to him, lost in the haze of desire. A finger probed his entrance, then slid in, cool and slick, moving slowly until it wedged its way in fully.

"How's that feel, baby. You want me to move?"

Capable only of whimpering, Zach pushed against Sam's hand, craving more fullness inside him. That night they'd spent together resurfaced, and Zach wanted to recapture that magic and the way Sam made him come alive.

"More, harder." Zach knew he babbled, didn't know what he was saying. All he knew was he wanted Sam. "Please don't leave me."

"I won't. Let it go. I'm right here. Give it up. Go on."

And Sam withdrew the one finger only to slide back in with two for a moment. Zach could feel the orgasm building inside him and tried to hold off, wanting to prolong the closeness, but he was useless against the force of his body. It ripped through him like a freight train, shattering him into oblivion, until he struggled back to reality, gasping for breath.

He lay still for a moment, registering the stickiness on his chest. "I want you so bad," he whispered. "I need you."

"You've got me. Now hold on." Sam rolled on a condom and slicked himself up. He leaned over, and the head of his cock nudged Zack's hole. "Put your arms around me." The head of his cock pushed inside, and Zach could've cried with relief.

If possible, it was better than the first time they were together. Zach barely registered the initial burn before Sam's cock sank so deep, it filled up every achingly empty space in his body. Zach felt consumed, enveloped, and enervated, his body in tune to the music and rhythm of Sam's movement inside him.

He loved it.

With his hands braced on either side of Zach's shoulders, Sam never took his eyes off Zach, not even when he moved, thrusting hard and deep, so deep Zach knew long after Sam would be gone he'd forever be imprinted in Zach's body and soul.

Sam strained and pushed against him, and Zach responded, shifting his legs up to his shoulders, giving Sam better access. Sam pressed his hands onto the headboard of the bed, changed his angle, and hit Zach's prostate, sending an electric current zinging through him again.

"Oh God, please, please," he twisted underneath Sam, whose face looked oddly serious and vulnerable, driving into Zach harder and faster until Zach forgot where he was, what day it was, and almost his own name. Crazy colors flashed before his eyes and he split apart, his skin flayed raw and tingling to the touch.

With not quite a cry or a grunt, but a sound of desperation, Sam threw his head back and came, filling the condom with liquid heat, then shuddered and fell on top of Zach, the air forced out of him in a whoosh of shocked breath. Sated and limp as Zach was, the old trembling began. Sam immediately rolled off and lay on his back next to Zach, still breathing heavily.

It was times like this Zach wanted a man who wouldn't mind cuddling. Sometimes a person simply needs to be held. There was so much inside him he'd yet to reveal to anyone, but he wasn't yet there with Sam.

Too early for that. Zach shifted in the bed, wishing for human contact, skin-to-skin, a touch, a caress. He wondered—would Sam pull away if he moved closer to rest his head on Sam's shoulder? How sad it was that you could make love with a person, take them inside your body yet still be so uncertain of the workings of their heart. All his life he'd waited to be wanted by the right man, yet, at twenty-nine, he was no closer to figuring out who it might be than when he'd been nineteen.

So when Sam took Zach's hand in his and laced their fingers together, Zach's surprise was so great, he almost missed what Sam whispered to him.

"I'm not running away. So whenever you decide to talk some more, I'm here."

Chapter Fourteen

A couple of weeks later, Sam and Henry met in the park to play ball. It was nice that it was relatively empty so early on a Sunday morning, and once they'd finished tossing the ball around, they sat on a bench under the shade of a large oak tree and caught up with each other's news. Henry had some new project lined up for him, but he didn't want to talk business. He was more interested in ferreting out whatever information he could about Zach.

"I tell you, there's something else besides Zach living at home. Young, single, and rich doesn't live at home with mommy unless there are other issues." Henry handed him a bottle of water from the cooler they'd placed under the tree.

He and Zach had spent almost every evening cocooned together in his apartment since the day Zach had cornered him at the pastry shop. Last night, before he'd left Sam's apartment to go home, Zach casually asked him if he'd like to join him and his friends for brunch, and explained how they met at least once a month to stay in touch. Sam agreed and looked forward to getting to know more about the two men who shaped Zach's life. Maybe he could talk to them and find out what lay beneath Zach's surface that frightened him so much.

Oddly protective of Zach now that Sam knew him better, Henry's comment rankled, even more so remembering the time he and Zach had spent together yesterday. They'd watched a movie on Netflix, ordered in a pizza, and made love. However unassuming to the rest of the world Zach might seem, Sam liked being the only man who knew the hidden talent of Zach's wicked mouth and tongue, and the way Zach moaned Sam's name right before he came apart in his arms.

That appealing quality—Zach's sweetness and complete unawareness of his looks—turned Sam on more than he ever thought possible. He couldn't have been more different than the previous men in Sam's life.

Six months before meeting Zach, Sam had reached a dead end—retired, angry, and somewhat sad—and figured this was how his life was meant to be for him. That's when his desperation to feel the touch of someone—anyone— drove him to a bar to pick up a stranger. Stupid, foolish, and dangerous, although of course he'd used protection.

After he came home, drained, hurting, and faintly disgusted with himself, Sam vowed to remain celibate. And so he had until he walked up to the bar in Atlantic City and got drawn in by blue eyes he couldn't forget and a sad but sweet smile.

"I don't think it's so strange." He chugged down half the bottle of water and wiped his mouth on his sleeve. "Zach's a family man, and his mother is a widow. It's only natural he'd want to be close to watch over her."

A speculative gleam entered Henry's eyes. "You seem to know more about him than you did last time we talked." He tossed his empty water bottle into the recycling bin. "Something you'd like to share?"

Like hell he would. "Don't know what you're talking about." He blinked at Henry and finished his water.

"Don't you bat your eyes at me like you're trying to be all innocent and shit." Henry's grin turned crafty. "Tell me, there's something going on between you two, isn't there?"

Time to go before Henry attacked him like a jackal with a carcass. Sam hefted his gym bag on his shoulder and settled his baseball cap on his head more securely.

"I gotta go. I'll call you about that new job you mentioned."

Before Henry could respond and pounce on him for details about his relationship with Zach, Sam sprinted out of the park and jogged down the block. It was nine thirty and he needed to shower and change before meeting Zach in about an hour. It surprised Sam how much he was looking forward to not only spending even more time with Zach, but also meeting his friends. It was a step back into the social life he'd shunned for so long.

Thinking back to how he'd spent the last few months, holed up in his apartment with only the television and takeout to keep him company, Sam hadn't realized how narrow and gray his life had become. Isolationism was never the answer and didn't aid in recovery. Without Henry stopping by to haul his ass out at least once a week, Sam was certain he would've formed a permanent and unhealthy attachment to his sofa.

He entered his apartment and headed straight for the shower, washing off the sweat and grime of the one-on-one basketball game he and Henry had played. The hot water beat down on his sore muscles like tiny massage fingers, and by the time he'd finished, Sam wouldn't have minded spending the day stretched out in bed, Zach beside him, underneath him, or on top of him.

No one could fault him for that reasoning. Grinning to himself, he brushed his wet hair and pulled on shorts and a shirt. Zach had said he'd be by around eleven, so Sam figured he still had enough time to check his emails. He scrolled past the advertisements for penis enlargements, Viagra, and triple-X hook-ups. Damn, he needed a better spam filter.

One email that wasn't junk stopped his scrolling short. Why the hell was Andy emailing him? They hadn't spoken since the breakup when he'd moved out to be with the other guy. The bell rang, and when he checked his watch it was exactly eleven o'clock. It had to be Zach to pick him up. For some vague reason Sam felt guilty knowing Zach was outside waiting for him while he sat in front of the computer with an email from Andy staring him in the face.

Common sense kicked in then, and kicked him in the head. The man was a serial liar, and Sam wasn't about to jeopardize the tentative beginnings of whatever he and Zach might be building together, to hear some bullshit spun by a master storyteller. Without sparing a second thought, he pressed Delete and hurried to let Zach inside.

"Hi."

He held the door open, and Zach passed in front of him to enter the apartment.

"Almost ready to go? Marcus is already at the restaurant, and Julian just texted me that he and Nick are on their way."

With Zach gazing up at him expectantly, an inexplicable sense of guilt swelled in Sam's chest and without knowing what else to do about it, he took Zach by the shoulders and kissed him. Almost immediately and without any hesitation, Zach sank against him, sliding his hands up Sam's chest, and tangling his fingers in the hair curling at the nape of Sam's neck.

"Mmmm." Zach virtually purred into Sam's mouth, then broke away to kiss along his jawline before nuzzling into the curve between his neck and shoulder. "What brought that on? Not that I'm complaining, of course."

The curve of Zach's lips imprinted his smile against Sam's shoulder, and he held Zach tighter against his chest. The delight in holding someone who felt so special, so *right* in his arms was such a new experience for him, Sam wanted to grab on to Zach, keep him close, and not share him with anyone.

"Why not?" Sam slid his arm around Zach and steered him into the living room where they sat on the sofa next to each other. "You look good, and I wanted to kiss you."

"Well," said Zach smiling up into Sam's face, his eyes sparkling behind his black-framed glasses. "Who am I to deny you that pleasure?"

This was the way he liked to see Zach: happy, light-spirited, and eminently desirable. "Good," said Sam, returning the smile. "Because I'm about to do it again." He bent and took Zach's mouth like he owned it. Zach grabbed on to his shoulders, his hands splaying across Sam's back, and returned the kiss with equal fervor. Sam could taste Zach's need in his kiss.

For the next few minutes their mouths pressed together, hot and hard, tongues wetly sliding and teeth clashing, nipping at each other's lips until they drew apart laughing and gasping with their rising passion and from the knowledge they had to put a hold on their groping, but only until later.

And Sam didn't stop to question how secure and happy he felt, knowing there was going to be a later.

"Come on," said Zach, pulling him toward the door. "We need to go, or we'll never get out of the house."

"Wouldn't be such a bad thing," said Sam, swatting Zach on the ass. He grabbed his phone and keys and locked the door behind them.

*   *   *

Instead of walking, they decided to take the train and had to wait almost half an hour in the hot and airless subway station, so by the time he and Zach reached the restaurant, Sam was sweaty, irritated, and thirsty. That didn't stop him from smiling however, when Zach slipped a hand in his and gave it a slight squeeze, which he returned.

"There they are." Zach waved at the table of men, his voice light with happiness. "You remember Marcus. And Julian is the blond and his boyfriend is Nick."

Sam remembered all of them. Julian eyed him with a serious, assessing gaze, while Nick seemed friendlier and more welcoming.

"Hi, everyone. Sorry we're late, but you know the trains." Zach sat in the chair next to Marcus, leaving Sam to sit in between him and Julian. "Everyone remembers Sam, right?"

"Well, if I didn't, my jaw does," said Marcus with a rueful smile. "How's it going, Sam, or need I even ask, since I haven't seen Zach this happy in I don't know when." He turned to Julian. "Right, Juli?"

A faint smile touched Julian's lips, but his dark green eyes held a hint of wariness.

"Nice to see you again." In contrast to Julian's cool acknowledgment, a genuinely warm smile of friendship touched his face when he spoke to Zach.

"Zach, how are you? How's your mom?"

"She's good, thanks." Seemingly unaware of any tension between Sam and Julian, Zach picked up a roll from the bread basket and began to butter it as he spoke.

"Every time you send her something, it's like her birthday.

I really appreciate it." Zach bent to murmur in Sam's ear. "Julian always sends beautiful silk scarves for my mom. It's the only women's fashion he designs, and my mom gets the exclusive before he puts them up for sale."

"That's really nice of you, Julian." It was obvious to him how much of a family these men considered themselves, their lives entwined with one another. Knowing how important these men were to Zach, Sam had hoped he too could become their friend.

Instead, Julian flicked a glance over Sam, and tilted his head in silent acknowledgement, then turned to speak to Nick.

Last time Julian was much friendlier. Sam had done nothing to the guy—why was he treating him like a pariah?

About to open his mouth to speak, Zach gripped his thigh in a warning squeeze.

"Don't say anything. It takes Julian a while to warm up and trust people. It's nothing personal. He's overprotective of the people he loves. Give him a chance to get to know you."

In the end, it was Nick who broke the ice.

"I hear you and I have a lot in common, Sam." Nick accepted a tall, foaming glass of beer from the waiter, who'd arrived with another round of drinks. Sam waited until the waiter took his and Zach's order and retreated, before responding.

"Well, yeah, we're both uniform—at least you still are," he said, a pang of regret searing through him. Sam wondered if the shame would ever leave him. "I'm retired now."

Nick finished drinking his beer and leaned back in his chair. "There's that, but I wasn't talking about our jobs." His eyes crinkled with good humor, and he grinned. "I was talking about punching Marcus. I did the same thing the first time I met him."

Zach collapsed against Sam, shaking with laughter. It took Julian, who couldn't maintain his stony coldness in light of that hilarious moment in their shared history, a moment to catch his breath before he could speak.

"I wish I had a picture of Marcus flat on his ass on the dance floor of Sparks. Priceless."

"I don't know what's so funny." Marcus huffed and rubbed his jaw as if it still ached. "I'm the aggrieved party here." He blinked and sulked in his seat.

Sam noticed Marcus's gaze roaming the restaurant, his foot tapping under the table, and fingers drumming the table. The man was never at ease with himself or his surroundings.

"Poor baby." Zach patted Marcus on the shoulder, then sat back to let the waiter place his mimosa on the table. "I'm sure you found someone to kiss it and make it all better."

"Well, yeah." Marcus tossed back his drink in a single gulp and signaled the waiter for another one. "That's never been an issue."

"I know," Zach muttered under his breath. "That's the problem."

Sam made a mental note to ask Zach what Marcus's story was. He had a sense there was a shit-ton of ugly emotion buried underneath Marcus's shiny, beautiful exterior.

"We never did get the story," said a somewhat friendlier Julian. At least his cold, standoffish demeanor had vanished. "Why did you pop Marcus in his beautiful mug?"

"You're all having entirely too much fun with this conversation," said Marcus, grumbling.

"It was actually very sweet," said Zach, nudging Sam, his eyes bright with happiness. "I'll let Sam tell you."

Sam understood Zach was pushing him to speak so as to include him and give him face time with the guys. Zach believed in harmony and avoiding confrontation, much like Sam himself, which was why they both had been taken advantage of in their relationships. It wasn't obvious from appearances, but the two of them were much more alike than either had realized at the start. Considering they'd both pretended to be people they weren't in real life, it wasn't surprising.

"I'd come to Sparks that night when we all first met in the diner to talk to Zach. I couldn't understand why he brushed me off and made it sound like he barely remembered me, when we'd spent an entire evening together."

"And hooked up it seems, let's not forget that salient point, shall we?" Marcus chimed in, obviously attuned to the conversation, despite his concentration appearing to be elsewhere. "That certainly shocked the shit out of me for sure."

Sam didn't pay much attention to Marcus since he'd already been through this with him the night at Sparks. It was Julian he now had to win over. And becoming a part of this group and fitting in as seamlessly as Nick did was something Sam wanted. The reason—something so alarming yet at the same time so wonderful—wasn't anything Sam had expected or thought would ever happen to him. It made him catch his breath for a moment and think. What was important to Zach had now become as important to Sam.

"It seemed apparent, at least to me from the way they were dancing, that Zach and Marcus were a couple." The way Marcus had ground his hips against Zach still rankled Sam, yet he logically understood it was Marcus and therefore acceptable behavior to Zach. "I couldn't understand why I was told to come. Zach tried to explain, but I didn't like how Marcus grabbed Zach; I thought maybe he was physically abusing him. Then when I found out you guys had bet him to sleep with someone when he went to Atlantic City, I'd had enough and left."

It was the truth, but there were some things Sam hoped the others would let lie. Things he and Zach should talk about in private. Like why Sam knew—without Zach having to say a word—that Zach had been abused at some point in his life. He wouldn't pry, knowing when Zach felt comfortable enough, he'd tell Sam everything.

"Thinking Zach was abused and by me, that's fucking crazy." The disbelief in Marcus's voice was genuine. "It must be that police officer mind that always thinks something bad is going down."

Interesting. Why wouldn't Zach tell his closest friends? It made no sense to Sam, but when he looked into his own personal life, he had no desire to talk about Andy and the shit that went down with him, forcing him into retirement. Keeping his mouth shut, Sam leaned back in his seat, resting his arm along the back of Zach's chair, and continued his story.

"Yeah, but I didn't know that so I left. Zach turned bulldog and came after me the next day, following me to my neighborhood pastry shop."

"Zach? Followed you?" An obviously shocked Julian shook his head in disbelief as he stared at Zach. "Seriously? You followed him?"

"It's not as bad as it sounds." Zach laughed weakly. "Sam had mentioned the name of his favorite pastry shop to me, and I knew where it was." He shifted in his seat. "I went there to see if he'd show up and even ended up speaking to the owner, Mrs. Caruso." He nudged Sam. "She loves you, by the way. Sang your praises to the heavens."

Warmth settled in his chest. "She's a lovely lady."

"Sounds like you and Zach are perfect together. All the old ladies love him too," Marcus interjected.

Zach flushed and once again, Sam experienced that protective rush toward him.

"There's nothing wrong with being kind to people without expecting anything in return."

"It's been my experience that everyone expects something

eventually. There are very few saints in this world, and the ones who profess to be one are boring." Marcus gave them all a grin full of charm and deviltry. "I prefer the sinners. They know how to have all the fun."

"Back to Zach and Sam, please." Julian arched his brow. "We already know you're a debauched sinner."

"You're no fun any longer, Juli. Maybe I need to tell Nick some stories of the good old days, huh, so you can remember you aren't any better than me because you found true looove." Marcus's voice teased, but Sam sensed the tension between the two friends.

Nick snickered and patted Julian on his shoulder. "We get it, babe. Neither one of you were innocent when you were younger. We're lucky we found each other again, and it seems maybe from what I'm hearing Zach and Sam are more than friends?"

Zach stiffened next to him, and Sam draped his arm around Zach's shoulders, signaling to everyone, Zach included, where he belonged.

Sam's gaze found Zach's startled one. "I'd say that's a safe assumption, wouldn't you?"

Chapter Fifteen

"I was glad to finally meet everyone. I thought it went really well, didn't you?"

The early afternoon sun beat down on them as he and Sam trekked back from the city to Carroll Gardens. By mutual agreement they'd decided to go back to Sam's house, even though Zach knew his mother would wonder where he was. Under normal circumstances he'd go home, and she'd pour him a coffee while he filled her in on everyone's gossip. A vague, uneasy guilt rose within him, knowing that she was waiting for him, and he'd chosen to be with Sam.

"Um, yeah." He pushed the sweaty strands of hair off his forehead and adjusted his glasses. "I knew they'd like you." A surreptitious glance at his watch showed the time at a little after two.

"You seem distracted, what's wrong?"

They'd come to a corner and had to wait for the light to change. Traffic whizzed by with so many people going places and doing things. Zach wished he could persuade his mother to do more than volunteer at the senior center a few times a week. True, she kept herself busy with that, but everything else rested on his shoulders. Again, the guilt pricked him, and much as he wanted to be with Sam, he knew he needed to go home.

Waiting until they crossed the street, Zach motioned to the children's park, set back from the street. The heat had kept many people away this afternoon, and there were empty benches in the shade of the trees that flanked the outskirts of the park.

"Can we sit for a minute?" He pointed to the park, and placed his hand on the latch of the iron fence.

"Sure, what's wrong?"

Zach remained silent and entered the park, Sam trailing behind him. He picked a bench far enough away from the other people to give them privacy and sat, staring at the children running through the glittering, watery spray of the sprinkler. What he wouldn't give to be a little child again, able to have a fresh new life ahead of him.

"We've already had the discussion about me living with my mother, and you didn't understand why that should be an issue."

"Is that what this is about? Of course it's fine," Sam said, with a comforting smile.

Zach remained grave, and Sam's smile faded from his lips. "Zach, what's wrong?"

"I know we were supposed to go back to your house now, but I can't. After I meet the guys for breakfast I always go back and talk to her." His cheeks were on fire, not only from the sun but from embarrassment. Zach ducked his head, observing hoards of little ants swarming around the sticky remnants of a discarded popsicle stick at his feet.

At twenty-nine he should be more independent, but his mother relied on him; how could he make someone like Sam, so strong and independent, understand his obligation, when he barely understood it himself, and resented it as well? Shame pricked Zach's conscience at his ungrateful thoughts.

"She looks forward to it. She loves hearing all their gossip." He shrugged, focusing everywhere but on Sam's face. He didn't want to see Sam's disappointment.

The shadowed patterns of the leaves played against the concrete of the playground, while the ice cream truck's jingle repeated over and over until Zach thought he'd go out of his mind. Any minute now he'd stand up and thank Sam for coming and say good-bye.

"You're awfully far away. Can you come sit next to me?"

Without hesitation, Zach moved closer to Sam on the bench. Zach's body, strangely attuned to Sam's now, fit easily into that comforting space against the hard length of Sam's hip and thigh. Sam took his hand and laced their fingers together, resting their entwined hands on Zach's thigh. After so many years of being on the outside looking in on relationships, Zach was in the deep end of the pool, treading water. He didn't know whether to learn to swim and maybe sink trying, or race for the security of the edge and hold on to the familiar.

"There's no need for you to feel embarrassed to tell me you want to go back and see your mother." Sam's fingers brushed above Zach's knee, sending tingles of excitement through him. "I'll tell you what I'd like, though."

"What?"

"I'd like to come with you. Would that be okay?"

All the countless times Zach had walked home from breakfast and passed couples in this park or walking hand-in-hand down the street, he imagined their conversations, the dinner plans and other mundane slices of life that made up their day, and longed to be them, to be a part of the one-plus-one equation.

To be whole, not a half.

Sam wanted to meet his mother; Zach couldn't wrap his head around that announcement. "Yeah, it's okay." Not trusting himself to look at Sam, he stared out at the children running around the playground.

"You sound a little hesitant. Does your mother know you're gay?"

Funny how they'd been so intimate with each other, yet never thought to discuss their families or any personal details of their lives. At once, all the bubbling joy burst and drained from his body.

"No. I've known who I am since I was a kid, but never talked to my parents about it. Once my father died, I figured my mother had enough to handle without me springing that on her."

That brought a frown to Sam's face. "Do you really think she'd be upset? She may surprise you and be stronger than you give her credit."

Perhaps Sam was right. He'd held back about his sexuality for so long; because over the years she made so many subtle hints about him dating and getting married, he assumed she wouldn't be happy if he came out. But maybe Sam was correct and she'd treat it as the perfectly normal occurrence it was.

"I'm not sure. I never wanted to bring it up to keep her from getting upset."

It was peaceful there at the park, Zach decided. The annoying ice cream truck song now sounded like a joyful tune remembered from childhood. They sat for a moment, still holding hands, watching the little children at play. One beautiful girl in a pink bathing suit came over to them. Her brown skin glistened from running through the sprinklers, and her green eyes were round with curiosity.

"Are you married?" Her curly hair was bound in two fuzzy braids on either side of her head.

Zach glanced up at Sam, whose lips twitched in amusement, before giving the child an easy smile. "No, we're friends."

"My mommy says boys can marry boys now, and I can marry a girl if I wanna."

"That's true."

"People look at her and my daddy funny, and it makes me mad." A man's voice called out, and she glanced over her shoulder and squealed. "Oh, there's my daddy. Byeee." She took off across the playground, her chubby little legs pumping.

Zach watched her fling her arms around a large blond man whose tattoos covered his arms and legs. Standing next to him was a willowy black woman, her long, wavy hair gathered in a ponytail down her back.

Sam stroked his cheek with a light touch. "She's a real cutie."

Zach had always wanted a child—boy or girl it didn't matter. He wanted to adopt, hoping to give a better life to someone who might need him as much as he himself needed someone to love.

"Yeah, she is."

"Should we go to your house now so I can meet your mom?" Sam's hand cupped his jaw, forcing Zach to look into his warm, hazel eyes. "I bet she'll surprise you and be happy to meet me."

"I'm honestly not sure. She and I are very close, and though she says she wants me to have a life, she's fearful of change and clings. I should've tried to break away years ago, but as you might have guessed, I don't like conflict, so it was easier to let it ride."

"But that's changed now, hasn't it?"

Sam slid a comforting hand down his neck to rest on his shoulder.

"Yeah. And I know it's going to be hard for her, but I need our relationship to move to a healthier level, one where she's less dependent on me and treats me as an adult, not Zach, the child." He gnawed on his lip. "She's so emotional; I hope she doesn't end up hating me."

"Impossible." Sam's hand tightened on his shoulder. "Who could ever hate you?"

Something fluttered in his chest at Sam's words, his heart twisted dangerously. It terrified and excited him simultaneously. The caution he'd lived with all his life stepped to the forefront, and Zach heard the warning ringing in his ears.

Be careful. You don't really know him. You don't want to get hurt again.

But this time Zach pushed back. Fear couldn't be granted a home inside him; it was an unwelcome visitor he'd allowed to reside, behaving like a squatter in his blood, brain, and heart all these years. And where had it gotten him—hiding in a basement, alone and lonely, living vicariously through his friends' lives, while wishing for courage to break through his walls.

Time to move past Nathan; Zach wasn't the scared little freshman any longer, desperate for love, thinking any attention is good attention. He squeezed Sam's hand. It was warm, large, and solid. Comforting. Sam was a real man without any need to put others down and hurt them to feel better about himself.

"Yeah." Zach smiled up into Sam's face. "I hope you're

right."

They waved good-bye to the little girl riding on her father's broad shoulders and laughing with glee, and exited the park. The walk to his house took only twenty minutes or so, and as Zach approached he could see his mother had been planting. Bright red and pink geraniums flourished in the white stucco pots on the front stoop, and the rose bushes were in full, glorious bloom, reaching to the top of the front parlor windows.

Sam slowed down in front of the house.

"Do you know what you're going to say to her?"

It probably would be a good idea to think about how he planned to tell her. After all the years of waiting, she deserved an explanation.

"Uh, not really. I was always younger than everyone in my class, so she never pushed me too much about dating; only a few comments here and there. I know she's dying for grandchildren. That's one thing she isn't shy about telling me."

"I think," said Sam in his quiet sober voice, "above all else, you must be honest and trust her to behave how she always has with you. With love and kindness. From what you've told me, I don't anticipate there being any issues."

"I hope you're right," said Zach, thinking, *if not now, when*? The time had come.

Making no move to go inside, Sam leaned against the waist-high, wrought-iron fence. "Is that something important to you? Kids, I mean."

Taking a deep breath, Zach spoke from the heart. "Yes. I have the money and time to give to a child. And I want to adopt. Having my own isn't as important to me as giving a second chance to a child who never got a first."

"That sounds like a plan."

He nodded. "Eventually."

Zach passed by Sam to open the gate, but Sam placed a hand on his arm.

"I think that's a wonderful thing you want to do for a child."

Zach licked his lips. "You do?"

"Yeah," said Sam, sliding his hand up Zach's shoulder to cup his face. "I do. But then again, I'm thinking you're a pretty wonderful guy, and I don't know why you're alone."

The tip of Sam's thumb rested against Zach's lips. "But now you're here. Are you planning on going anywhere?" He touched his tongue to the pad of Sam's thumb, listening to the sharp inhalation of Sam's breath.

The question hung between them in the air, heavy with meaning. Sam's eyes darkened and he stilled, his hand remaining on Zach's face.

"No. I'm right here, and I'm not planning on going anywhere else."

Something shifted between them then, their connection firing hotter than it had before. From the start, even back to that first night in Atlantic City when they knew nothing about one another, Zach had bared himself to Sam in a way he never had prior, not even with his best friends.

And now? Now it seemed like the beginning of a future he'd never imagined possible. All thanks to a little bet and some help from his friends.

"Let's go inside."

Zach led the way, acutely aware of Sam's hand resting on the small of his back. He opened the front door and called out, "Mom?"

"Back here, sweetheart. In the kitchen."

With Sam trailing behind, still touching him, Zach headed to the back of the house. "She's always either in the kitchen or the backyard with her flowers."

"Beautiful house. It looks pretty old but well restored."

"My father bought it when they were first married, before the neighborhood was 'hot.' When I made my money, the first thing I did was restore the house for her."

They entered the kitchen, and Zach spotted his mother at the wooden table, a full pot of coffee sitting in the center.

"Where were you? Is everything okay? I put the milk away—oh." She stopped speaking at the sight of him and Sam. Her gaze focused behind him, and Zach stepped to the side.

"Sorry I'm late. I want to introduce you to someone." His mother couldn't stop staring at Sam, a look of confusion on her face. "Mom, this is Sam Stein. Sam." He gave a gentle squeeze to Sam's arm. "This is my mom, Cheryl Cohen."

"A pleasure to meet you, Mrs. Cohen. Zach has told me so much about you."

His mother's smile failed to reach her eyes, but only someone who knew her well would notice.

"He did? How nice. Please sit and have some coffee. Zach, get Sam a cup."

Zach pulled out another mug from the cabinet, listening to his mother quiz Sam. Suddenly this didn't seem like such a great idea.

"So tell me, Sam, since my son hasn't found the time to tell me anything about his personal life, how long have you known each other?"

The guilt was what he expected. Zach should never have allowed this to go as far as it had.

Zach slid into the chair next to Sam and poured him a cup of coffee. "Mom, please. He's my friend; I don't think you need to interrogate him."

"Who's interrogating? I only asked a simple question.

You bring someone new home, and I'm not supposed to say anything?"

Amusement not anger danced in Sam's eyes and for the first time in hours, Zach relaxed. For once, things might work out well for him.

"We met the weekend Zach went to Atlantic City, but only reconnected recently back in the city." Sam sipped his coffee. "I went to breakfast with him today and met his friends."

"Oh." Mentioning Zach's friends guaranteed to bring a smile to her face. "You met the boys? Aren't they the sweetest?"

"They seem like a great group of guys."

Cringing, Zach almost groaned out loud. His mother acted as if this was high school and Sam was picking him up for the prom. He sneaked a glance over at Sam and was surprised to see him engaged and not at all annoyed.

"What do you do, if you don't mind me asking?" She refilled Sam's coffee cup and her own, leaving Zach out to his surprise. He took the pot and poured his own cup.

"I'm retired from the police department, and now do private undercover work." Sam drank more coffee, his smile fading around the rim of the cup.

"Retired? But you're so young." Her hand clapped over her mouth. "Oh, were you injured? Did you get hurt and have to retire? Are you on disability?"

"Mom." Mortified, Zach raised his voice to her for the first time. "Stop asking Sam such personal questions." Especially since Zach himself didn't know the answer. There was so much about Sam he didn't know: whether his parents were alive, if he had brothers or sisters, his past lovers, although Zach wasn't sure about bringing that up.

"Sam seems like a very nice man. You don't mind, do you?" At his shrug, she patted Sam's hand, then stood and took her cup to the sink. "You see? After all, we're family here. There're no secrets."

Wincing, Zach drained his mug and joined his mother at the sink.

"Mom," he whispered, low enough for Sam not to hear over the running water. "Please stop asking him all these personal questions. I didn't bring him here to be questioned."

"Why is he here?" Her hands methodically washed her cup, even though it was clean.

"Um, I, um." Fumbling to explain, the coming out conversation didn't seem so easy right now. "I knew this was a bad idea," he muttered to himself. "I never should've brought him here."

Her lips trembled. "You're ashamed of me, aren't you? I'm sorry I'm such a burden." She placed the cup on the counter but left the water running.

"Of course not. I could never be ashamed of you; you're my mother." And he meant it. His mother was loving, kind, and gentle; he knew she'd be accepting. But knowing it inside and saying it out loud to her were two separate things. You could never be certain until the words were spoken and your soul laid bare.

"So what is it? What are you holding inside that has you tied up in knots, looking sick to your stomach?" She placed a hand on his arm, and he gave her a questioning look.

"What?"

"Is it Sam?" She glanced over at him sitting at the table. "Is he your boyfriend?"

The mug he held crashed in the sink, breaking into half a dozen shards. "Wh-what?" He licked his lips in nervous anxiety. "My boyfriend?"

She turned off the water and led him back to the table and Sam. "Sit." She pointed at the chair. "Instead of having this conversation over the kitchen sink, I think we should sit down like adults, don't you?"

Her tone brooked no objection and like the obedient child he was, Zach complied. He met his mother's eyes over the expanse of the old wooden table, but there was no condemnation, only love.

"Sam. I'm sorry to put you on the spot, but are you and my son dating? And if you're trying to make a good impression on me, lying wouldn't be a good thing right now."

Shooting him a stunned look, Sam rubbed his chin. "Ahh."

"It's not for Sam to answer, Mom. Maybe I shouldn't have brought him here without talking to you first, but it's hard for me to explain this on my own, and Sam's become a big part of my life recently, so it's time you met."

She loved Julian and Nick, and Zach long suspected she knew Marcus was gay, but didn't feel it was her place to talk about his sex life. His mother was a believer in true love in all forms for all people, so his hopes were high that coming out to her now wouldn't break their relationship.

So here at this kitchen table where he was told of his father's death, he finally opened his heart to his mother.

"I'm gay, Mom. I didn't plan on telling you today, but maybe it's time already." Sam's hand crept into his, and he grabbed on to it for dear life. "No, not maybe, it is time. I'm twenty-nine years old and still scared about what my mother might say when I tell her I'm gay."

Her gaze darted from Sam back to him, and Zach could swear that with her unerring sixth sense, she knew how hard his hand squeezed Sam's.

"You were scared of me? What I might say to you?" Blinking furiously, she wiped her eyes with a tissue she pulled from the pocket of her shorts. "You're my child, I love you. You remind me so much of your father, did I ever tell you?" She touched his cheek with shaking hands.

"No, Mom. I didn't know that." After he died, she'd put away all the pictures of his father and never took them out again, claiming it hurt too much to see him every day when he was never coming home again.

When his mother would go to sleep, Zach would quietly search through the house, looking for the pictures, any picture of his father he could keep. Except for a hazy memory of laughing blue eyes and dark hair, Zach had no recollection of what his father looked like.

"You do. And he would've been so proud of you, like I am and always will be. Nothing could ever change that." She cupped his jaw. "Nothing. Do you understand me?"

The trembling in his body didn't cease; in fact he shivered from it. "I didn't want to disappoint you. I know how much you wanted grandchildren, want them, I mean."

The chair screeched as she abruptly stood, and he flinched from her emotional outburst. "Don't ever say you've been a disappointment to me. You're the only thing that's kept me going all these years. My everything."

That was the problem. Being with Sam now, wanting to explore where the tentative beginnings of their relationship might take them, meant he had to set boundaries with his mother where there'd never been a need for them before.

"I can't be that for you anymore, Mom." His broken whisper rang in his ears. "I can't be your everything. I need to find out who I am, and find my own everything."

Stricken, she gaped at him and Sam, who sat steady by his side, continuing to hold on to his hand with a firm grasp. "I thought you loved me."

"I do. And it's because I love you that we have to let go of each other." He released Sam's hand to grasp hers. "Our relationship isn't healthy, you have to see that."

When she said nothing, he continued to speak in a rush, the words flowing out of him fast, like a river overflowing, waiting a lifetime to be set free.

"I was so young when Dad died, I didn't know what to do or how to help you. And I knew you were falling apart, and I had no one to turn to. Only Marcus talked to me, but I wanted my mom."

"And I wasn't there. I let you down."

It killed him to have this talk, but his hope was if they put it out between them, they could move forward. No more hiding.

"In a way. But then I grew up and never tried to help you, because it was easier to simply stay here and make excuses. It made you happy. So, I'm as much at fault as you are. I let you down as well."

"I'm sorry."

"Mom, don't—"

She continued as if he didn't speak at all. "I thought I was doing the right thing. I never expected to raise a child alone. And yet you were so smart and had Marcus as a friend, so I thought you were handling everything."

"I did, I am. You know that now."

"But at what price? You're my son; you should be able to tell me anything. To be afraid to tell me you're gay…you know I'll love you no matter what. I can't believe you didn't trust me enough."

Zach couldn't let his mother blame herself for his mistakes.

"It had nothing to do with trust. I didn't tell you because I didn't want to burden you. And I know now that was wrong, so all I can do is say I trust you with my life. My mistakes were made out of love, not from a desire to hurt you. To shield you from more pain and confusion you might have felt at a time when you couldn't handle any more."

"You were the child and yet you tried to protect me."

"I think we all make mistakes out of love, because we anticipate the negative. It's fear of the unknown, which never makes for the wisest decisions."

Before he could add to that thought, his mother surprised him.

"You're right. We're programmed to think the worst, instead of anticipating the best. It's a trait that isn't confined to children either. Adults are some of the worst offenders, myself included."

Now that it was out in the open, he found the freedom intoxicating, yet he knew he needed to spell out boundaries that had never before been set.

"There are parts of my life I won't be sharing with you, but," he hastened to add, "it doesn't mean I don't love you, because I always will." He reached up to brush away her tears. "My wanting to be with someone—with Sam—can't and won't change the fact that you're my mother and I love you."

"When did you get to be so smart?" She sniffed, letting go of his hand to wipe her streaming eyes with a tissue.

"I had a good teacher," said Zach, smiling with relief. The day he'd always feared had come, and they'd all survived; the apocalypse had fizzled out. "She taught me about the heart's infinite ability to love."

They smiled into each other's eyes, the only sound coming from the comforting tick of the clock on the counter. Then Sam's hand touched his thigh, bringing with it a prickling awareness of his lover. "I hope you and Sam will be friends?"

Zach watched as Sam smiled at his mother across the table. "I know I'm looking forward to it." The grin Zach loved, the one that lightened Sam's face broke free, and Zach's heart squeezed tight. "It's been years since I had homemade chicken soup."

An answering light dawned in his mother's eyes. "Finally

someone to cook for." She smiled at them both. "It'll be wonderful to see Zach happy. And if you're the reason, then I know I'll love you."

No one had mentioned love, but neither he nor Sam was about to get into that conversation now. New beginnings and happiness were perfect.

Chapter Sixteen

There was something exciting about walking home with a person you couldn't wait to get into bed with, knowing you'd be ripping each other's clothes off as soon as you got past the front door. Sam tightened his grip on Zach's hand and increased his stride.

"I'm looking forward to getting back to my house. I can't wait to get you into bed."

Instead of the laughter he expected or even a kiss, Zach stiffened and stopped on the sidewalk, pulling away so they were standing face-to-face.

"Is this only about sex? I thought there was more to it." With a frustrated push of his finger, Zach slid the glasses back up on his nose and scowled.

God, Sam could eat him up, he looked so pissed. Tonight

Zach wouldn't be frustrated or angry after they fucked. Sam would make sure he would be wearing nothing but a smile and those glasses. Nothing had ever gotten Sam so hard so fast as Zach's big blue eyes behind those black frames, and the adorable, pissed-off expression on his face was icing on the cake.

And Sam loved cake with lots of icing.

"What's wrong with sex? We have a great time in bed together." Sam pointed down the block. "We're almost at my house, come on." There was no need to have this conversation on the street in public. He'd been horny all day. They could talk until morning about their feelings, but first he wanted to get laid. "And besides, I told you and your mother, in case you've forgotten, that we were dating. And dating implies sex." He began to walk down the block.

Zach fell into step with him but continued to argue his point. "It may imply sex, which we can debate at another time because I'm not sure how much I believe that, but there are other more important things when one dates another person."

"More important than sex?" Sam scratched his head. "What are you talking about?"

"Uhh." Zach let out a frustrated growl. "I feel like I'm talking to Marcus. I don't know anything about you, and you seem happy to keep it that way."

Suddenly uneasy with the way the conversation was heading, Sam attempted to lighten the mood. "Not much to know. I'm boring."

"It was important to me to tell you that I still live with and take care of my mother. That would've been the perfect time for you to tell me about your family, but you didn't." Zach sounded miserable. "I don't know anything about you, except you're a retired cop, and every time someone mentions that, you change the subject."

Sam gritted his teeth. "I don't believe in rehashing the

past. What's the point? It's finished, you can't change what happened, so why torture yourself over things?"

"Why would you torture yourself? Sometimes a person with a new perspective can make all the difference." Zach touched his arm, but he remained unyielding. "Maybe it wasn't as bad as you think."

The hell it wasn't. "Number one, I don't want to have this conversation. Number two, I certainly don't want to have this conversation on the street." They'd finally reached his corner, and he pulled out his keys. "Can we please go inside?"

Considering he once thought Zach to be compliant and a bit of a pushover, the man could be stubborn as hell.

"What's the point? We'll go inside, and I'll go to bed with you, but in the end, it won't mean anything. I might as well be making love to a stranger."

They stood in front of his house. His apartment was one of five that made up the townhouse, with his being the smallest and cheapest. The landlady liked having an ex-cop in the building and gave him a pretty deep discount on the rent, and in return he kept an eye on things for her and made the small repairs she needed.

"I understand what you're saying. Let's go in and we can talk."

Zach gave him a skeptical look. "Talk talk? Or talk as a euphemism for sex?"

Earlier in the evening, the answer would have been the second choice. But with how important this now had become to Zach, Sam was at war with himself: shut Zach out and he'd lose him, probably for good; open himself up and all the shit he'd stuffed away for the past year would rise up to expose him and lay him bare.

Before he could stop himself, Sam reached out his hand to Zach. "Talk as in talk. If you have questions, I promise to try and answer them."

What Sam would've liked to see from Zach was a smile in return for what he said, but when none was forthcoming, a moment of fear kicked in that Zach would walk anyway. Relief flooded through him when Zach gave him a nod, grim though it was, and followed behind him into his apartment.

Keeping a respectable distance away from Zach, Sam headed into the kitchen. "Do you want a drink?" He knew he needed a beer for what was ahead.

"No, thanks," called out Zach, who remained in the living room.

His elbows braced against the countertop for a moment, Sam regrouped his scrambled brain and parsed together what he would and wouldn't say. He could talk about his mother and the death of his father; that was a neutral subject and wouldn't take too much time. As for work, retirement, Andy...he'd have to see how it flowed. The thought of telling Zach why he retired nauseated him.

After a quick, bracing gulp of beer, Sam went to the living room and found Zach sitting on the sofa, staring into space.

"Hey. You're sure you don't want anything?" He stood by the arch in the doorway not yet entering the room.

Late afternoon sunlight fell across the room, missing Zach in his position on the sofa, hiding his face in the shadowed dimness. In the short time they'd been together, Sam had learned Zach's eyes reflected every emotion inside him; they truly were an insight into his heart and soul. Right now he'd lay bets they were dark with sadness.

"No. I'm good," he said softly. Zach shifted into the sunlight. "Look. I'm sorry I forced you into this. I don't have the right to push you into something that for whatever reason makes you so uncomfortable."

Sam sat on the opposite side of the sofa from Zach. "It's important to you. I'm not good at this kind of stuff; talking about personal issues. That's more my best friend Henry's job. He loves all that stuff, him and his wife, Heather."

"You've known him a long time?" Zach wound the tassel of the sofa's pillow around his finger. "He's the one you went to Atlantic City with, right?"

"Yes to both. I've known Henry since we were teenagers. He's like my brother." The tension in his chest eased some. He could do this, keep the talk light and easy. "He runs the computer security firm I do jobs for and was the one touting your brilliance to me." Sam grinned. "I think he has a bit of a fan boy crush on you."

"Me? That's crazy," Zach scoffed, then grew serious again. "Do you have any brothers or sisters? Parents?" The question hung in the air.

The prick of a guilty conscience hit him when Sam remembered he hadn't called his mother in a few weeks. They had an odd relationship, so different from the close-knit, loving one he'd seen between Zach and his mother. At one time it had been, and if Sam searched his memory, he could dimly recall late-night kisses and hugs from her.

Always dressed in the clothes Sam knew were more for young women in their twenties, Barbara Stein fought the aging process like a five-star general waging a war. And it was for her—the march of time and creep of age was an everyday battle for her, leaving little time to parent her bewildered, lonely son. After his father died, her time was spent in the gym exercising, at the salon getting hair extensions, facials, and whatever else they sold to keep her on the singles scene, hopping from man to man, each one richer than the last.

"My father died when I was fourteen; young, like you. And also like you I was an only child."

"What about your mother? Is she alive?" Letting go of his hold on the pillow, Zach tucked his feet underneath him on the sofa, settling onto the armrest. He looked expectantly at Sam.

"Yeah. She lives in Florida, so I don't get to see her too much." Not that either one of them made an effort. Desperate about money after his father died, she brought a succession of men through his life, none of them leaving any permanent mark. Some were nice to him, trying to curry favor with his mother, some ignored him, and most only wanted him out of the way. All of them demanded his mother's time, and she freely gave it to them, as they were the ones financing her lifestyle with their gifts of expensive clothes, jewelry, and dinners.

The one thing she never made time for was her son.

"I tried to make my mother go to Florida; I thought she'd like me to get her a house there in the winter, but that didn't go over too well," said Zach wistfully.

"Maybe it will be different now that you've cleared the air."

"Maybe, but I think she'll still want to be close to me. Years of habit won't change overnight."

That smacked of unfairness to Sam, but he could hardly criticize Zach's mother, knowing how close they were. Treading carefully, he hoped his answer was nonjudgmental. "You'll probably need to sit down with her and talk again. Today was a good beginning, though."

Zach blinked and glared at him. "You've managed to steer the conversation away from you back to me again. Nice try."

"It wasn't deliberate. Ask me something else."

"You know," said Zach, a glimmer of humor returning to his eyes, "I'm not here to interrogate you. I only wanted to get to know you better. I'm kind of a novice at this myself. Having Julian and Marcus as friends didn't make for the best role models for healthy relationships."

"I imagine Marcus has never had a relationship with anyone."

"Oh, he's had hundreds of relationships; the problem is they all last only one or two days. He loves everyone." Zach's good humor faded. "I wish I knew how to help him. He refuses to talk about himself or anything personal. He's always been like that."

"Then you'll have to wait. Forcing him to talk will ruin your friendship. When he's ready, he'll come to you. But Julian and Nick seem like a solid couple."

"Yeah." Brightness lit Zach's face. "They knew each other in high school and only recently got back together. I'm so happy for Julian. He loves Nick so much, always has."

Sam liked this happy, smiling Zach, until he asked casually, "Have you ever been in a serious relationship?"

Fuck. Thoughts darted everywhere in an effort to figure out what to say and not say.

Apparently Sam no longer had the blank cop face it took years to perfect, as Zach now stared at him, tense and unsmiling.

"You don't have to answer me." He shifted on the sofa and stood. "I think I'm gonna go. I have stuff to do. Work…" He headed to the front door.

The drifting sadness in Zach's voice, the finality of him walking toward the door, snapped Sam out of his lassitude. If Zach left now, Sam knew he wouldn't see him again, and that was unacceptable. He rushed to block Zach's departure, standing close enough to feel Zach's breath blow hot against his neck.

"Don't go."

"There's no point," said Zach tiredly. "You shut down on me as soon as I mention a former lover. I never thought you were a virgin, Sam. I'm only trying to discover how and if we fit together."

"We do. Better than I have with anyone, ever." Honesty was the only way with someone like Zach. His kind of caring was obvious from the moment they met. Sam supposed it was what drew him to Zach in the first place. Being in his presence imbued a person with his warm and gentle spirit and steadfast loyalty. It made him a man impossible to forget.

"Tell me. Tell me how. Not with your body." Zach pulled away when Sam leaned down to kiss him. "I already know the sex is amazing. Talk to me. Let me know what's in your head. You have to know by now I'm the least judgmental person you'll ever meet."

"I used to be happy." His voice caught, and he cleared his throat. Shit. Could he really do this? If he wanted to keep Zach, yeah. And he needed Zach. He didn't know how it happened, or why it was Zach and not any other man, but he wasn't questioning the vagaries of fate. Things were and shit happened.

"I was in a relationship for almost two years. We were total opposites but laughed about it, saying we complemented each other's differences. And all that was fine until he got tired of me."

Somehow he'd ended back on the sofa, Zach pressed up to his side.

"Andy started hanging around with his single friends; he never liked Henry and his wife, thought they were boring. He became all about the party scene and the clubs. He'd go out when I was on shift or too tired. I didn't care 'cause I trusted him, and clubbing was never my scene."

"We have that in common," said Zach, smiling into the curve of Sam's neck. "I'm all about the sofa, Netflix, and some Pad Thai."

That sounded pretty fucking awesome to Sam right about now. The only thing better would be fast-forwarding to later tonight when he hoped to be naked on this very sofa with an equally naked Zach riding him. The thought sent a flush of pleasure racing through him, and he slipped his arm around

Zach, hugging him close.

"I think that can be arranged later, what do you say?"

"I say keep—" Zach's pocket vibrated and rang. "Hmm. That's Julian. He never calls unless it's important."

"Go ahead and take it."

Shooting him a disapproving look, Zach touched the screen to turn on his phone. "We aren't finished yet."

The image of Zach impaled on his dick still fresh in his imagination, Sam leered at Zach. "I know."

"Idiot." He spoke into the phone. "Julian, what's up?"

Not wanting to eavesdrop in case the conversation was personal, Sam stood, but Zach grabbed him by the arm.

"You're WHAT?" His voice rose in excitement. "When? Just now? Was it planned?"

What happened? mouthed Sam.

"Nick and Julian got engaged." Zach's face shone with happiness, and he nodded while listening. "Yeah, of course I'll be there." Flashing a quick look at Sam, he bit his lip. "I'll ask him."

"Ask me what?"

"Julian and Nick are having a party to celebrate at their loft tomorrow night. It seems Nick planned everything as a surprise for Julian."

"That's great, but what do you need to ask me?" Sam couldn't imagine.

"They want to know if you'll come. To the party with me, I mean."

Completely taken by surprise, Sam gaped at Zach. "Me? I didn't think Julian even liked me, are you sure he meant to invite me to his engagement party?"

Zach said something inaudible into the phone and shut it off. "One thing you need to know is Julian never says what he doesn't mean; he doesn't lie or hide the truth. They want you there, and I'd really like it if you'd come with me." The hopeful smile made him impossible to resist.

Sam shared Zach's smile. "I'd love to." He tugged Zach close, resting his hands lightly on Zach's slim hips. Nestled close together, their bodies fit, settling into place like it was meant to be. Zach rested his head against Sam's shoulder and that felt perfect as well. Scary perfect. "So we have the whole rest of the afternoon and tonight together. You know what I think we should do?"

"I can only imagine," said Zach, the sarcasm evident in his voice. "Do I have three guesses and the first two don't count?"

This teasing and joking was nice. Normal, relationship-nice to be with Zach and make plans like a real couple. He trailed his hands down Zach's back to cup his ass. "Well, you do owe me."

"Mmm?" Zach hummed against the curve of his neck. "I owe you?"

The man was driving him wild, planting tiny kisses along his collarbone, licking up his neck. It took an incredible strength of will for Sam to not simply fling Zach over his shoulder and take him to bed, but having begun to tell his story, he had a sudden desire to free himself of his past. Sam wanted Zach to know Andy had been exorcised from his life and he was ready to move forward. Together.

"Yeah. You promised me a walk on the beach in Atlantic City. Now, I'm not driving to the Jersey Shore tonight, but how about the boardwalk on Coney Island? We can walk on the beach there and have a hot dog at Nathan's or some fried clams."

When Zach didn't answer right away, Sam grew nervous. "It's nothing fancy like the Hamptons where your friends probably go but—"

Zach cut him off with a kiss, wrapping his arms tight around him. "I can't think of a more perfect way to spend the day."

Chapter Seventeen

When Sam mentioned going to Coney Island, Zach wasn't prepared for what that meant. It had been years since he'd been there; as a child he'd go with his parents and they'd spend the entire day there. His mom would stay under the umbrella reading, and he and his father would hold hands to jump the waves or walk down to the rocks, swinging pails, looking for shells.

As an adult, his usual beach visits involved nothing more than solitary walks along the shoreline, his pants rolled up while the water lapped around his feet. He'd spend his time staring out at the endless horizon or into the depths of the water, wishing he had someone there with him.

Now he did and Zach couldn't help the excitement trickling through him. He and Sam had packed up Sam's car with a blanket, a cooler of beer and water, bags of chips and fruit, and headed out. Sam's hands looked strong and sure on the wheel, and Zach lost himself a bit staring at his fingers. He wanted them on his body, stroking him, touching him, penetrating him.

Conversation flowed easily between them; Zach relayed the story of Nick and Julian finding love after all their years apart and the company Julian had started, creating beautiful bandages for burn victims.

"Those are amazing stories; both Nick and Julian finding each other again and Julian creating such a meaningful business. Most people in that industry don't care about anything except for pretty faces and perfection. Julian must be a very special man."

"He is; they both are." They rode in silence for a while before he spoke again. "People spend so much time worrying about what might happen or could happen, they forget to live in the present, in the now, and they miss so much."

"How about you?" Sam shot him a quick look when he switched lanes on the Belt Parkway. "Do you think about what might happen in the future too much?"

Staring out of the car window, Zach pondered Sam's question. The future. Up until now his future mirrored his past: time stretching endlessly, one day to the next, with him vicariously enjoying his friends' successes. "No," said Zach. "That wasn't my problem. I never thought or planned for the future because I didn't think I had one worth a second thought. It was always going to be my mother and myself."

A muscle in Sam's jaw tightened and his brows drew together as if in anger, but he remained silent, continuing the drive along the parkway, passing under the Verrazano Bridge. The afternoon sun glinted along the water, seagulls diving down to skim the surface. Multicolored kites soared in the sky, and Zach watched in wonder as their handlers deftly controlled the strings, their flashy tails swooping high against the backdrop of the clear blue sky.

"I haven't seen the kite flyers in years. I've forgotten how watching them is like watching an artist perform a ballet in the sky."

With an unexpected turn of the wheel, Sam pulled the car off to the side and into the small parking area reserved along the side of the road for people to park. A delighted thrill rose within Zach when Sam turned off the engine and turned to him with a wide smile.

"Wanna try it?"

"Are you serious?" His excitement grew and like a kid he couldn't stop throwing out questions to Sam. "I've never done it before; you have a kite? You know how to fly one? I always wanted to try."

Without answering, Sam got out of the car and opened the trunk. It took a minute or two of rummaging while Zach alternated between wanting to shout for him to hurry up and hoping it would take forever so he could enjoy the anticipation. Even Sam's muffled cursing as he shoved aside the items in the trunk couldn't detract from Zach's happiness on this gorgeous summer day.

"Aha!" Sam's head poked around from the side of the opened hood. "Finally got it. I wanted to make sure I didn't rip the tail." Zach remained silent and motionless, wanting to capture everything he could about this moment. The tang of salty air, the slap of the water against the rocks, the cries of the children pointing to the kites mixing with the raucous call of the gulls overhead—all of it imbedded itself in his mind, smoothing over the scars he once thought a permanent fixture on his heart.

Now, all that resided there was Sam.

"Are you okay?" The slam of the car's hood knocked him out of his daydream, and he came to, with Sam holding on to his shoulder, a concerned look on his face. "You had such a strange look on your face, like you'd seen a ghost or something."

Impulsively, Zach reached up to kiss Sam. "No ghosts; not anymore at least." He kissed him again, resting against Sam's broad chest. "Only dreams from now on."

Giving him a funny smile, Sam hugged him briefly, then displayed the kite. It was bright red, edged in yellow. The long, trailing tail was red, black, blue, and yellow. His excitement growing, Zach watched as Sam expertly unwound the string from the ball and stood with his back to the road, waiting.

The wind had been picking up gradually, and Zach's hair blew across his forehead, becoming trapped between his face and glasses. Irritated, he brushed it away, and Sam slipped his arms around him from behind and spoke into his ear. "Take hold of the string with me. Let's fly together."

With Sam's strong arms around his shoulders, Zach took the string and the kite tugged hard as it took flight. His heart pounded when Sam's hand covered his, and the two of them moved in concert, sending the kite dipping and soaring in the sky. With some subtle hand moves, Sam made the kite swoop and cut through the air, like it was dancing amidst the clouds.

Zach couldn't help but laugh; the joy of being alive poured through him, setting his heart jumping to a rhythm it had never played before. He had no capacity to put into words the swell of emotion blooming sharp and bright in his chest.

"We're losing the wind; I'm gonna bring her in, okay?" Sam took control of the string, and Zach, still unable to speak, nodded and stepped back, content to keep his secret to himself. Sam pulled the kite down and wound the string back around the holder. They walked back to the car.

"That was fun, huh?" said Sam, placing the kite in the backseat of the car. "I hadn't done it in a while, but I was hoping we'd get a good enough wind so I could break it out and show you some moves."

"You were great. Very impressive. I always wanted to try it, but never thought to ask my parents when I was a kid. I didn't think to do it as an adult, but maybe I'll try now."

"I could teach you," said Sam, leaning in for a kiss. "We could fly together."

Zach blinked and could only nod.

They pulled back onto the Parkway and with the traffic it took about twenty minutes before they exited and found a spot near the beach. Sam balanced the small cooler on his hip, Zach took the bag with the towels and blanket, and they trekked across Surf Avenue to the original Coney Island Nathan's.

Zach sniffed the air, the unmistakable smell of hot dogs, greasy burgers, salt water, and suntan lotion combining to form the quintessential New York City summer beach aroma. Nothing in the world was like it.

"Come on," he urged Sam, hurrying to an empty table he spotted outside. "Let's grab that table."

Sam grunted, hefting the cooler, and followed him, setting the cooler down on the cement in the shade under his chair. "I'll get us the food. Be right back."

Already seated, Zach merely nodded and leaned his head back to catch the rays of the sun. Sometime today, Zach didn't know when, the rules of his life had changed. His willingness to live a secondhand life, content to sit on the sidelines, had vanished, leaving in its place a man who, though imperfect, recognized his own self-worth.

It might have been an epiphany, late in coming but still viable and no less deserving. For years he'd been lectured and yelled at by his friends to live a whole life, not one hidden away. They'd done so without the knowledge of why and what had brought him to that point.

Now, it was time. Watching Sam approach, balancing a tray laden with hot dogs, fries, and fried clams, beers sloshing over the rims of huge plastic cups, Zach sensed it was his moment, placed before him to be seized tight and never let go. It was time for him to give up his shame and embrace this new, exciting future.

Forever was too long a time to live with regrets about a past that couldn't be changed. And who's to say that past didn't shape him into becoming a better man in the end.

"I don't give a damn if it's bad for me, nothing is better than this stuff." Sam popped a piece of fried clam in his mouth, chewed and swallowed, then moaned in ecstasy. "Fuck, that's so damn good and greasy. Ha." He gulped down the beer.

The fries were hot and crispy, and the hot dog had that delicious snap to it with the mustard and sauerkraut piled on. He and Sam munched through their food as if any moment someone would appear to snatch their fun away. At the end, all that was left was little red plastic forks, paper holders for the fries and clams, and some ketchup-and-mustard-smeared paper plates.

"Damn that was almost as good as sex." Sam leaned back and stretched out. Zach eyed his thick thighs and hairy legs and wanted to climb him like a ladder.

"Oh, yeah?" Zach asked lazily. "I prefer sex. Unless we're talking about eating in bed." He raised a brow at the dark expression on Sam's face Zach now recognized as rising lust and quirked a smile. "I'm all for eating in bed."

"Don't start what you can't finish. At least until later."

Laughing at Sam's pitiful excuse for a threat, Zach tossed a crumpled napkin at him. "Let's go to the beach. I want my walk by the water."

They cleaned up their trash and threaded their way past the crowds to walk onto the boardwalk. Though crowded, it was late enough that the families with young children had started packing up, getting ready to brave the drive or subway ride home with sunburned, sun-exhausted children. Zach didn't envy them.

"There's a good spot." Sam pointed to a large swath of empty sand. "Let's go there."

The closer to the ocean, the stronger the pull it had on Zach. His toes dug into the warmed sand and neither the hawkers selling water on the beach nor the loud music playing from a nearby radio detracted from his enjoyment. This was where he was his happiest. Something about the water and the sand called to him, and he made up his mind, this would be the year he'd buy that dream house by the ocean he'd always wanted and fall asleep listening to the quiet shush of the waves.

They shook out the blanket and set it out on the sand, along with the towels. Sam placed the cooler on one end to keep the blanket from flapping in the breeze.

"Good, right?" Sam kicked off his flip-flops and held out his hand. "Let's go to the water." He wiggled his fingers and flipped down his sunglasses with his other hand. "We can walk off all that food, and I can feel more virtuous than if I sat on the sand like a blob."

The sun beat hot on his shoulders through his thin tee shirt, and Zach dropped the now-empty bag on the blanket. The sound of the waves and Sam standing, waiting for him with an outstretched hand, framed by the bright blue sky and soaring waves, made for a perfect picture. He jammed a cap on his head, kicked off his flip-flops, and took Sam's hand. "Let's go."

The sand burned on their bare feet and both he and Sam raced to the ocean's edge to cool off in the encroaching tide. Wordlessly they stood, the water lapping cool against their ankles, their toes sinking in the wet, mushy sand. To Zach's surprise, Sam inched his foot close and tickled Zach's toes with his own.

"You have such a peaceful look on your face." His thumb stroked Zach's palm. "Like everything is right in the world."

"It is when I'm here. That's what the beach does to me," he admitted. "Like I told you before, the happiest memory I have of my father and me was at the beach. I'd like to think he would have still loved me the same, even when I told him I was gay."

Every month he'd drive out to the cemetery to visit his father's grave. Zach would sit on the bench he had placed there and talk to his father about his life, and how much Zach still missed him. His mother's insistence on visiting the grave weekly when he was young had given him a different perspective on life than that of most kids his age. For more than half of Zach's life, death had played a significant part.

Sadness, like a veil drawn over Sam's face, chased away the smile and humor from his eyes. "I never got the chance to know my father well. He was away for most of my life and died on the job."

"What did he do, was he a cop as well?"

"He was an undercover narcotics agent with the FBI."

"Oh, Sam." Zach slipped his arm around Sam's waist. "I'm so sorry. It must've been so hard on you and your mother."

"She didn't care," he said, bitterness rising off his words to hang like an accusatory cloud between them. "It took her a whole month of mourning before she moved on with her life, leaving me and my father's memory behind." His jaw flexed tight. "I could never forget him though. Even though he was home so infrequently, it was like a holiday when I'd wake up and he'd be there. He'd take me to the park and play ball…"

"It sounds like he loved you very much."

Sam shrugged, digging a divot in the sand with his toes. The tide rushed in, smoothing it back to its original, unblemished surface. If only the human heart and spirit could be healed as easily. "I dunno." For the first time he sounded unsure to Zach; like a lost little boy searching for help.

"How could you think not? You're a big strong guy; you became a policeman. I'm sure he would be proud."

The spray of the water hit them then, and some screaming children rushed past, kicking up the water as they threw themselves into the waves. Moving closer to Sam, Zach watched the lines deepen on his face and the clenched jaw indicating his internal struggle. With a gentle touch, Zach rubbed Sam's back, between his shoulder blades. He tensed at first, then relaxed, humming with approval under his breath.

"Sounds like we both have some unresolved issues that need discussing, but for now we should put them on hold. What do you say?" Zach continued stroking Sam's back, fingers digging into the muscles of his shoulders, dipping down to trace the vertebrae of Sam's spine.

Like a cat in the sun, Sam arched into his touch. "Feels good."

"I give good back rubs." Zach squeezed Sam's shoulder. "If you're nice, I'll treat you to one later."

Giving him an amused smile, Sam said nothing, continuing to stare out at the water. Sensing from the troubled expression on his face Sam was working something out in his head, Zach remained silent, giving the man his space. No longer at its zenith, the sun still remained hot in the sky, and Zach contemplated taking off his shirt to cool down.

When it seemed apparent Sam wasn't ready to talk, Zach pulled off his shirt and after tossing it on the sand, waded into the foamy surf. He had no qualms about getting his shorts wet; they were mostly nylon and would dry quickly. Besides, they were at the beach; how could he not go in the water?

Small waves buffeted him, but Zach jumped them with ease, going deeper into the water until it was up to his chest. The familiar sense of peace stole through him, and he laughed from the sheer joy of being in his favorite place on earth, closing his eyes and turning his face up to the sun and its warmth.

Without warning, he was knocked under water, a wave sweeping him off his feet. He choked, lost his glasses, and his mouth filled with salt water. Flailing about, terrified, Zach couldn't breathe. He swallowed some water and battled upward through the pull of the current. Was he going to die now, after finally making peace with his life? Frantic with alarm, he kicked his way back up to the surface.

Strong arms pulled him up to the surface, and he coughed and spit up salt water before dragging in deep breaths of air. Plastered up against Sam's wet shirt, Zach looked up into his concerned yet furious face and smiled weakly.

"Thanks."

Sam crushed his mouth over Zach's in a harsh, desperate kiss, and Zach sagged against him, his arms clamped around Sam's neck. The hard, almost angry way Sam held him, instead of sending Zach into a panic, reassured him. If Sam didn't yet understand, Zach did. Sam's fear personified the deep emotional connection he had yet to put into words in the way their mouths fused together, and his heart hammered against Zach's.

The air turned chill, and Zach shivered, despite the heat pouring off Sam's body. Sam broke their kiss and hugged Zach close to his chest. "Let's get you back to the blanket. I'm sorry I couldn't get your glasses."

"It's okay; I have other pairs at home." He shivered again.

Half dragging Zach through the water and sand, Sam brought him back to the blanket and draped the extra towels over him, until Zach found himself buried in a mountain of terrycloth.

"Stop," he protested. "You saved me from drowning, and

now you're going to smother me." He rubbed his head with one to stop the water from dripping in his eyes and down his face.

"I, I got scared." Breathing heavily, Sam sat near, but not close enough to touch him. "I thought you were drowning and then I grabbed you—"

"It's fine. *I'm fine.*" Zach reassured Sam and tossed the wet towel behind him on the blanket.

"I heard you yell, and it was the scariest sound I ever heard in my life." Sam's chest heaved. "Then you got knocked over by the wave and disappeared, and I thought I was gonna lose you." He scrubbed his face with his hands, and Zach was close enough to see his pale skin, slightly wild eyes, and wet hair flat against Sam's head. "To know your last words would be you crying out for help almost killed me. I couldn't let that happen."

Asking for help had never been easy for Zach. He'd learned to internalize his suffering or to skate by his feelings without ever touching below the surface. Telling Julian and Marcus wouldn't have served any purpose; they'd never liked Nathan or understood his dogged devotion to him. But they'd been born with a sense of self-worth and swagger. Zach was convinced he was shy from birth. Some people are natural leaders and others tend to follow along in their wake. Zach had always been a follower, until Sam showed him how to walk together, side by side.

"He used to hurt me," said Zach, blurting out the ugly truth he'd kept hidden all these years. "My *boyfriend* in college, who I was so thrilled to have, would verbally abuse and humiliate me. I thought I loved him; I let him make fun of me in front of other people, knock down my self-esteem any time I'd get praise." Ashamed at what Sam must think, Zach studied the wet sand clumped between his toes. "Nathan said I was too sensitive and couldn't take a joke. Then he started in on the physical. No one knew."

"You never said anything to anyone; not even Marcus or Julian? They never guessed what was happening?" Sam's questions were kindly, though Zach could sense the seething anger banked behind his voice.

"I was lucky Marcus and Julian wanted to be friends with me." He huffed out a self-conscious laugh, but even after all these years, a small part of Zach still harbored the conviction that he wasn't good enough.

"I was scared and ashamed, so no, to answer your question, I never said anything; what man would? In my eyes I wasn't a real man to let myself get pushed around like that. It took me years to get past it." The lump in his throat made it virtually impossible to swallow without pain, but he forced himself to hold Sam's troubled gaze. "That's why it was perfect hanging out in my basement where my mother basically left me alone. When Marcus and Julian pushed me to come to the club and meet guys, it made me want to shrivel up and hide. I didn't want to get close to people and let them touch me; why would they want to?"

All that seemed like it had happened to a different person so many years ago. Perhaps it had, because Zach could no longer see himself as that helpless ever again.

"But I want you to know when you touch me, I don't ever want you to stop. That's a whole different kind of scared."

Chapter Eighteen

The sun sat in the sky, its heavy presence like a juicy, overripe peach throwing the sweetness of its late afternoon rays over the water and sand. The fiery glow heralded the end of another summer day to be tucked into the memory books; but Sam could see in Zach's unfocused eyes he wasn't admiring nature's beauty, nor did he want to remember his past.

There was no hiding from it though, our past shapes our future, and Sam could no more disassociate himself from his own failed relationship than Zach could. Each of them handled it differently, and in their own self-destructive ways. Zach, who hid away and believed, despite all his achievements, that he wasn't a man worth getting to know, and him, by cutting off social contact completely.

"Did you ever get any help?" Sam prayed Zach would say yes but didn't hold much hope.

"Yeah, I did, even though I already knew what they would tell me; low self-esteem, struggling with being gay, too wrapped up in his mother, blah, blah, blah." Grimacing, Zach tried to wiggle the sand off his toes.

"They can be very helpful sometimes; it's good to let it all out and have someone sit there and listen."

"They did nothing." Zach's eyes spit fire, his face tight with remembered pain. "I sat there and spilled my guts to them, and all they did was tell me how I need to get to the unresolved issues of my sexuality. I have none. I've never doubted who I am." He dug his heels into the sand, burying his feet. "I needed someone to tell me why I still panic sometimes when people touch me; why a person can call me invisible when I sit in the room with them, why I never make an impression."

His face stony with hurt and anger, Zach jumped up and walked back to the shoreline, his silhouette forlorn against the backdrop of the pounding tide.

Shocked at that outburst, Sam scrambled to his feet and caught up with him. Zach said nothing as they continued their walk along the ocean's edge.

"I don't think you really still believe that about yourself anymore. Maybe you went to the wrong person."

The tide came in and the water swirled around their ankles, spraying up their legs. Sam took Zach's hand and held it tight, afraid he might be losing him to the shadows of his past.

"No, you're right, I don't. It was so hurtful at the time, and it fed my insecurities for years. I don't doubt myself as much, but I don't ever think I'll have the self-confidence my friends do."

They walked up the rapidly emptying beach; gone were

the screaming young children and loud salsa music from the radios. It was them, the seagulls, and the waves.

"Who says you have to?" Sam stopped and faced Zach. "No two people are alike, that would be boring as hell. It would be a universe where everyone acted the same and eventually looked the same. Who wants a world full of robots?" He tightened his grip on Zach's hand and tugged him closer. "I don't need you to change; you fascinated me right from the start."

Zach blinked and wet his lips. "Me? I didn't do anything."

Heedless to the water pooling around their legs and the rising tide, Sam cupped the nape of Zach's neck, sliding his fingers through Zach's salt-roughened curls. "That's the point. You don't have to do anything. You're you. And *you* will always be enough for me."

Their lips met tentatively, unsure and soft, but then with increasing fervor, their mouths remembering the hot scorch of past kisses. Zach melted against Sam, and he responded by taking Zach's mouth harder, their tongues pushing together, breaths merging.

It was easy to lose track of both time and place holding a half-naked Zach in his arms, the languid stroke of his tongue like wet silk against his own, but the rising tide and setting sun intruded. With great reluctance, Sam pulled away from Zach, admiring his swollen lips and unfocused expression. Keeping him close, Sam ghosted his fingers along Zach's stubble-rough jawline and over his mouth.

Zach smiled, lips curving against Sam's fingers. "That was nice. Unfortunately, I'm going to have to go home and change clothes."

Alarmed, Sam had no intention of letting Zach leave his bed tonight. Tonight Sam would hold him close and show Zach with his body, if the words fumbled and stalled, how much Zach meant to him. From the first it seemed he'd underestimated the man. What had started out as a light and easy hook-up on a weekend away had led to a friendship and now an entwining of lives. The littlest thing Zach did occupied the biggest part of Sam's head and heart; he could no longer separate the two when he was with Zach.

He'd fallen into a love affair without even realizing it.

"Uh, you can pick up some clothes on the way back to my place. I think we should leave now and continue this conversation at my house."

Zach blinked and rubbed his eyes. "I've told you everything. I know I have a problem." He drew a design in the wet sand with his toe, and Sam saw it was the beginning of a heart, before the tide rushed in again to wash it away. "I was thinking I might start seeing the doctor Nick goes to; he's helped him so much with his recovery after 9/11."

Personally, Sam thought that was a fantastic idea, but it wasn't his decision to make. The best he could do for Zach was support him and be there for him if asked.

"That might be good; Nick seems to be pretty happy, from my impression." Sam slipped his arm around Zach's waist, and they began walking back to the blanket. The

beach was deserted for the most part. Only a few couples remained, and from past experience as a cop who once patrolled this area, Sam knew they were waiting for night to fall to get down to having sex.

"He is," agreed Zach, slipping his shirt over his head. "He had a fear of elevators and enclosed spaces from being trapped, and Dr. Landau slowly brought him back to where it isn't a problem anymore. Or," Zach corrected himself, "not so much of a problem that he can't work through it."

"I'm glad for him."

They shook out the blanket, then folded it up, Zach stuffing it back in the bag. Sam hefted the cooler onto his hip and teased Zach. "Do you need to hold my hand since you can't see where you're going?"

Zach rolled his eyes and pushed him playfully. "Wise-guy. After all you ate today, you're big enough that I can see you."

The trek back to the car took less time since the dense crowds had disappeared. Sam dumped the cooler in the trunk along with the bag from Zach and slammed down the hood. He slid into the front seat and started the engine.

"So, we'll head back to your place, and you'll pick up your glasses and some clothes, right?" Maneuvering out of the parking spot, he joined the line of cars heading out from the beach and back onto the Belt Parkway.

"Sure."

Traffic was stop and go all the way back to Downtown Brooklyn, and Sam spent the majority of his time yelling out the window at the drivers cutting him off and muttering curses under his breath. When Zach stopped chiding him after the third, "Fuck you," Sam figured he'd finally given up in exasperation.

"You're cute when you're trying to get me not to curse, you know that?"

No answer. Sam sneaked a quick look to the side, only to see Zach asleep, his mouth slightly open and head tipped to the side and resting on his arm. Unexpected warmth stole through him; he suddenly wished he could keep driving for hours, just to keep Zach so comfortably relaxed.

Sam wanted to be the man who Zach turned to on a miserable day, to be the man who Zach would call with happy news he couldn't wait to share. He wanted Zach in his bed, his life, his heart.

Fuck. He was in love.

*　　*　　*

"That wasn't so bad." Sam unpacked the cooler in the kitchen sink and popped a few grapes that had survived the trip into his mouth. "You told your mom I had to stay outside with the car so I wouldn't get a ticket, right?" He threw out the unsalvageable fruit and put the containers in the dishwasher. "I wouldn't want her to think I didn't want to come inside and say hi."

Zach lazed against the doorway, yawning. "Uh-huh. She had an ice cream social at the senior center she was helping with, so it turned out she'd be out anyway." Scratching his head, he wandered back into the living room and flopped on the sofa.

Holding two beers, Sam joined Zach on the sofa. "Move your feet."

Raising his brows, Zach lifted his feet, immediately placing them back in Sam's lap once he'd sat down. With a slight grin, he held out his hand. "One of those is for me, I hope?"

Sam handed him a bottle and joined Zach in taking a sip. "So," he began, unsure of how to bring this up. "You showed me yours, so it's my turn now."

"Hey." Zach sounded so serious. "It's not a contest. If you're not ready to talk, it's okay. I'm not going anywhere."

"It's not a big deal; I'm making more of it than it is. I lived with a guy for two years, and when I found out he cheated on me, we broke up." That wasn't too bad. He swallowed some more beer. "Things happen, and we both changed. Like I told you before, he became a big partier and that started becoming more important to him than spending time with me. I'm a homebody; I don't need to go to clubs to find someone to prove anything, or wiggle my ass at some kid, hoping he'll want to fuck. Sorry." He saw Zach's wince at his terminology.

"It really bothers you when people curse, huh?"

Turning red, Zach shrugged.

"I'll try to remember."

"I know it's strange; it's the way my parents raised me, and it's always stuck with me." Zach slanted a smile at him. "On you it can be kind of cute, but yeah, I'd prefer it if you didn't." He took a sip of his beer and closed his eyes.

Sam settled back into the sofa, wondering if it was too early to go to bed. It had been a long-ass day, and he wanted to spend a good part of the night exploring Zach's body. He smoothed his hand up Zach's leg, enjoying the play of muscle.

"When did you break up?"

His hand stilled for a moment, then continued its exploratory trail toward Zach's knee. "A little over six months ago."

"That also when you retired, right?"

"Yeah." The conversation was treading on dangerous ground. The only person he'd ever told about that night was Henry. He'd have to trust in his faith in Zach that he wouldn't make a snap judgment and instead listen to the mess Sam made of his life.

He drew in a deep breath. "I retired because I fucked up at work and couldn't come back from it. And yeah, fucked up is the only way to explain it, so sorry, but I'll have to offend you. I let my personal life interfere with my job, and it almost got my partner killed."

Henry had always been on his side, but he wasn't so sure Zach would understand. Sam glanced over at him and discovered he needn't have worried. The look on Zach's face—a combination of sorrow and heartbreak—broke down Sam's barriers for good, and the words he'd held to his heart came tumbling out.

"It hadn't been good between me and Andy for a while. Like I said, he'd gotten into partying and was out more often than home. Actually,"—Sam rubbed his chin and shifted his gaze over to Zach, hoping he wouldn't take what he was about to say the wrong way—"Andy reminds me of your friend, Marcus."

"No." Zach's tone was very definite. "For all his insanity, Marcus would never cheat; he hates people who do. He has a strong moral ethic for couples, he just doesn't believe in settling down himself."

Sam shrugged. "Anyway, it had been too many nights of Andy coming home drunk or high, smelling like sex, sweat, and unfamiliar aftershave." He couldn't forget that last night when Andy thought sucking Sam's cock like it was a dripping ice cream cone on a hot summer day would be enough to offset the cheating.

It wasn't. Sam had had enough.

"I got tired of the excuses, the attempts to use sex as avoidance for the real problem, which was simply that we didn't love each other anymore."

That was the saddest part of all. Someone he'd once said I love you to and meant it had carelessly thrown it all away for the excitement of a fresh, hot mouth and a willing ass. But he'd also been to blame, not seeing the warning signs or ignoring them, if he was being honest with himself.

"I've never been in a real relationship, so I'm not the right person to talk to about this, but it seems like you wanted to create a home, maybe a family, and he wasn't ready to settle down."

Sam faced Zach. "You're right, but how can anyone be sure that it's going to last, that the person they love won't change?"

"I don't know." Zach leaned his head on Sam's shoulder, and Sam tightened his arm around him. "I don't think you can; life is all about change. Growth, maturity, discovering things about yourself you never knew." He sighed, a quiet expulsion of breath Sam barely felt drift along his arm. "But what did this have to do with your retirement and your partner?"

"Andy disappeared after our fight, and I didn't hear from him in over a week. Even though I knew we were finished, I still worried about him. He didn't answer his phone and no one had seen him."

It had been a horrible week. Sam knew Andy was so melodramatic he was prone to grand gestures, and he'd feared he'd try something stupid or outlandish to get attention or prove a point and wind up hurting himself.

"One night we were covering some undercover detectives on a buy and bust. My partner was near our detectives, and I was across the street, when I got the first phone call from Andy in over a week."

Zach's brow furrowed. "I'm surprised you were allowed to have your cell phones on."

Humiliation burned through Sam. "You're not. It's a violation of command discipline. My first mistake, one of many that night."

Shifting around on the sofa so they sat face-to-face, Zach took both his hands. "You answered it, didn't you?"

Sam nodded. "I was afraid he was doing something stupid, and the suspect was already twenty minutes late for the buy. I took my eye off my partner to answer the call. It was only for a second, but that's when the shots started."

"Oh, Sam."

He barely heard Zach; his mind was fixated on a replay of that night. "I started shooting back, and all I could hear were sirens and screams. When I searched for my partner he was on the ground, gushing blood. A bullet had lodged in his thigh, and they weren't sure if it had nicked the femoral artery."

He found himself in Zach's arms. It was the first time in forever he'd been held, and Sam allowed himself a moment to sink into that almost forgotten comfort.

"Did he die? No, you said you almost killed your partner,

so he's still alive, right?"

Not trusting himself to speak, Sam nodded, fighting to draw his breath past the dryness in his throat. Still holding on to Zach, never wanting to let go.

"So it all turned out okay then." Zach rubbed his back in slow circles.

Hard to explain to civilians—it's not okay to unload your weapon unless absolutely necessary; you never want to shoot or hurt another human being. And most officers never do; in his twenty years, that was only the second time Sam had ever fired his weapon in the line of duty.

"No, it didn't," he said flatly. "Someone saw me on my phone; taken a picture in fact and forwarded it to my commanding officer. But because I was the right age and had a spotless record, they allowed me to retire without bringing me up on departmental charges."

"Oh."

The disappointment in the timbre of Zach's monosyllabic response hurt like hell, more than he thought it would. Fearing Zach's disapproval, Sam did what he knew best and withdrew, schooling his expression to careful, numb neutrality.

"Luckily, Santiago—my partner—came out of it okay. I spoke to him about it before I retired."

"I'm sure he didn't blame you."

Sam harsh laugh was nothing if not incredulous. "Of course he blamed me; they all did and with every right. I screwed up, and he survived only by pure dumb luck." Regret stung his heart, but Sam refused to let it break him.

"Forgiveness is a wonderful thing, it shows heart and compassion. I'm sure Santiago must have forgiven you."

Sam agreed begrudgingly. "He said he did…"

"But you don't believe it because you haven't forgiven yourself. You have a need to beat yourself up bloody until your suffering exceeds the pain you caused your partner."

He had nothing to say because Zach was right, so he sat in stony silence.

"You tell me I shouldn't hide away and I'm worth more than I think, yet here you are, doing the same thing yourself."

"It's not the same; you were a victim. I caused my own problem by not following the rules. And it cost me everything." His voice caught. "All I ever wanted to be was a cop; I didn't know anything else. It was hard enough being gay on the force; at least I thought my personal life was settled at last. But even that failed and now I have nothing."

"Are you sure about that?"

Zach's eyes drew him in. Pure and honest, they shone with a bright clarity he hadn't seen until now.

"What do you mean?"

"I don't know if you're being deliberately obtuse or if I'm saying it so badly you honestly don't understand." Exasperated, but with a hint of laughter on his lips, Zach kissed him. "You have me, you big idiot. Don't you realize it by now?"

Chapter Nineteen

Not normally the aggressor, the time seemed ripe for Zach to take care of Sam, to show with his body what he held in his heart.

"It's taken years for me to get to the point where I would want to be held and touched," he said, fingers ghosting over the scratchy stubble of Sam's jaw. All that roughness pressing up against him weakened Zach with burgeoning desire. "And yet it hadn't ever been right until you were the one doing it. And each time we're together is better than the last. It still scares the hell out of me."

His lips brushed Sam's, his tongue tracing the strong line of Sam's jaw. "But not having you is no longer an option."

"You've got me, baby. I'm right here for you."

His heartbeat accelerating, Zach dipped his head down

FELICE STEVENS

for another kiss. Sam's lips tasted like hope and desire and everything Zach had ever wanted. Caught up in their escalating fire, they pulled off each other's clothes, running into the bedroom and winding up lying naked and panting on the bed.

With a sureness he'd never exhibited before now, Zach kissed a path down Sam's chest, pausing to lap and tease at his nipples. Hearing Sam groan under his lips spurred Zach on, and he shifted south until he was faced with Sam's cock.

He was beautifully hard, the tip wet and glistening. Zach ached to feel it inside him, but first wanted a taste of Sam in his mouth and swirled his tongue around the thick head. Sam touched his shoulder with his fingertips.

"Zach…"

Hearing Sam sigh his name, Zach cast his gaze to the head of the bed and smiled at the sight of his lover. Slack-jawed and with a blissful grin curving his lips, Sam was beautiful. Closing his eyes, Zach enveloped Sam's cock in his mouth, sliding his lips down the thick shaft. He tasted of promises to come and warm nights; of aching desire and passion.

He tasted like forever.

"Zach." Sam's strangled voice coupled with the warning trembles beneath his lips and fingers signaled Sam's impending orgasm. With one final suckle and kiss, Zach withdrew and sat back on his heels. The hardened expression Sam normally wore like a mask had slipped, exposing a vulnerability Zach hadn't counted on.

"I—I want you." He licked his lips, and Zach's cock jerked in response. "Inside me."

Excitement shot up Zach's spine, his blood running hotter than ever before, but he faltered. "I've never…"

"Yeah?" Sam quirked a brow. "Good." And he smiled broadly, reaching out his hand. Zach took it, and Sam yanked him down for another bruising kiss.

202

"Where are your condoms?" Zach hardly recognized the commanding voice as his own, but today was a day full of change, and this was another step in his metamorphosis.

"Drawer," said Sam, voice raspy with need.

Zach scrambled to the night table drawer and pulled out a strip of condoms and bottle of lube. He scooted back to Sam and with shaking fingers, ripped the foil and rolled the condom down on his cock, then drizzled lube over it. Sam opened his legs, offering himself up, and with the utmost care Zach pushed himself inside Sam's body, inch by inch. The sensation was unexpected: like sinking into a soft, suede-like fire clutching his cock. He couldn't hold back his groan of satisfaction.

"God," said Zach. "God *damn*." His hands gripped Sam's hips, then skated up his ribs and chest. "This is…amazing

Zach held on to Sam's shoulders, angling his body, leaning his torso almost flush against Sam's chest, the penetration so deep and overwhelming he began to shake from the fire building inside him. He rolled his hips, thrusting deep, as the sweat dripped off his body, mixing with Sam's.

"Harder," Sam said, gasping for air as Zach pumped inside him. Slippery fluid leaked from Sam's rigid cock trapped between his stomach and Zach's. Zach closed his eyes to ride the rising wave of hunger inside him.

"Open your eyes." Sam heaved upward to meet his thrusts.

The exquisite pleasure-pain of pressure on his cock submerged Zach into an almost somnambulant state. Feeling as if he was drugged, Zach opened his eyes to find Sam's piercing gaze fixed on him. Zach's breath caught in his throat; Sam was so happy, the wary look in his eyes wiped clean, rendering him years younger. Unable to resist the teasing smile on Sam's lips, Zach laced his fingers through Sam's and captured Sam's mouth. Their teeth clashed and tongues slipped and slid against each other. They broke apart, Sam whispering against Zach's lips. "You're mine."

His heart lurched with happiness, beating a furious tempo. He could only kiss Sam again until they had to break for air.

Zach reached in between their bodies and grasped Sam's cock in his hand, rolling his thumb over the head, smearing the fluid leaking from the slit. Sam groaned and tightened his inner muscles around Zach's cock.

With another roll of his hips, Zach thrust deep within Sam, while at the same time squeezing his dick. His breath caught in his throat, the waves of hot pleasure radiating through him from every nerve ending.

His eyes shut tight, Sam shuddered and groaned, spilling his release over Zach's fingers. Zach stiffened and pulsed hot and hard inside Sam's passage, then sagged against Sam's chest, his body limp and boneless. Plastered with sweat, they lay together, Zach's face buried in the curve of Sam's neck. Eventually, he softened, and pushed up and off Sam's chest to lie next to him. Zach's hands trembled while removing and disposing of the condom and he took a few gulps of much-needed air to stop his head from spinning. After crawling back into bed, he splayed his hand over Sam's chest, the rapid beat of Sam's heart beneath his fingers settling down to its normal rhythm.

"Mine," Zach whispered to Sam before they slept.

*   *   *

"Are you sure you don't mind? I feel funny arriving separately." Zach fiddled with his tie. He hated wearing formal clothes, but Julian had hired a professional photographer for the party and wanted to take pictures of not only himself and Nick, but he insisted Zach and Marcus come early to have their pictures taken as well.

"Don't be ridiculous, I don't mind at all." Sam brushed aside his concerns, lounging on the bed. "It'll give me a chance to get to know your mom better."

With a final tug at the tie, Zach scowled at the mirror. "I hate wearing ties; I feel like I can't breathe."

"You look pretty hot, not gonna lie." Sam met his eyes in the mirror. "Although I like you better out of the clothes than in them."

And much as he loved Julian and Nick, Zach yearned to be alone with Sam even more. Wistfully, he glanced down at the bed, wishing he could join Sam. The pull to touch him ran hot like a fire through his bloodstream. "I, uh…" Zach licked his lips. "I have to go. You'll be there at six, right? My mom will be back from the beauty parlor in an hour, and that'll give you guys plenty of time to get to the loft."

Sam jumped off the bed and pulled him in close for a kiss. "Stop worrying, everything will be fine."

And for once, Zach didn't think twice, falling into Sam's strength. "Okay," he said, his mouth hovering over Sam's. "I trust you."

*   *   *

Three quarters of an hour later he entered Julian and Nick's loft, amazed at its transformation. A bar had been set up by the expanse of windows, and long rectangular tables flanked the wall, set with snowy-white tablecloths. Servers waited patiently behind a line of silver chafing dishes to dish out the delicious-smelling food.

Julian, spotting him from across the room, beckoned. "Zach, come." Nick and his entire family congregated around him, along with his assistant, Melanie. Several of Nick's work colleagues were there, as well as the young recovering burn victims Julian had featured in his fashion show this past winter.

Zach passed them by, giving them a brief smile if they recognized him. He didn't expect them to, as he'd made only a brief appearance at Julian's show. When he reached the small circle of Nick and Julian's family, Julian hugged him, his breath sweet from the champagne.

"Can you believe it? I'm getting married."

A lump formed in Zach's throat; he couldn't help the rush of emotion at his friend's happiness. He knew he was a sentimental softie like Marcus teased him. But he also knew how long Julian had loved Nick and thought he was gone forever. Zach's happily-ever-after quotient filled to overflowing, and he blinked furiously, tears wetting his lashes.

Julian held him close. "I know. And I know it will happen for you one day, because you, more than anyone, deserve to be loved by a wonderful man."

With the heel of his hand, Zach rubbed his eyes dry and smiled at his best friend. "This night is about you and Nick, not me. I can't tell you how happy I am for both of you." Nick came up behind Julian and slipped his arms around him.

"Thanks, Zach. And thanks for coming early. We wanted to get family pictures before it got too crowded." He glanced over Zach's shoulder. "Ah, there's the photographer." After a brief smile and a kiss for Julian, Nick hurried off.

"Where's your mom?" Julian drained his glass and set it down on the table they stood next to. "She's coming, right?"

"Sam's bringing her" said Zach, wishing Sam was with him now. "I thought it would be a nice way for the two of them to get better acquainted."

The gleam in Julian's eyes brightened, and he waved to Marcus from across the room. Marcus sauntered up. "What is it?"

"You introduced Sam to your mother?" He nudged

Marcus. "Did you hear that? Zach introduced Sam to Cheryl."

Marcus's dark brows arched high. "You did? But you never told her you were gay, right?"

"You guys know my mom." Warmth flooded through Zach at how easily his mother accepted his sexuality. From his work with runaway teens at the LGBTQ centers he volunteered at in the city, Zach knew firsthand it could've been so much worse. "She only wants me to be happy."

That speculative gleam hadn't disappeared from Julian's eyes. "And is Sam making you happy?"

"I hope you're using protection, dear," teased Marcus.

"You two are as bad as the old ladies at the senior center. Don't you have better things to do than obsess about my sex life?"

"Aha! You admit it." Marcus crowed in triumph. "Our Zach is finally having sex."

The man could exasperate a nun. "Excuse me. I haven't said hello to Nick's parents yet. I don't want to be rude." Turning his back on his two friends, he joined Nick, his parents, and a man he didn't recognize, presumably the photographer given the expensive camera he had around his neck.

"Mr. and Mrs. Fletcher, congratulations."

"Oh, Zach, thank you." Nick and his mother shared the same kind smile. "And thank you for coming early to take pictures with us. We wanted to make sure all Nick's and Julian's closest friends were here to celebrate."

"I wouldn't miss it. My mom is coming later, in about an hour."

To his shock, Nick's mother leaned in and whispered to him, "I heard you met a nice man of your own. I'm very happy for you."

Heat crept up his neck. "Um, yeah. Thank you."

"Zach." Katie hugged him. "I'm so happy you're here."

Taken by surprise, he froze, unused to such close personal contact by someone he considered a stranger. Katie drew back, and he fumbled an excuse.

"Sorry, you, um, took me by surprise." Lame and pathetic, even to his own ears, but it was the best excuse he could come up with quickly. Apparently falling in love hadn't solved all his problems; he was still the same awkwardly shy Zach he'd always been.

"It's okay," said Katie, flashing him a grin that held a wealth of understanding, and Zach remembered Katie worked as an ADA in the sex crimes division of the District Attorney's Office. The verbal harassment, taunts, and humiliation he'd endured paled in comparison to what she saw on a daily basis.

"How do you do it?" he blurted out, then stopped, horrified that he asked such a question from a virtual stranger.

"Do what?" Her smooth brow furrowed, then she nodded, as if she understood. "Oh, my job?"

"Yes. Isn't it hard to deal with so much violence every day? I can't imagine the suffering you see from the victims."

"It's hard, but I look at it from the other direction." Together they walked to a quieter corner of the loft. It amazed Zach how comfortable he felt with Katie; like she was an old friend or even the sister he'd never had. Julian was lucky to have a family like this.

They sat on the broad windowsill that overlooked Delancey Street. The sky was a midnight blue, the moon filtering out from between the clouds. So many people crowded on the street below; Zach remembered how desolate and run-down this area was when he was growing up and his parents took him to the Lower East Side to buy fresh pickles from Guss' Pickles. He shook his head at the memory popping up in his mind.

"Not only do I get to put in prison people who hurt others

who are weaker than they are, but I'm helping the victims." She tucked a lock of hair behind her ear, and her colorful earring swung forward. "They can breathe easier knowing some lousy bastard who hurt them or their children won't be able to anymore."

If he thought too hard on it, he'd never have the courage to ask; plus, they were isolated enough, and Katie seemed as though she'd keep what he said confidential.

"Did you ever have a case where a man was the one abused? It would have to be physical abuse though, right?"

She held his gaze with steady blue eyes. "Men can be abused as easily as women, Zach. And it doesn't mean they're weak or that they deserved it." Her hands formed fists and rested on her thighs. "I've seen cases where a man was assaulted by his female partner. The problem is most men are too ashamed to report it. And while every case I've personally dealt with has been physical abuse, it almost always starts with the victim being verbally abused."

Now, so many years later, Zach could take that step back and be thankful Nathan left when he did and had never taken it further with him. Remembering the scared, shaken boy he'd been in college, growing up as sheltered as he'd been, Zach wondered if he would've had the courage and the guts to stand up for himself had the verbal taunts turned to anything more physical than the nipple twisting and pinning him face down in the bed. Had it escalated to serious violence, would he have said anything, to anybody?

Zach suspected not.

"It's empowering for the victims as well, am I right?

"Absolutely." She was about to say something when the photographer approached the two of them.

"Katie, we're ready for you."

"Okay." She stood and gave Zach a kiss on the cheek. "Any time you want to talk, feel free. I feel like we're all family now, Zach. It's nice to have more brothers."

Touched yet uncomfortable under her knowing gaze he smiled and nodded.

"Oh, so this is Zach." The photographer's assessing gaze raked Zach up and down. "Julian told me you're the computer whiz."

"I'm into development mostly."

He stroked his short-trimmed beard. "You, Marcus, and Julian have all been *friends* for a long time. That's so interesting."

The emphasis on *friends* made the photographer's words sound obscene, an insinuation that there was something sexual between him and the others. Zach answered back with a rare spurt of anger.

"There's nothing interesting about having people in your life you care for and count on."

"Well said, Zach." Katie gave his arm a little squeeze.

"Hey, I didn't mean anything by it. I'm Andrew, by the way, Andrew Trachtman." He held out his hand.

"Zach Cohen."

If pushed for a reason, he couldn't say why, but the touch of the man's hand made Zach feel dirty, like he needed to soak it in some hand sanitizer and rub until his skin turned red and raw. It was unusual for him to have such a visceral reaction to another person, and he jerked his hand free, muttering an apology.

"I can't wait to take your picture, Zach. The blue of your eyes and shirt against the black-and-white backdrop..." His grin turned slightly feral. "Stunning."

"I think we should get started," said Katie. She shot Zach a troubled look. "Follow me, Andrew. My brother and Julian will tell you the shots our family wants."

Andrew winked at Zach and gave his shoulder a squeeze

before he joined Katie. "I'll see you in a few, Zach. Save your smiles for me."

"Whoa, that guy wants your ass. Better make sure Sam doesn't see him flirting with you." Marcus leaned on the wall nearby, a grin teasing his lips. "We'll have one dead photographer, and I know Julian wouldn't like blood all over his nice wooden floors."

"Don't be an idiot. He was being friendly."

"Friendly, my ass. I know a player."

Marcus had a point.

"It doesn't matter. I'm not interested."

Because it was a loft, the elevator opened directly into the apartment, and Zach's reprieve, in the form of his mother and Sam, appeared.

"There's my mom and Sam. See you later," he said, but not before he heard Marcus mutter, "Bet your ass, you will."

Putting the whole unsettling incident out of his mind, Zach hurried to his mother and Sam. "Hi." He bent down to give his mother a kiss, but his eyes were on Sam, drinking in his face, broad shoulders, the strength in his arms…desire swept through Zach, so rich and so strong he felt physically weak from its pull on his heart.

"Hi, darling. Sam was so lovely; he picked me up at the beauty parlor and took me to the florist so I could pick up a plant for the boys, a little gift. I couldn't walk in empty-handed. We've been having the best time on the way over here."

"Is that so?" He hugged her. "I'm so glad you're getting to know each other." Over his mother's head he mouthed, *Thank you*, to Sam, who stood a bit awkwardly, holding the potted plant.

And when Sam smiled at him through the green leaves, so easy, warm, and sweet, a crescendo of happiness rose within Zach, finally silencing the self-doubt and fears of insignificance that had once played a never-ending tune within his head. Zach knew how the sorrows of life could get so hard they pushed you back until you fell, limp and exhausted from all the effort. You'd rather remain alone, hiding in bed under the covers, and no coaxing with promises of pots of gold at the end of the rainbow would help, if you never believed in rainbows to begin with.

It only takes a minute sometimes to make that one decision that can change your life, though at the time you didn't know it. Zach knew about life and its fragility—like sand on the beach, slipping easily through a person's fingers, fading like a dream half-remembered.

Love was no different. Love can burn hot and fierce as the sun for years, only to end in smoking ruins. But if love is recognized and treated like the precious gift it is, it can be life's greatest reward, that golden prize at the end of the rainbow, the victory at the top of the mountain.

Returning Sam's smile, his heart beat fierce and proud in his chest with the knowledge he'd won that elusive prize, made it to the top of the mountain through a hard-fought battle. He was in love with Sam, and tonight when they were together, he'd tell him.

"Let me go say hello to Marilyn and Brian. I know how happy they must be with Nick getting married." His mother bustled off to Nick's parents, leaving him and Sam standing together, smiling into each other's eyes.

"Hi." Sam placed the plant on a low table that had been moved to the side to make room for easy mingling between guests. "This place is beautiful. You'd never know it from the outside of the building. That's what I love about New York. When you think you know everything, there's always a surprise to prove you wrong."

"Like people, right? You think you know them, and

it turns out you've prejudged them, and they're complete opposites of what you thought."

Sam's eyes darkened in response, and he rested his hands at Zach's waist, drawing him close. His lips skated over Zach's cheekbones, coming to rest at his temple.

"I know I did with you, and it almost cost me everything."

A weak laugh escaped Zach; his heart pounded so hard, Sam must certainly feel its jumping rhythm against his own chest. "Not likely. I'm the bulldog who came after you. I wouldn't let you go, remember?"

Sam drew his nose down Zach's cheek, the soft expulsion of his breath fanning against Zach's cheek. "You think I don't remember?" The faint touch of Sam's lips brushed across Zach's. "I never forget what's mine."

A thrill shot through Zach at Sam's possessive tone; his hands slid up the broad expanse of Sam's back, and he leaned into his favorite spot, the curve of Sam's neck, inhaling his scent. The knowledge that he was responsible for the rapid tempo of Sam's heart and the slight hitch in Sam's breath was a powerful aphrodisiac, and it made Zach possessive and handsy.

"You're mine as well, remember." He massaged Sam's shoulders.

"Break it up you two or get a room," drawled Marcus, joining them. "My eyes can't take all this lovey-dovey crap." He smirked. "Gives me hives."

"Better get a doctor to check that out." Zach elbowed him.

Marcus surveyed the room. "You didn't get your picture taken yet, right? I think the photographer is still with Nick's family."

"Nope." Hand in hand, Zach walked with Sam to the bar so they could get a drink. "I figured we'd be last."

"From the way the photographer was ogling your ass, I'm going to guess you'd be first." Marcus smirked. "Sam better watch out."

Beer sloshed over Sam's cup as he hastily placed it back on the bar. "What the hell does he mean?" His eyes darkened as his gaze bore into Zach.

He didn't have anything to feel guilty about; the photographer had made him uncomfortable from the beginning, and he had no intention of responding to his blatant innuendos.

"Nothing." If a look could kill, Marcus would be supine on the floor with a bayonet sticking out of his chest. "He"—Zach pointed to Marcus—"is being an annoying idiot."

"Hey, it's not my fault the guy hit on you, telling you how pretty your eyes were." With his own eyes wide and innocent, Marcus said, "Here he comes now. He can tell you himself." With a smug grin, Marcus leaned against the bar, arms folded.

Frustrated over Marcus's teasing and annoyed with Sam for thinking he'd welcome another man's attention, Zach pulled Sam over to the side.

"You know Marcus is baiting you. Don't fall for his game; he loves doing this to everyone." Sliding his hand up Sam's arm, Zach lowered his voice so only the two of them could hear. "I'm not interested in anyone else."

"Zach, are you ready to have your picture taken?" The photographer stood behind Sam, sporting a big grin. "I know the camera is going to love you."

He wanted more time to tell Sam he was being ridiculous; after the weekend they'd just had there was no need for Sam to think he'd look at anyone else, but this was Julian and Nick's night, and he had no right to take away from their enjoyment.

"Give me a minute, please."

Sam had gone from red-faced and angry to pale and unmoving. He didn't look well at all. Zach barely gave the photographer a nod, concentrating on Sam and the sickly look on his face.

"Sam, what's wrong?"

Eyes wide with surprise, the photographer now ignored Zach and took Sam by the shoulder and spun him around.

"Sammy?"

Frowning, Sam twisted out from under the photographer's grasp. "Hello, Andy."

Andy? Sam's ex-lover Andy? Zach thought he might be sick.

Chapter Twenty

"Sammy? Holy shit, it is you."

Before Sam could take another breath, Andy had crushed him to his chest. Shouldn't Andy's arms have felt familiar? They'd shared a bed and a home, and it had only been a little over six months since they'd been apart. Instead, his scent, that light cologne he always favored, smelled alien, his lips felt wrong, and the stubble on his chin irritated Sam's cheek.

If he were the same person he'd been six months ago, Sam would've been happy to talk to Andy; maybe even suggest a dinner to see if there was still a spark to rekindle their relationship. The six months apart would have been a good break for them both. But he wasn't that man anymore.

Sam didn't want Andy. Sam wanted Zach.

But Zach had disappeared and was now across the room

with his friends who'd surrounded him like the fucking Great Wall of China. That pissed Sam off; they had to know he wasn't the enemy.

He pulled away from Andy. "What're you doing here?"

Andy hefted the expensive camera around his neck. "I'm filling in. The guy Julian hired got stuck at LAX this morning, so he called me and asked if I could take the job."

"And your boyfriend?"

"We broke up a month after I moved to D.C. I never should've left the city."

"Guess it wasn't meant to be." Though Sam no longer loved him, he couldn't help the dart of satisfaction at hearing Andy words.

"I have to do these pictures, but I'd like to talk later."

"I've got nothing to say."

"But I—"

Sam held up a hand. "When I wanted to talk to you six months ago, you couldn't be bothered. Well, sorry, but I'm busy."

"With hot little Zach? You're hooking up with him now, nice." Andy gave him a wink. "Maybe we can have a threesome—I bet he and his two friends shared at one point."

"Go take your pictures." Disgusted by Andy, Sam took his beer and sat down, ignoring the socializing around him. He drank his beer steadily, still a bit unsettled from his encounter with his ex. From his vantage point on the sofa he watched Andy photograph the group, growing angrier and more annoyed seeing Andy's hand linger on Zach's shoulder or hip when he placed him in the position he wanted him to stand. At one point, Andy leaned over and whispered in Zach's ear, and Sam crumpled the empty plastic cup in his hand.

Unwilling to let Andy molest Zach any further, Sam

strode across the room. Vibrating with suppressed tension, Sam hovered on the outskirts of the group, reluctant to create a scene in front of Nick's family and Julian, yet equally incapable of standing by to let his ex hit on Zach. To his complete frustration, he couldn't catch Zach's eye; he wasn't sure whether or not Zach was avoiding him deliberately, or if he was imagining it.

Why the hell was he so off-kilter? He'd never been possessive or had a jealous streak with guys he was with before, yet seeing Andy brush against Zach's hair with the back of his hand on the fucking pretense of adjusting the lights made him want to bash his ex's face in. No one touched Zach but him.

"Easy, killer." Marcus spoke in his ear.

"I don't trust him." Sam answered back.

"I know you're not talking about Zach, because he's the most trustworthy person you'll ever meet."

"Of course I don't mean Zach. It's Andy."

"You know him?"

"He's my ex. I know what he's capable of."

"But you know Zach, and you know what he's not capable of."

Sam turned around to face Marcus. "What are you talking about?"

"Zach, the man who loves you, is the most decent person I've ever met. Do you know how fucking lucky you are? The fact that he's fallen in love with you means he's given you everything. His trust, his heart. That's it for him; he's not ever going to look at anyone else. Zach is not capable of cheating on you or hurting you intentionally."

Sam gazed into Marcus's dark eyes. "You love him, don't you?"

"I'd give my life for him, but he'd never ask for my help.

I do love him," he said, glancing over at Zach, then back to Sam. "But not like you can."

Sam understood and surprisingly felt pity for Marcus. Others might see only the fast life and handsome exterior, but he saw beneath that gloss and recognized a sad and lonely man.

It was like looking into a mirror before Zach had come into his life. Marcus was able to hide his emotions behind the partying and the sex, whereas Sam, who couldn't be bothered with the bullshit, simply withdrew, content in solitude.

"One day, my man, someone's gonna crawl under your skin."

"I'd better stock up on bug spray then. I hate crawly things."

They shared a laugh. "It'll happen; you'll be going along, minding your business, then *bam.* You'll fall in love."

"I don't plan on it."

To Sam's surprise, Marcus slung an arm around his neck, and they stood watching Andy take his pictures.

It made Sam feel accepted and a part of Zach's group. He needed to introduce Zach to Henry and Heather, he mused. They would love him.

"That's just it. You don't plan. It just happens; and then you look around and you're living life again, and you wonder how you ever thought being alone night after night made you happy."

Marcus withdrew his arm and checked his phone, a small smile curving his lips. "I'm never alone any night. Excuse me a minute." He walked off texting.

Sam forgot about Marcus and focused his attention back on Zach again. A pure-white screen had been set up, and Sam had to admit Andy, for all his failure as a human being, was an excellent photographer. Marcus was called, and, having finished with his texting, or sexting as was more likely, he joined the threesome. Andy posed them in a group with their arms around each other, and the joy on all their faces was palpable.

Julian whispered to Zach, and the man shrugged, his face a mask of seriousness.

"Sam." Julian waved him over. "Come here."

A little surprised, Sam joined the foursome at the screen.

"We'd like a picture with you as well." Julian leaned on Nick, whose arms wrapped around Julian's waist. The two men were a perfect unit; Sam couldn't imagine one without the other, yet he recalled Zach recounting the story of all the years they'd spent apart.

"Me?" He caught Zach's eye. "Are you sure?"

But it was Julian who answered, not Zach. "We have a feeling we'll be seeing you at family functions from now on, so yes, we're sure."

Shooting a troubled look at Zach, who'd withdrawn and stood silent, Sam decided to ignore whatever was weighing on Zach's mind. He'd speak when he was ready.

"I'd be honored; thank you. I'd love to be included."

"Okay, Sammy." Andy took him by the shoulders and placed him next to Zach. "Stand here next to your cute boyfriend."

A prickle of resentment rose within Sam at Andy's snide tone. The hell Sam would let his ex be dismissive and rude to Zach. He held his rising anger in check, not wanting to make a scene, vowing to deal with Andy later, and bent down to whisper in Zach's ear.

"Ignore Andy; he's being a dick."

"It doesn't matter." Zach adjusted his glasses. "Let's get this done."

What the hell? What was he so pissed about? At that

moment, Andy started calling out instructions, and Sam's concentration focused solely on the shoot. He'd deal with a temperamental Zach later.

But somehow, later never came. In the following hours, Sam never once found himself alone with Zach, who'd specifically maneuvered himself to be surrounded by at least one or two of his friends or Nick's family members. It seemed he and Nick's sister Katie had forged a friendship, and along with Julian's assistant, Melanie, formed a tight little circle of their own.

Even now, the three of them sat at one of the small round tables set up for people who preferred to sit and eat and not mingle. Sam looked about and spotted Cheryl sitting with Nick's parents and several other older couples, presumably Nick's relatives, since Zach had told Sam Julian had no family of his own.

The delicious food and beautiful backdrop of the night sky through the tall windows were wasted on Sam. Instead, his concentration was fixed on Zach who gave the appearance of a happy party guest, all smiles and laughter. "Looks like you're on the outs," said Andy, from behind.

"Shouldn't you be working? I'm sure Nick and Julian aren't paying you to chat up their guests."

A teasing grin broke across Andy's face. "I'm on a dinner break," he said and popped a cheese cube in his mouth. "Want some?" He held out a forkful of pasta. "You used to like it when I'd feed you across the table."

Those days were a million years ago; Sam struggled to remember what it had been like with Andy and could only come up with emptiness. In the beginning they'd had hot sex, but after a while it had burned itself down, and they couldn't revive the embers of that dying fire. They hadn't bothered to try.

"No thanks."

FELICE STEVENS

The afternoon he and Zach spent yesterday, flying the kite and then at the beach, was all he wanted. In the end it came down to him and Zach. He loved Zach, and it was like the ocean, a force of nature, forever changing in its form yet always the same. Powerful, deep, and strong.

He hadn't told Zach he loved him; maybe that's why he was acting so strange tonight. Sam knew he wasn't good at these things, but even he knew, much as Zach loved Julian and Nick, it might be bittersweet to watch his friends get married, thinking he might never find that lasting love himself.

Andy placed his plate down and leaned against the wall. Dispassionately, Sam took in Andy's tanned, lean body, expensive watch, and designer clothing. His chestnut hair gleamed under the recessed lights; he looked straight off the pages of a magazine—charming, rich, and successful. But Sam knew the Andy he thought no one saw; his vacant eyes told the story. No warmth touched their deep-brown depths. Sam could only imagine how many men he'd gone through in the time they'd been apart.

There was nothing between them now, Sam realized, except faded memories.

"Listen, why don't we get together after the party, and we can have a drink. You know, reminisce for old times' sake." The smile Sam once thought charming, now reeked of insincerity.

Perhaps Andy still believed Sam would fall back into bed with him, and truthfully, if he were single and not with Zach, who knows what might have happened. Nights were long and lonely without someone to hold.

But now Sam had a taste of what real life was like—a man who cared for him, the tentative beginnings of a friendship with this tight-knit group of men who fiercely protected their own, and a sense of family he hadn't even realized he wanted. You can't want what you didn't know existed.

"Sorry, but I'm busy."

Andy glanced over to where Zach sat with Nick and Julian who'd now joined him and the two women. "With Zach? He's a cutie. Well, what about the three of us?" He gave Sam a wink. "I do him and you do me." His eyes narrowed. "I wouldn't mind a taste of that ass."

Almost choking on his fury, Sam muscled Andy up against the wall. "Don't talk about him like that. He's not one of your club hook-ups."

"Whoa, Sammy. Going all Papa Bear on me, huh? Anyone would think you're in love with the guy."

"I am, you dumb fuck. Maybe if you stopped thinking with your dick for once and looked beyond it, you'd understand."

A bewildered expression crossed Andy's face. "I didn't think you'd find someone so quickly. I thought—"

"I know what you thought." He had nothing left for Andy, not even pity. "You thought I'd be waiting for you to come back, didn't you? That I was a boring fool and you were the only part that made me interesting. You never thought I'd move on and someone would want me."

Andy's jaw clenched in a mulish expression. "You never wanted to do anything or go anywhere. I liked to go out, and you were an old married man sitting at home watching TV and making dinner plans with your friends."

In all their time together Sam couldn't recall an honest conversation between them. Now that their emotions were no longer vested, they could be free to speak the truth.

In a gentler tone, Sam urged Andy to understand. "We never should have stayed together as long as we did; you know it as well as I. It was good in the beginning, but it had died out between us way before that final night."

"You're probably right," said Andy, his eyes thoughtful, and to Sam's surprise, a bit wistful. "But we did have fun.

You can't tell me it wasn't good in the beginning."

"It was," said Sam, passing by Andy and giving his shoulder a squeeze. "But it hadn't been for a long, long time. And now I'm interested in the future, not the past. Good luck and I'm glad we had the chance to say good-bye."

The future was all about Zach, and it was time to let him know it. Anticipation threaded through his veins as he approached Zach and the group.

"Hey, mind if I join you?"

"Take my seat," said Julian standing, Nick joining him. "Nick and I need to mingle, especially since some of his family members are leaving soon." They walked away leaving behind Marcus, Katie, and Melanie, in addition to Zach.

"So that was your ex, huh? Doesn't seem like your type." Marcus lazed back in his chair, a drink dangling from his hand.

Forgetting the good will of their previous conversation, Sam bristled. "No offense, Marcus, but what do you know about me? And Zach and I talked about Andy. He knows everything."

"I didn't know he was back in New York," said Zach diffidently.

"Neither did I." He had nothing to hide, yet he was on the defensive. "He wasn't the photographer Julian and Nick hired; he's filling in for a friend who got stuck at LAX."

Marcus drained his glass. "Is he staying in New York?"

"I didn't ask him. Look—"

"I'm sure he wanted to get together, you know, for old times' sake." Zach rubbed his thighs with the palms of his hands in a classic nervous gesture Sam recalled from his police days. "You should, you know. You guys were so close for so long."

The crooked smile he gave confused Sam.

"Why would I want to do that? What's wrong with you?" Life was too short to sit around and play mind-fuck games.

"Nothing. I figure you could catch up with him, and I can hang out with my friends."

The fakeness of Zach's smile blinded him, and Sam frowned. This was a new side of Zach he hadn't seen, and he didn't like it.

"Excuse us, please," Sam took Zach by the arm. "We need to talk," he whispered to Zach, pulling him to a standing position.

The two women wore identical confused expressions, but Sam didn't care; he'd leave it to Marcus to explain if they asked. From the sly grin curving Marcus's lips and the approving light in his eye, Marcus understood what Sam was about.

"There's nothing wrong," said Zach in a furious hiss when they finally reached a quieter, more private space in the loft. "I'm fine. Besides, I have to go soon; I need to get my mother home."

"Your mother is doing fine, stop hiding behind her as an excuse." Sam's gaze traveled through the loft until it found Cheryl happily ensconced in a conversation with Nick's mother. "I'll make sure she gets a ride home, but you're coming with me. We have things to discuss."

"I'm going home. We don't have anything to talk about, everything's fine."

The mulish tilt to Zach's jaw surprised Sam. For someone people claimed was sweet and amiable, Zach could be a goddamn hard-ass. But, Sam admitted to himself, he liked when Zach transformed into a demanding lover, showing his strength, taking control. The times he'd pushed his and Sam's limits resulted in the most explosive sex Sam had ever had.

It was a side of Zach Sam had only seen in their bedroom

and one Sam wanted to explore in greater depth. But only if he could get Zach back to his house, and they could be alone.

"Zach. Please." It took every ounce of Sam's strength not to drag Zach up against him and kiss him until he couldn't breathe. Now more than ever, Sam had to set things straight so Zach would never have cause to doubt his feelings. He knew Zach had never exerted himself; he'd simply gone along with the crowd in an effort to please, never once voicing his own wants and desires.

He understood that life; for years Sam had wallowed in a miasma of uncertainty, his relationship floundering, but he hadn't had the strength of will or reason to move on. He wasn't going to let what he felt for Zach have its life sucked dry, to end up withered and dead like a plant forgotten in the corner.

Who would've thought a silly bet would set off a chain reaction of events leading to this moment, where he knew for certain he'd discovered the rest of his life. Sam had to make sure Zach believed him. He wasn't playing a game of chance—he was playing for keeps.

For forever.

"Remember how you chased me down after I walked out on you?"

Zach's stony expression softened, then grew heated. Sam pressed his advantage by touching Zach on his arm and sliding his hand up to curve around the nape of Zach's neck. The smoothness of his skin acted as a balm, soothing Sam's soul. Merely touching Zach now brought him a peace he'd forgotten existed.

"I won't let you run away from me," said Sam, the words coming directly from his heart. "If you leave, I'll only follow you, no matter where you go. Come home with me. Please."

Zach's uncertainty twisted Sam's heart into a painful knot in his chest. He cupped Zach's jaw with his hand, his fingers resting on Zach's face. Zach's eyes held his, glimmering hot and fierce with an emotion Sam hoped he was able to convey back. When Zach nodded, Sam's breath escaped him in a whoosh of exhalation.

"Let's go."

Chapter Twenty-One

Did he make a mistake? Conflicted, Zach found it hard to relax in his seat on the drive back to Brooklyn. When he'd said his good-byes to Julian and Marcus, they each told him the same thing: *"Don't jump to conclusions. Listen to what Sam has to say."*

It was his mother who had surprised him the most. He'd approached her with trepidation, afraid of her reaction to his leaving with Sam and sending her home in a car.

"Nick's parents have graciously offered to take me home, so don't worry. I'll be fine; you go off with Sam and enjoy yourself."

"Really? I, uh, I may not come home tonight, or I might be very late, so don't wait up for me."

The shock must've been evident on his face, for her eyes

danced with amusement.

"I think I can handle it. If I'm not mistaken, there might be many nights like these ahead."

After staring in disbelief for another moment, Zach gave her a kiss on the cheek. "Nothing's changed you know."

"Oh darling, everything's changed, but it's all good. Being here tonight and seeing how happy Julian finally is made me understand how I've cheated you."

"Mom, no—"

"Yes. Now listen to me." She drew him off to the side and in bemusement he went, uncertain as to what other things she'd say.

"You go with Sam and you find that happiness you deserve. For years I held you back, don't tell me no, I know what I did," she said when he opened his mouth to protest. Her expression remained clear, her eyes unwavering in their honesty. "I see the damage I did and how wrong I was. I look around and see Julian so happy now with Nick, and I want that for you. You deserve a relationship and a family. You deserve everything."

"I love you, Mom."

"I love you too, but you have a man now and a chance at happiness and a good life. Don't waste that love; grab it, hold it tight, and treasure it. You never know how long you'll have it. Go with your heart."

Her words reverberated in his head during the drive back to Sam's. While he understood what she was saying, seeing Sam with his former lover brought back all his old insecurities crawling through his head, whispering how he'd never measure up to a man like Andy, making him question why would Sam want him, now that his old lover was back.

He'd sat pretending to listen to his friends, all the while surreptitiously eyeing Sam with Andy across the room. He could barely choke down his hurt watching Andy put his hand on Sam's chest, and Sam accepting his touch. The food had tasted like sawdust in his mouth, and he'd pictured his future once again bleak and lonely.

His mother spoke of love, Zach thought bitterly, but who needed it if all it brought was this searing doubt and fear twisting through his nerves, leaving him tense and on edge? No wonder Marcus disparaged emotional ties; in the end, he might be the smartest one of all.

And yet…Zach glanced over at Sam's profile, silhouetted in the dim interior of the car, and wondered. Yesterday, after the kite flying and the walk on the beach, Zach had never felt as close to another person as he did with Sam. He even dared to think maybe Sam would say he loved him.

Was he wrong letting his old self-doubt eat away at his newly acquired yet still shaky confidence? Andy's return didn't mean Sam would want to resuscitate their relationship; last night Sam made it clear not only with his body but with his words the relationship was dead and he wanted Zach.

Mine. Zach would never forget hearing Sam say the word to him.

"What?" Sam shot him a look.

"Nothing."

Sam gripped the steering wheel, working his jaw as if holding back on words threatening to spill out. They hit every green light coming off the Brooklyn Bridge, and in less than ten minutes, pulled into the parking spot in the front yard reserved for Sam's car. Silently, he trailed into the house behind Sam, his frustration growing.

"Why did you bring me here if you didn't want to talk to me?"

"What did you mean in the car?" said Sam, ignoring his question.

Confused, Zach ran through the minimal conversation they'd engaged in. "What're you talking about? We barely spoke."

Sam spun around and backed him flat up against the wall; not touching him but making it impossible for Zach to move. There was no fear—instead Zach's breath caught in his throat and a curl of desire streaked through his blood, hardening his cock. An unreadable expression remained on Sam's face, his hot breath fanning against Zach's cheek.

"Mine." Sam's lips hovered close to his. "You said 'mine' in the car. What did you mean?"

Oh. Damn. For the first time Zach wished he was more like Marcus, with a string of curses ripe and ready to go. Had he really said that out loud?

"Uh." He licked his lips. "I, I don't remember saying that."

"But you did," said Sam, his voice a low growl of promise. "Did you mean it, like you did last night? Like I meant it." The touch of his lips intoxicated Zach, his brain short-circuiting into overdrive, spinning him away.

Zach gasped, the touch of Sam's fingers sending aching jolts through his body. "Do you still?" It was becoming harder to stand on his feet, and he sagged against the wall, trapped between it and Sam's large frame.

"Still what?" Sam nuzzled at Zach's neck.

Stifling a moan, Zach said hoarsely, his voice full of need, "Still want me?"

The warmth of Sam's face molded against his own; they stood in the moonlight of the room, holding one another. Sam's lips whispered a trail of heated kisses down his neck, coming to rest in the hollow of his throat. "I never stopped."

Zach's blood beat strong and hot. "I thought—"

"Don't." Sam's mouth hovered over his. "I can't listen to you say you thought I didn't want you anymore when that's the furthest thing from the truth."

Words unsaid hung in the air, waiting to be spoken, yet Sam stayed quiet. The painful silence resonated through the apartment, and Zach waited, hopeful his instincts hadn't proved him wrong.

"Andy is gone. I told him there was nothing left between us. That I wanted you." His lips brushed Zach's. "That I loved you."

Finally—the words that created magic from the madness of it all.

"I didn't know."

"I'm sorry for that." Sam took him by the hand and led him to the sofa where they both sat, Sam pressed up next to him. "I shouldn't have held myself back, but I'm not good at this."

Zach smiled at Sam's frustration. "This? What, saying I love you, or kissing me? Because you have the kissing thing down pat, so there's no complaint there."

But Sam didn't smile back. "I want to make this right because I know how much the words mean to you, and I don't want to fu—screw it up."

With each word, Zach's heart squeezed a bit tighter. It wasn't possible to love Sam more than he did at this moment; the absolute honesty and his tentative voice slayed Zach to his core.

"I never thought I'd get a chance at love. I hid away. Not even my friends could bully me or talk me into changing."

"That bastard did a number on you," said Sam, running a hand down Zach's arm.

Hot ribbons of need ran across Zach's skin, his body awakened from its long dormancy, blooming back to life. "But you've changed all that and given me back trust. Trust not only in you that you wouldn't hurt me, but trust in myself as a man."

Sam gripped his shoulder, and Zach stared into his unsmiling face.

"What?"

For all outward appearances, Sam presented a tough, hardened ex-cop; always watchful and in control. That wasn't the man in front of Zach now. The harsh grooves in his forehead smoothed, and Sam's vulnerability was on full display for the first time for Zach to see. The tightness in his chest returned, along with a welling up of love from a place so deep inside him, Zach hadn't ever delved that far down before.

"Tell me. You haven't said it yet, and you're not the only one who needs this. I need to hear it as much as you do."

Zach slid his palm up Sam's chest to rest above his heart. "I love you. I know life isn't a movie, and that we aren't promised happy endings all the time. But we have a chance now, out of the craziest of circumstances to create something together, and I want to grab hold and keep it close."

"You love me." Sam covered his hand with his own.

"I do. And you love me."

A smile broke across Sam's face. "I do. I love you. I gave up on trusting life to behave the way I wanted it to, so I did nothing. From the moment you burst into my life that night in Atlantic City, I had zero control."

It was as if they'd made private vows to each other; words didn't need to be spoken aloud. "You make me lose control too." Zach had never felt so reckless or as free.

Sam's mouth found his, and it was soft and hot, his lips sweetly tender. The tip of his tongue traced the seam of Zach's lips, and instinctively Zach opened, allowing it entrance. The hot wet velvet of Sam's tongue swept inside Zach's mouth, probing deep, and Zach, the persistent ache inside his chest swelling to pounding desire, slanted his mouth against Sam's, drinking him down. The hard ridge of Sam's erection pressed against Zach's thigh; in a sinuous motion Zach twisted so he rubbed against it, while never breaking contact with Sam's lips.

The pleasure built, and they stayed on the sofa kissing, Zach continuing to slide against Sam's cock until Sam broke away, panting slightly, his mouth wet and glinting. "Let's move this to the bed. I can't do what I want to do to you out here."

Zach could barely stand for the trembling of his legs; he needed to lean on Sam to hold him steady. They stumbled to the bedroom, kissing and shedding their clothes as they went, leaving a trail behind them. By the time they reached the bedroom they were panting, naked, and the hunger to feel Sam inside him was almost unbearable.

"Hurry." He clutched Sam's arm and pulled his head down for another searching kiss. His cock, stiff and aching, slid along the equally hard length of Sam's erection, and Zach whimpered from the exquisite torture of the pleasure-pain of his desire.

To his surprise, Sam didn't rush to push him on the bed. Instead, Sam continued to kiss him; long, languorous kisses that left Zach breathless and shaking. Hunger pooled in his belly, and he clung tighter to Sam, wanting to meld their bodies together until it would be impossible to separate them.

Sam lifted him up and placed him on the bed, then straddled his hips, his face still an unreadable mask. Zach lay still, body aching, his heart pounding like the ocean waves crashing against the rocks.

"What's wrong?"

"Nothing. I'm looking at you lying there, so fucking perfect, thinking one day you'll wake up and wonder why you made the mistake of getting involved with a washed-up ex-cop like me."

Through half-opened blinds, gleaming bands of

moonlight striped the room. The pale light shifted, throwing Sam's solemn face into stark relief.

"I don't see that person. I only see the man I love, who catches me if I'm falling and holds me tight. I'm not perfect. I'm nothing close to it, no one is."

"I don't want you to have regrets."

"How could I regret you? It would be like denying the best part of me." Zach reached up and brushed his fingers against Sam's roughened jaw. "I love you so much, Sam. We're here for such a short time, we have to make sure we recognize love when we find it and not wait to live and make our memories. Any regrets I have would be in not making my memories with you."

"Oh, baby." Sam groaned and dipped his head down. Zach grabbed on to his shoulders and eagerly met his lips, opening his mouth to Sam's probing tongue. Sam's cock lay warm and heavy against Zach's stomach, and the pull to take Sam inside his body proved too irresistible for Zach to wait.

"Now." Nothing further needed to be said between them. He lay back and opened his legs, offering himself up to Sam. After prepping himself with both condom and lube, Sam positioned himself and pushed inside.

"God," said Sam, sliding in, inch by inch. "So fucking perfect."

Bearing down, wincing against the initial pain, Zach breathed out, accepting Sam, drawing him deep inside. Looking up at the play of emotions on Sam's face, the strength in his tight jaw, the ripple of muscles across his shoulders, a surge of lust shot through Zach, and he shifted underneath, forcing Sam farther into his body, clenching his cock tight.

A dark groan escaped Sam's lips. "Jesus Christ, you're killing me."

Feeling the pulse and surge inside his own body, Zach ached, wanting Sam harder and deeper. He gripped Sam's thigh, urging him on, pushing up against his thrusts, locking his ankles against the small of Sam's back.

"Harder; there," Zach whispered as Sam changed the angle of his thrusts, brushing up against his prostate; sparks of electricity flew up and down Zach's spine. A quivering began deep in his core, and Zach fought against it, wanting to stave off the ferocious orgasm he sensed building.

They rocked together, Zach weakening from the struggle of holding himself together. There was no stopping it; like a dam bursting, Zach's orgasm ripped through him, pinwheels of white light spiraling before his eyes. This was a tidal wave he'd gladly drown in and, sinking into the soft, welcoming darkness, Zach recalled the French phrase *petite mort*—"a little death"—and knew it to be true.

He closed his eyes and succumbed.

Too shattered to move, Zach still knew exactly when Sam had reached his point of no return. The formidable muscles of Sam's back flexed and his body stiffened; his cock pulsed hard, spilling hot and heavy inside the condom.

They lay gasping, clutching at each other, Zach's face pressed up against Sam's neck, his lips tasting the salt of Sam's sweat on the surprisingly smooth skin of Sam's shoulder. Neither one of them made a move, not when their breathing returned to normal nor when their heartbeats regained a stable rhythm. They were both aware of the hard journey they'd undertaken to reach this moment, and each was loath to move apart.

Sam picked up his head, a lazy smile curving his lips. "Hey." Without waiting for Zach to respond, Sam kissed him. His lips played over Zach's, soft and gentle; there was no need for gnashing teeth or probing tongues. It was a kiss of tenderness and sweetness. A kiss that spoke of early mornings and late nights. A kiss of forever.

All the years he'd stayed at home, shunning the shallow

clubs and meaningless parties his friends invited him to, it was a moment like this Zach knew he wanted and held out hope for; a forever man and a forever love. He'd imagined someone who shared his dreams of family and togetherness. These past months watching Julian—who Zach had always thought of as so hardened and withdrawn—find Nick and fall back in love with him had proved it wasn't an impossibility.

Now, to have Sam here in his arms, whispering his love, restored Zach's faith in himself and his dream of happiness. Perhaps everything in life did happen for a reason; he was meant to go through his trials with Nathan to come out stronger and more resilient.

He winced at Sam's withdrawal and rolled over on his side, enjoying the pleasurable ache. Sam returned from the bathroom with a towel, joining him back on the bed, and Zach delighted in the loving strokes of Sam's hands on his body. There was something to be said for being petted and stroked Zach thought, admiring the lines of Sam's broad shoulders and chest.

"Thanks." Zach kissed Sam and stretched out next to him, thinking how nice it would be to share his bed every night.

"You're staying here tonight."

Not so much a question but a demand. Zach grinned, knowing Sam couldn't see his face and decided to tease him.

"You're pretty bossy. A guy likes to be asked, you know."

Obviously, Sam didn't get the joke; he rolled on top of Zach, his eyes dark in his face. "You're mine and you belong here. End of story."

"Yes," said Zach, cupping the back of Sam's neck to draw him in for a kiss. "I'm yours."

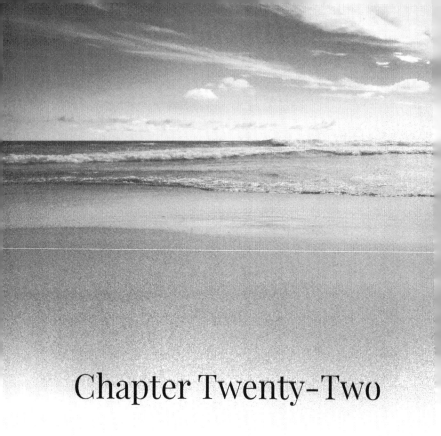

Chapter Twenty-Two

He could kill Zach. Looking across the table at his lover's wide smile and hopeful eyes, Sam regretted that they were about to get into their first fight. Considering they'd spent the last month practically inseparable, it was bound to happen, but Sam hated to see Zach unhappy. This, however, couldn't be helped.

Now that he thought about it, Zach wasn't as innocent as he wanted Sam to believe. He probably gaged Sam's reaction to the news he'd just announced, and that was the reason he called to have Sam meet him at Caruso's bakery, instead of at Sam's apartment. Zach figured Sam wouldn't lose his temper and bellow like an enraged elephant. Or throw things.

"You did what again? I know I must've misheard you."

Zach sipped his cappuccino and licked the foam off his

top lip. Normally Sam enjoyed doing that for him, but he was too angry right now.

"I called your mother down in Florida. It didn't seem right that you hadn't spoken to her in months and yet you've become so close with my mother."

Breathe in, breathe out. The warm smell of almonds, roasted coffee, and vanilla should have relaxed him; by this time, he'd have consumed a few cannoli and an espresso, but his appetite, even for his favorite sweets, had deserted him, which proved how upset he truly was.

The funny thing about it was he liked Cheryl. Once she'd seen how Sam truly cared for Zach, she herself began the tentative steps of getting back out into the world, forming social relationships with the other volunteers at the senior center. With gentle encouragement, Sam had no doubt she'd soon have a rich life, one that didn't revolve around Zach.

But Cheryl Cohen was not Barbara Stein. His mother had never given a damn about anyone but herself. One night he'd mentioned to Zach she lived in Florida, and that they were somewhat estranged. He laughed bitterly to himself. Yeah, right, estranged. More like she barely knew she even had a fucking son. Never in his wildest dreams did he think Zach would take it upon himself to not only call and speak to his mother, but fly her up to New York all expenses paid and arrange for them to talk.

"I asked you to call her so many times but you never did, so I figured I'd help."

"Didn't you think," said Sam, trying hard to keep himself together so he wouldn't end up in jail for killing his lover and trashing the bakery, "maybe there was a reason why I don't speak to her?"

The concept of strife within families was foreign to Zach, who'd always known he was loved by his mother and father.

The sweet smile on Zach's face faltered. "Well, I kind of

thought—"

"No," said Sam, shaking his head. "You didn't think. Let me ask you a question. Did you introduce yourself as my boyfriend to her? Say you were my lover?"

"Um, I said I was a close friend." He screwed his face up in thought. "She didn't really ask me any questions."

No surprise there. She probably stopped listening after she heard the magic words "all expense paid."

"Are you trying to tell me something? Like, you've never told your mother you're gay?" Behind his glasses, Zach's blue eyes blinked at Sam in disbelief.

If he wasn't so annoyed with Zach, he'd kiss him for looking so adorably bewildered.

Just then, the bell tinkled over the door, and Sam heard a familiar voice over his shoulder.

"See, I told you he'd be here. Sammy, where the hell have you been hiding yourself?"

Henry circled around the table to stand in front of Sam and Zach, his arm around his wife. Sunlight glinted on the spill of Heather's long red hair over her shoulders, gilding the freckles dotting her cheeks. Her blue eyes lit up with curiosity.

"Sam Stein. You haven't called us or visited in over a month, and now I see why." Her bright gaze traveled from Sam to capture Zach's. "Hi, I'm Heather, Henry's wife."

"Uh, hi, I'm Zach, Zach Cohen."

Sam loved Heather and had been meaning to call and bring Zach and his best friends together, but time had slipped away; time that had been spent with Zach—making love, walking on the beach, or teaching him how to fly a kite. Sam hoped Zach wouldn't retreat into the shell he'd only recently emerged from. He wanted his friends and his lover to get along.

Sam needn't have worried, as Heather was the warmest

person he'd ever met. Henry brought over two chairs, and within minutes, she had them all laughing at some crazy stories at her job as a dental hygienist.

"I told her: Babe, the only cavity you ever have to worry about filling is mine." He winked at them. "And I return the favor on a nightly basis."

"Oh God, Henry, you're so bad." Heather smacked him on his shoulder. "Now Zach is going to think we're some kind of sex fiends."

The natural banter between them restored Sam's good humor. So what if Zach spoke to his mother? It didn't mean she was hopping on a plane tonight. Considering it had been well over a year since he'd last seen her, the possibility of her being anxious to visit him seemed remote. He relaxed and took Zach's hand in his lap, toying with his fingers. Zach threw him a smile.

Henry sat with his arm across the back of Heather's chair, playing with a curling tendril of her hair. Mrs. Caruso bustled up and kissed them both on the cheek.

"Ah, my favorite couple. See? I brought you the cappuccino and the little fruit tarts you like. And for you, my beautiful girl, I have the tiramisu you love, all fresh."

She set the plates in front of them and returned with forks and the coffees. Standing back from the table, she surveyed the four of them with a satisfied look in her eye.

"This is what I like to see, my two handsome boys and my gorgeous couple who one day if I live to see, will maybe bring me a baby." Without waiting for an answer, she returned to sit behind the counter.

"She never stops, does she?" asked Henry, picking up his fork and digging into Heather's tiramisu. "Here, babe." He offered Heather the cake.

One thing Sam loved about his friend was that he never let people's opinions matter. When Sam came out as gay,

Henry didn't blink and never treated him any differently. The moment Henry met Heather in college he fell for her, and when he introduced her to Sam for the first time, Sam understood why. Her beautiful face was only outshined by the sweetness of her heart; Henry didn't care she wasn't a size four; he loved every curve of her body. If Sam wasn't gay, he'd want a woman like Heather.

"You don't go to the lifestyle coach anymore, Sam?" She licked her fork clean of the custard.

Except for that.

"I'm fine. No more blocked chi."

Henry snorted. "I'll bet nothing's blocked anymore."

Henry bit into his fruit tart and chewed with gusto, unable to keep that shit-eating grin off his face.

"Shut up, Henry."

A quiet snort of laughter came from Zach's direction, and Sam nudged his thigh. "What? You too? You're supposed to be on my side."

"I am." Zach bit his lip, but Sam saw the struggle it took for him to keep his laughter under control. "This reminds me of Marcus, Julian, and me at breakfast. Marcus always baiting Julian, and Juli telling him to shut up." A wistful expression crossed Zach's face. "I miss them. We haven't had a chance to get together for a while."

"Julian and Nick are busy planning their wedding; I'm sure once everything settles down, things will get back to normal." He nudged Zach's knee with his and returned Zach's grateful smile of understanding.

"I know; you're right. And that'll give us a chance to prepare for your mother's visit."

"What?" Henry choked. "Barbara's coming to New York?" He swallowed a gulp of his cappuccino. "When? Sign me up for a ringside seat. This is one not to be missed."

Death by cannoli. Sounded like the perfect name for a murder mystery, although there'd be no mystery as to who would kill Henry. Once he told his story, Sam believed no jury would convict.

It was impossible to even fake a smile without looking like Death's head. "Zach invited her. I had no idea she was coming." All his earlier good will disintegrated; he no longer had confidence he'd be seeing his mother later than sooner. "When is she arriving? Please don't say tonight." He needed at least a week to prepare himself. Henry and Heather sat across from them, their gazes ping-ponging between him and Zach.

"No, of course not."

Thank God.

"Tomorrow night."

"Kill me now."

*   *   *

"I don't know why you're so worried. Everything's going to be fine."

They'd spent the entire morning cleaning his apartment in preparation for his mother's visit, and Sam was grouchy and tired. All he wanted was a beer, the sofa, and Zach.

To his credit, Zach had taken care of everything; he'd thrown out all the mysterious items that had taken up residence in the refrigerator and scrubbed out the bathroom. They'd taken a trip to the city and bought new sheets and a comforter for the bed and new towels.

It had been something he'd meant to do since Andy had left but hadn't bothered, since house things didn't matter to him. Too many nights in the past he'd fallen asleep on the sofa, watching whatever he found mildly interesting and never made it to the bed. He hated sleeping alone anyway.

But he understood Zach's discomfort, waking up in a bed Sam had shared with another man, drying himself off with towels that man had used. Though Sam had no attachment to anything, he knew Zach was more sensitive and aware of things like that.

And Sam discovered he liked shopping with Zach. He didn't throw things in the cart, but rather took the time to think about things like colors and textures, asking Sam's opinion on the softness of sheets. It made it seem as though they were beginning a new life—together.

And Sam liked that as well.

His mother's plane wasn't due in until nine that evening, and Zach had ordered a car to pick her up at the airport. They returned home, the trunk of the taxi stuffed full with their bags, and Sam lugged some of them inside, while Zach paid the driver. His hands laden with the rest of the bags, Zach trudged up the steps, following him into the apartment. They stood in the small entranceway, the mountainous pile surrounding them.

"Damn, we bought a lot of stuff."

"You needed a lot of stuff," said Zach, pulling open the first bag and taking out a set of dishtowels. "Not only hadn't this place been cleaned in ages, but you don't have a single fork and spoon that match." He opened a box full of cutlery. "Now we can eat like adults, not frat boys who stole all their utensils from a fast-food restaurant."

"Hey," said Sam, enjoying the sight of Zach arranging his kitchen. "It's not like I had dinner parties or anything. It was only me."

"Well, now it's us." Zach returned to kiss him, and Sam held him close, deepening the kiss. Zach burrowed into him, and Sam walked him backward until Zach's back rested flat up against the wall.

"Us, huh?"

"Yeah, us. You and me, right?"

Truth blazed from Zach's eyes. This wasn't the same man Sam met those months ago in Atlantic City at the beginning of the summer. Back then, a fog of uncertainty coupled with acute dejection had hung over Zach. He'd looked like a man who'd been kicked down by life hard.

But now those blue eyes that had so mesmerized Sam from the start shone bright with an optimistic inner light. And Sam remembered something else.

"Right. And you know what else?" Sam rubbed his crotch over Zach's and was rewarded with a smile that spoke to his dirtiest fantasies.

"What?"

"I still want you up against this wall, wearing only those glasses and that smile."

"Then do it."

Shocked, Sam stared at Zach, the dreamy expression in his eyes replaced by one of rising hunger. Sam's body hardened in response.

"Yeah?" His voice rasped in his throat.

Without answering, Zach drew his tee shirt over his head and pulled down his shorts and boxers. His cock jutted out, already hard, and Sam recognized the flush of lust creeping up Zach's chest.

"Yeah."

Sam didn't need to be told twice. He kicked aside the shopping bags and knelt before Zach, holding his hips to steady him against the wall. The skin beneath his fingers was so smooth it begged to be touched, kissed…licked. Sam pressed his mouth against the slant of Zach's hip bone and inhaled the scent of him.

"Come *on*," said Zach rocking his pelvis forward.

At the sound of Zach's shuddering breath, Sam glanced

up and was transfixed: Zach's eyes were closed, his head thrown back, the black glasses askew. His mouth had fallen slightly open, and his breath came in short pants.

Jesus. Sam had hardly touched him, yet Zach looked ready to explode. And Sam's fantasy changed. He didn't want Zach up against the wall in a hard and hurried fuck. He had other plans.

"Hey."

Zach opened his eyes, his expression heavy with lust.

"Bedroom."

Without taking his hand off Zach's hip, Sam stood and gathered him close, then walked to the bedroom. Along the way Sam snagged a bag with sheets and a small, faux sheepskin throw they'd bought to put down on the wooden floors for the winter.

Before they'd left the apartment this morning, Zach had stripped the bed so all that remained before them now was the bare mattress with a mattress cover. Sam threw the furry rug on top of the mattress and pushed Zach down on it where he lay waiting, desire written in his open mouth, flushed skin, and panting breath. Sam had never felt so wanted; so *hungered* for. He stripped naked and joined Zach.

To his surprise, Zach rolled over, facing him. Their cocks bumped together, and Sam pressed against Zach as they kissed, the taste of Zach's mouth, always addictive, spiking a need deep within Sam for even greater intimacy.

Sam continued kissing down Zach's throat, licking and sucking the tender skin along the cords of his neck. Zach shifted restlessly beneath him, his hands reaching downward to touch himself, but Sam batted him away.

"No."

Zach stilled. "Touch me." Desperation echoed in his voice.

Sam gazed down on Zach spread out beneath him and couldn't hold back. He bent down and took Zach's straining cock into his mouth, swallowing him down to the base. Beginning the slow glide upward, Sam swirled his tongue around the thick head, flicking the underside while always keeping a steady pumping rhythm with his hand.

The earthy taste of Zach intoxicated, and he continued to suckle, listening to Zach's little gasps and moans. Sam loved those small, desperate sounds, loved that he was the one driving Zach crazy, and it spurred him on. He reached to cup Zach's balls, rolling them in the palm of his hand, and gave them a little squeeze. At the sharp inhalation of Zach's breath, Sam slid his fingers behind Zach's balls, and brushed the crease of Zach's ass.

"More." Zach moaned, his head thrashing on the bed. "Please."

His mouth still busy on Zach's dick, Sam flirted with the rim of Zach's hole, his fingertip sliding in just past the opening, then withdrawing. The first taste of Zach's precome trickled onto his tongue, and Sam sucked hard and at the same time pushed his finger inside Zach.

"Oh, God." Tremors racked Zach's body, his harsh cry echoing in the room as he came, sending streams of ejaculate down Sam's throat. This moment was Sam's favorite: drinking down the hot, salty essence of Zach that filled his mouth, while holding his shaking body close. He waited until Zach's cock softened in his mouth before releasing him and shifting upward to lie next to him.

The act of giving Zach pleasure had become an addictive craving, but the aftermath was what Sam loved. That closeness, the intimate touches of their lips and bodies brought him peace. He buried his lips in Zach's damp curls and sighed with contentment.

His eyes still closed, Zach lay limp next to him, a smile

curving his lips. "That was amazing." He opened his eyes. "Come closer."

Surprised, Sam rolled nearer, fitting his body into Zach's, and slid his hand over Zach's face to cup his jaw. He tugged him close and kissed him.

"Ummm." Zach hummed against his mouth, then wrapped his arms around Sam's neck and threw his leg over Sam's hip so their pelvises rocked together. Zach was all over him, nipping at his jaw, his tongue pushing in Sam's ear. Their sweat-slicked bodies moved languidly together.

It wasn't often Zach took the lead during sex, but Sam always enjoyed this aggressive side of Zach. He wanted Zach inside him again.

"Turn over."

"What?" He blinked, trying to read Zach's face, and the thoughts behind the slightly amused, yet wicked smile.

"I said, turn over." Giving his shoulder a shove, Zach kissed the corner of his mouth. "Don't you trust me?"

With his life. "Of course I do. You know that."

Zach raised his eyebrows, remaining silent, and Sam complied. The soft fur of the rug brushed up against his cock, warm and sensual, and Sam gripped himself, thrusting through his fist. With each stroke he squeezed the head of his cock, giving a twist on each upstroke.

Zach's warm hands smoothed up his back, followed by his even warmer lips. It felt so good to be touched. Sam had long ago given up the hope of being loved. Lost beneath the betrayal and the pain of his past, Sam now tasted something new and frightening. Something his forever, if he chose to accept the gift.

Forgiveness. Hope. Love.

He stilled, cheek pressed to the soft sheepskin, and lost himself in Zach's healing touch.

"Don't stop; keep touching yourself." The warmth of Zach's breath touched his shoulder. Little licks of fire raced beneath the surface of Sam's skin as Zach's kisses progressed from the top of his spine down his back, until he reached his ass.

Sam began to stroke himself again. He closed his eyes, imagining Zach's mouth sucking him, when he felt Zach press a kiss first on his right cheek, then the left. The breath stuttered in his chest at the first swipe of Zach's wet, warm tongue against the dip of his back.

"What the—?" He reached back to grab hold of Zach but flailed, finding only air.

"Quiet." Another pass of Zach's tongue, this time over his ass, and then Zach ran a finger down the crease and slid it between the globes of Sam's ass, finding his hole.

Every nerve ending in Sam's body lit up; all thoughts of anything but having Zach touch him again, right there, *right now*, fled his mind. He shifted back and spread his legs wider, his mind whirling in a dark vortex of desire.

"Zach." His voice rasped harsh, but Sam didn't care how desperate and needy he sounded. If Zach didn't touch him again, soon, things might get ugly.

"Hmm, you like that?" The tip of Zach's finger touched his hole, then circled the rim. "What about this?" His fingertip slid just inside, teasing Sam.

Fire seared through him once again, and Sam almost whimpered. The hunger to be touched soaked through him, drenching him to the core of his soul.

"Don't stop," he said, unashamed of his begging, needy pleas. "Please."

Then Zach's mouth was everywhere; his teeth nipped Sam's ass, then kissed away the sting, laving the skin. The roughness of Zach's stubbled cheek rasped gloriously against Sam's skin, increasing the pleasure and the pain. With firm hands, Zach massaged Sam's ass, then spread him wide, and alternated between lapping at his opening and ruthlessly spearing his tongue into Sam's hole, sending a sizzle of white hot electricity to short-circuit the portion of Sam's brain that still functioned.

"Fuck me. God damn." Sam's swearing increased exponentially with each teasing lick. "Right there, shit." Craving the friction, Sam pushed back against the wet stabs of Zach's wicked tongue, the sensitive nerve endings sparking with every thrust. Helpless against the burgeoning wave of passion racing through him, Sam writhed beneath the relentless, shocking onslaught of Zach's mouth.

For years he'd lived without this kind of passion, a life content with unexplored possibilities. Zach's fierce, loving touches incinerated all prior lovers'; any that had come before had been sex merely for the sake of release. What he had with Zach—sex as an extension of the love they shared—made each touch a memory and each kiss a lifeline to his heart.

A golden haze dropped like a curtain over his eyes, shimmering in his vision's forefront; his body clenched, and his head spun in dizzying circles. Sam's breath caught, and he let himself fly.

The force of his orgasm ripped through him, and he came, spilling great hot streams into his hand and onto the fluffy new rug. His free hand scrabbled for purchase against the mattress, and he became dimly aware of Zach enveloping him in a hug, holding his hand tight. Wetness dripped down his cheek.

"I love you." Zach's lips hovered over his ear, his body a warm and comforting weight on top.

"Love you too."

"I'm sorry I didn't speak to you before I talked to your mother," Zach whispered in his ear.

Sam smiled into the rug. "So you thought to make it up

to me by blowing my mind, huh?" He laced his fingers tight with Zach's.

Zach spoke against his shoulder. "The thought crossed my mind, yeah." He could hear the laughter in his voice and knew he wanted Zach happy every day. If having his mother visit would do that, he'd buy her a plane ticket every fucking weekend.

He rolled over, keeping Zach on top of him. "Hot sex will get you forgiven every time." Sam traced Zach's spine, trailing his fingers up each vertebra. It wasn't the same as the way Andy had used sex. This was give and take between him and Zach. He knew what he had in his arms was forever. Zach would never deceive him.

"You're so easy." Zach nuzzled into the crook of his neck and kissed him. "I bet if I threw in half a dozen cannoli, you'd be my slave."

He squeezed Zach's ass, then slapped it, laughing over Zach's outraged yelp. "Why don't you try it and find out?"

A quick glance at the bedside clock revealed the time— seven thirty. Shit. His mother would be landing in little more than an hour, and the place was still a mess. And he still needed to shower, although he liked having Zach's scent all over him.

Damn. He had it bad.

He smoothed the slightly reddened spot on Zach's ass where he'd smacked him. "I promise to kiss it and make it better. Let's take a shower; my mother will be here before you know it."

Zach scrambled out of the bed and walked toward the bathroom. "Well then, better move it, old man."

Old man? "Who are you calling old?" He jumped out of bed and raced after a laughing Zach, who shut the door in his face.

Sam wrenched the door open to find Zach had already

turned the water on and was getting in the shower. He held his face up to the water, letting it stream over his face and shoulders.

Sam joined him under the flow of water and pushed him up against the tiled wall. "If we had the time, I'd show you how this old man would fuck you until you couldn't move."

Droplets of water streaked Zach's face and hung like tiny teardrops on his dark lashes. He smiled up into Sam's face. "We'll just have to do it another time, right?"

Sam kissed him hard, then reached for the shampoo. "Yeah. Hold on to that thought until after my mother leaves." Since she'd be staying in his apartment, Zach wouldn't be sleeping over.

"It'll all work out. I know it." Zach took some of the gel and began to wash his hair.

An hour and a half later they sat in the clean apartment, listening for the car to drive up. Zach squeezed his hand.

"Don't worry."

"I'm almost forty years old; I was a cop for Christ's sake. I've lived through shit most people will never see, and yet…" It was hard to explain even to Zach, who hadn't told his mother he was gay, not out of fear of rejection but because of her own personal grief. Zach had always been certain of love. "I'm nervous."

It was embarrassing to open up like this; like cutting open your chest and exposing your guts and your heart. He knew Zach had meant well, but right now Sam could only concentrate on the negative.

Headlights swept through the front windows, and the sound of a car pulling up in front broke through his internal monologue. A car door slammed.

"She's here."

Zach took him by the shoulders and kissed him hard.

"It'll be fine."

"I know." He kissed Zach back, and together they went to the door. Sam opened it before his mother could knock.

She stood at the base of the steps, smaller than he remembered from his brief visit last year. Her long blonde hair was pulled back, held in place by huge dark sunglasses, and her heavily made-up eyes found his in the glow of the overhead fanlight.

"Sammy." A tentative smile touched her lips. "Hi."

Was it possible she was as nervous as him? The thought hadn't crossed his mind; somehow that made him calmer and all this easier to handle.

"Hi, Mom." He jogged down the steps to greet her. They didn't kiss or hug; it wasn't their way. "Here, come inside. I'll take your suitcase."

He hefted it and let her pass in front of him. The heady scent of her perfume drifted in the air. In typical brownstone fashion the stairs were wide and steep, without any railings. On the first step she wobbled a bit, and Zach hurried down to help her.

"Mrs. Stein, I'm Zach. We spoke on the phone."

With a grateful smile, she took his arm. "Yes, thank you. And thank you again for arranging this for me." Sam watched her lean on Zach's arm.

They proceeded into the house, and while Sam put her bag in the bedroom, Zach settled his mother into the club chair with a glass of wine. They'd already put out a platter of cheese, crackers, and hummus before she arrived. He took the glass of wine Zach handed him and sat next to him on the sofa.

"How was your flight?" Small talk for strangers who had little to say to one another.

"Good, thank you. Not even three hours." She gazed

into the depths of her glass of wine. Without taking a sip she placed it on the coffee table and laced her fingers together.

They sat in uncomfortable silence for a few minutes.

"Has it been really hot in Florida, Mrs. Stein? I imagine the humidity is worse than here." Sam could sense the desperation in Zach's voice to keep the conversation rolling. Anything to get him and his mother to speak. But Zach didn't know their history.

Without taking her eyes off Sam, his mother answered Zach. "It is terrible. I never turn off my air conditioner. And the tropical storms are the worst." Her lips curved in a brief smile.

"Do you remember how scared you used to be of lightning when you were little, Sam? You used to come into my bedroom and ask if you could sleep with me."

That was a surprise to him. "I have no memory of that, sorry, Mom." He took a sip of wine. "I'm guessing it was a very long time ago."

Perhaps she thought he'd remember or at least pretend to smooth over the awkwardness, but he couldn't. Her smile faded, and she removed her sunglasses from her head, placing them on her lap.

"Sam, why did your friend call me to visit? What's wrong?" Though she favored Zach with a brief smile, her attention focused solely on Sam. "Not that he doesn't seem nice, but who is Zach to you?"

"Zach is my lover." There didn't seem to be any need to pussyfoot around it. He wasn't a teenager anymore, worried whether his mother would love or accept him. Still, he couldn't keep the defiant tone out of his voice or harden the tilt of his jaw, as if girding himself for a fight. "I love him."

He heard her quick expulsion of breath. "I was wondering if you were ever going to tell me."

Shocked, he stared at her. "What?" His mouth hung open

with surprise.

Regret glimmered in her eyes. "I didn't know when you were a child, but when you never spoke about girls in high school or mentioned ever having a date, I suspected something. You never talked to me and were so angry all the time, so I left you alone." Her red lacquered fingers laced and relaced themselves in her lap. "Now I see how wrong I was."

"I wasn't angry at you, specifically. I was angry at the world; Dad for dying, and myself for the feelings inside me that I knew were different. All the guys were looking at girls and whispering; meanwhile I was having strange thoughts about men." The glass of wine in his hand shook, and Zach wordlessly took it away.

"I couldn't talk to you about sex—you were my mother. Dad was gone, and any time I thought maybe I'd talk to a teacher or guidance counselor at school, I'd hear someone making a homo joke, and I'd forget about it."

She raised her agonized gaze to him. "I failed you and I'm sorry. Your father and I got married so young and then he was away most of the time." Her eyes welled up with tears. "I was lonely all the time. After he died, I know I went crazy. I needed to feel loved again and did everything I could to make myself attractive to men."

Strange how perspectives can change with a little conversation and insight. If someone had asked Sam to describe his mother yesterday, the picture he'd conjure up in his mind would be that of a weak woman in denial of her age, dressing and acting inappropriately.

But after the most personal talk they'd ever had, she didn't seem like a desperate woman refusing to give up her youth by dressing in too-young clothes. Maybe her bright clothing and eye makeup gave her a sense of strength. Or maybe she hid behind the colors to keep the darkness of her thoughts at bay.

He was in no position to judge her.

Before Zach came into his life, his existence was pretty much colorless; a wash of neutrals that all blended together without any vibrancy or cheer. He dragged himself along with Henry and forced himself to play ball, but the truth was he would most likely have been content to be a couch potato for the rest of his life.

Everyone deals with grief in different ways; how he'd felt as a fourteen-year-old boy who'd lost the father he worshipped was different from his mother, who'd lost the man she loved.

"Did you and Dad have a good marriage? Did you love him? Did he love you?"

That question required his mother to take another sip of wine. "I loved him with the desperation a twenty-two-year-old girl loves a man who tells her she's beautiful and he wants her. I was so happy when we got married and I got pregnant right away. But then when he went to work for the FBI undercover and was away most of the time, it was as if we became strangers." Her eyes took on a faraway look. "He'd come home every three or four months and we'd sit quiet, like we'd forgotten why we were married. When we'd start to reconnect it was time for him to leave again."

She blinked and then smiled at him. "But he loved you. So much. Do you remember when he'd take you to the beach or kite flying?"

Sam couldn't answer, so he nodded; his throat was too tight to swallow, much less speak. Zach took his hand and squeezed it gently.

"Sam and I went kite flying the other day," said Zach. "It was my first time, but Sam was a pro."

"You still have your kite?"

"Yeah," Sam said gruffly, clearing his voice. "I hadn't flown it in a long while, but lately I've been thinking about him…"

"He wouldn't have cared."

His heart fluttered in his chest. "He wouldn't?" It became imperative for Sam to understand the little he could about his dead father, and this was one more sliver of his life.

"No," said his mother, shaking her head. "Nothing could ever change how much he loved you. I remember,"— she brushed the tears away with her fingers, smearing her makeup a little—"I once told him how worried I was raising you without him around. I wanted you to have a strong male presence." She smiled through her tears. "He said, 'Don't be ridiculous, Barbara. Sammy will be whatever he is, no matter if you or I raise him alone or together. It's what's in his heart that matters most.'"

All these years he never knew. "I'm so angry he isn't here."

"I am too. I was so angry after he died I went crazy, running after all those men, looking for a replacement. I was overwhelmed thinking no one would ever love me again."

If they were going to be adults and be totally honest with each other, he wasn't about to sugarcoat it.

"It was as if I lost both of you. Dad was dead, and you were too busy with other men." He shook his head, trying to frame together his patchwork thoughts. "The only times I saw you were when you came home to change for another dinner date. It wasn't until I met Henry that I found someone to talk to."

They'd never been this honest before; but then, they'd never talked. He fed off his resentment and lived in angry silence, while she led an equally lonely life surrounded by strangers and men who could never give her back the love she'd lost. He waited in silence for her to speak.

"We can't erase the past. What's done is done. That was my mother's favorite saying, and it's true. If I come away

257

with nothing else this weekend, at least let me know you'll think about forgiving me."

Sam didn't need to see Zach's face to know what he was thinking; he could hear the sniffles to his left. The choices were clear. Sam could hold on to his resentment, struggle through this stilted visit, and send his mother back to Florida, continuing the way they had been all these years. In doing so, it became clear that neither one of them ended up a winner. Or, he could swallow his bitterness and look at the situation through his mother's eyes and try to understand.

"I've spent most of my life angry; angry over my father dying when I was so young, and angry at you…"

"Sam."

No one, not even Zach, would stop him from finally saying his piece. He needed it, didn't anyone understand?

"I know what I'm doing."

"Let him talk, Zach." His mother's gaze held his. "I have a feeling he's been waiting all his life to say what he has to say."

"I was angry at you for checking out on me when Dad died, I hated you even. Then, when I grew up and you moved away, it seemed like the inevitable relationship anyway; you had your life and I had mine, and once a year we could stand each other enough for a short visit."

"Mrs. Stein, it doesn't have to be that way." Zach broke into the conversation. Sam almost smiled to himself that Zach had managed to hold back from speaking this long.

"I think my son made it pretty clear how he feels. I do appreciate what you tried to do." She gave Zach a wan smile.

"And yesterday, I fully intended it to stay that way," he said, surprising them both from their shocked expressions. Shit; he surprised himself with that one. But it was true. "I never expected it to change, but thanks to Zach it has. I think it's gone on long enough. We've beaten ourselves up over a past that can't be changed. But I've been through enough bullshit in my life, and I'm ready to move on. I've been taught recently I need to look to the future."

Zach's shining eyes and sweet smile of approval gave him the courage to continue.

"So if you can forgive me for being a less-than-perfect son, I can forgive you for what happened in the past." He hesitated a moment. "I think Dad would've wanted it that way, don't you?"

At his mother's nod, he went to her and finally gave and received the hugs that had been missing from his childhood. It might never be perfect, but it was good enough for him, and by the smile on his mother's face, it seemed to work its magic on her as well.

"That was beautiful." Zach threw his arms around Sam and hugged him. Then, as if he realized what he was doing, he swiped his arm across his face to dry his tears and let Sam go. "Sorry."

Sam kissed his cheek. "Don't ever be sorry for being yourself. I don't think my mother minds. After all, this only happened with your help."

"No. It's because you finally let love into your heart, instead of pushing it away."

Sam kissed Zach again and held him close. If it had to do with love, it was all because of Zach.

Chapter Twenty-Three

"Are you guys nervous?"

Zach couldn't believe tomorrow was Julian and Nick's wedding day. The past month had been a whirlwind of plans, tuxedo shopping, and menu planning, and he, Marcus, and Julian hardly had a chance to text and say hello, never mind meet for their weekly breakfast.

So when Marcus texted him early this morning with the surprising news that Julian and Nick wanted to meet for breakfast, he almost bounced off the bed with excitement. Of course that woke Sam up and Zach needed to soothe the grouchy beast, which necessitated some intensely hot sex.

Zach couldn't help but be amazed; to look at Sam now—unperturbed at the hubbub around them in the restaurant and sipping his drink—it was hard to imagine only several hours earlier he'd been face down on the bed, shaking and calling out Zach's name.

As if sensing Zach's eyes on him, Sam glanced over, and they shared a smile. He slid his palm down Zach's jean-clad thigh, resting it above the knee and it reminded Zach of how only last year he'd sat right here with his friends, depressed and alone, thinking how he'd never find someone to love.

Now, he not only had someone he loved who loved him back, but they were contemplating a future together.

Julian's fingers beat a rapid tattoo on the tabletop. "I am, but he isn't," he replied, indicating Nick with a tilt of his head. "He's so mellow about all this I hope he doesn't forget."

"Not likely, Juli. Not with the way you have everyone scheduled to the minute." Marcus dug into his scrambled egg whites. He grinned as he chewed, then swallowed. "Tell me, Nick, does he schedule you in for sex?" Marcus checked his watch. "Ah, 11:15, time for a blowjob."

Nick choked on his beer while Julian glared at Marcus. "Don't be an asshole." The glare turned to a smug grin. "Besides, I have no complaints."

Marcus put up a hand. "Stop. Zach's ears are too delicate for such gruesome details."

Nick snorted. "That's a crock of shit. Look at them— Sam's grinning like the Cheshire cat and Zach's happy for the first time since I met him." He lazed back in his seat and nudged Julian. "Looks like he handled his life fine without you guys interfering in it."

Heat crept up his neck from the force of Julian's penetrating gaze, but Zach didn't care anymore. The weight of Sam's hand rested warm and comforting on his thigh, and he placed his hand over it, sliding his fingers in between Sam's.

"As a matter of fact," said Nick. "I'll bet—"

"Oh, shut the hell up. Don't you dare mention that word

again." Marcus sat back in his chair, sulking. "You're the reason for that stupid bet. Now Zach gets a hot cop and you're forcing me to be celibate. It's unnatural."

"You're mad because we caught you trying to cheat with a waiter. Try and relax." Julian cackled with unrestrained glee. "All that frowning will give you wrinkles."

Though Zach wanted to laugh, he did his best to placate his friend. "It's not that bad. Maybe it'll give you a chance to take stock of your life."

"My life was fine. This is fucking killing me." Marcus faced him with a black glare. "And yeah, I'm going to keep cursing. If I have to stay celibate, it's the price you'll have to pay."

"It'll be worth it," said Zach. "Maybe you'll meet someone and actually talk first, instead of jumping right into bed."

"What for?" said Marcus, clearly horrified at the idea. "I've got nothing to say to them."

One day, my friend, Zach mentally shook his head in despair for Marcus. *One day you'll meet someone, and everything you thought you knew will be turned upside down.*

"I wanted to thank you guys for inviting my mother to your wedding. She's really touched, and it means a lot. To both of us." Sam raised his glass to Nick and Julian, and Zach had never been happier.

"Yeah. Barbara extended her trip, and she's staying with my mom." The two women had hit it off perfectly, and Barbara even accompanied Cheryl to her volunteer work at the senior center. Having her stay with his mother had been a stroke of genius on Sam's part. They now had all the privacy they could want every night.

"Leaving you free to stay with Sam, huh?" Marcus grinned. "Guess it all worked out for you in the end."

Sam squeezed his hand. "It worked out for both of us,

I'd say."

"Well, everyone." Julian and Nick stood. "We'll see you all tomorrow afternoon."

The wedding. Zach could hardly wait.

*   *   *

"To the grooms!" Marcus raised a bottle of champagne, declaring a glass wasn't good enough. "May you have a long and happy life together. Now go ahead and kiss."

To everyone's surprise, Julian grabbed a startled Marcus and kissed him full on the mouth. "Thank you. For everything, but most of all for being our friend." Nick hugged Marcus next; then he and Julian kissed to appreciative whistles and catcalls.

The music started playing, and Zach found himself carted off by Marcus to the center of the dance floor, where Julian and Nick were already dancing with their arms wrapped around each other.

He looked around for Sam, who simply smiled and tipped his champagne glass at him, then turned to speak to his mother.

Marcus held him close. "Your mom seems happier now. She likes Sam, right?"

Since they were kids in the playground, Marcus had always looked out for him, so the question didn't seem strange to Zach.

"Yeah, she loves him."

"So do you, right?"

Zach knew Marcus had thrown the question out there to finally hear him say it.

"Yeah." There was no reason to deny it. "And he loves me as well. I only wish you could be as happy one day."

Marcus pulled back and shot him a wry look. "Why does everyone think pairing up exclusively is a guarantee for happiness?" A bitter laugh escaped him. "If I learned one thing in my life, it's that one person is never enough to satisfy. I hope that's not the case for Juli." He held Zach close, and they swayed together for a moment before Marcus spoke again.

"You know I've always loved you. But I could never be the man you deserve." Zach froze, his heart twisting painfully. He couldn't believe this was Marcus, unburdening himself for the first time in their many years of friendship.

"Knowing myself, I'd only disappoint you in the end. I couldn't do that to you or me; losing you wasn't something I was willing to risk. Our friendship means too much… everything to me."

"Me too," said Zach finally, forcing the words out. "And I love you like my brother."

He and Marcus held on to each other, awash in memories. Feeling a tap on his shoulder, Zach looked up to see Sam standing there.

"Mind if I cut in?"

With a brief squeeze of his shoulder, Marcus stepped back. "Not at all. I was only the warm-up. You're the main attraction." He disappeared into the crowd.

And once Sam held him, Zach forgot anything else except the sensual pleasure of being touched by the man he loved. For a while they moved together to the sounds of the big band music Nick and Julian had chosen; Zach said nothing, utterly content to spend the rest of the evening right here in Sam's arms.

"You know what would be nice?" Sam whispered in his ear.

"Yes, but I can't do it in public." He smiled against Sam's cheek. "Marcus would approve, but Julian and Nick might not understand."

"Keep whatever you're thinking in that brilliant mind of yours." Sam chuckled and Zach grinned. "I think we should each dance with our mothers, especially since mine is going back to Florida in a week."

Wow. He did not expect that at all, but the more he thought about it, Zach knew it was the perfect idea. A quick glance to the sidelines revealed his mother and Barbara Stein standing together watching them with identical smiles on their faces.

"I love it. And then in mid-dance we switch partners."

They walked off the dance floor holding hands and stood before their respective mothers. Zach held out his hand.

"Mom, may I have the pleasure of this dance?"

Her eyes filled but she held herself together and nodded. "I'd love to." They walked to the dance floor, and it thrilled Zach to know Sam and Barbara were only a step behind.

Zach gazed down into his mother's eyes. "Having fun?"

"It's a beautiful wedding, and Julian and Nick are so happy. I only hope you and Sam could be as happy as they are."

"Don't." Zach shook his head. "I don't want their happiness, I want my own for Sam and me. But," said Zach hastily, "I understand what you mean, and I love you."

His mother remained silent, and they danced together for a while listening to the music. "I love you too, and I'm not upset."

"You're not?"

"No. You know, I've been speaking to the therapists over at the senior center, and they've been very helpful making me see how I can better my life and become a more independent person."

"That's the best news I've heard in years, Mom." He kissed her cheek, and they hugged.

Life hadn't been fair to either of them, but no one was guaranteed smooth, untroubled waters. A silly bet made more to tease Marcus than get Zach a boyfriend had set the course for the firestorm of events leading up to this moment; Zach in love with Sam and his mother on her way to better health and a life separate from his.

"May I cut in?"

Zach blinked, and Sam came into focus with Barbara by his side.

"Of course. I'm happy to dance with the two most lovely ladies at the wedding."

He whirled Barbara around, and the two of them laughed about her bad dates; he teased her that he'd give her a family discount for his dating website.

Dinner was a boisterous affair with Marcus making racy toasts and calling for the grooms to kiss every five minutes.

"If I can't get any, I might as well know that Juli and Nick are having as much fun as possible."

"I think lack of sex may be making Marcus delusional," said Zach, leaning back into Sam's arms. Julian and Nick cut the small cake and fed each other from the piece, leading to more applause and picture-taking.

"Can we go?" Sam's breath touched Zach's temple. "Its wrapping up and I want to take you somewhere."

"Yeah?" Zach smiled up at him. "I guess so. The guys won't mind." He looked over his shoulder at Nick and Julian who were drinking champagne, their eyes only on each other.

"I don't think they'll even miss us."

Chapter Twenty-Four

"Come on." Sam took his hand, and they threaded their way through the crowd, stopping only to kiss both his mother and Sam's good-bye. Curious now, because Sam seemed like he was in such a hurry, Zach peppered him with questions.

"Where are we going? You're in such a hurry; can't we go home and change first?" Zach loosened his tie and undid the top button of his shirt collar when they exited Sparks. The sun shone bright with a late-afternoon glow against the scattered clouds, and a light breeze rustled the leaves on the trees.

"Nope. No time." Sam handed his ticket to the valet Marcus had arranged for. It took only a few minutes before Zach spotted Sam's car pulling up in front of the club. "Let's go."

The valet opened his door, and Zach slid in the seat. Sam started the engine and drove away, refusing to answer any of Zach's questions.

"You can sit over there and sulk all you want, but I'm not gonna change my mind." A tiny smile played on Sam's lips. "You're so impatient. Save it for the bedroom."

"Not gonna be anything going on in there either if you keep being so annoying." Zach stared out the window, watching the scenery change as they drove over the Brooklyn Bridge, crossed over to the Gowanus Expressway and then merged onto the Belt Parkway, heading to Long Island.

Excitement grew steadily within Zach as the miles rolled on and the water came into view. When Sam pulled into the now-familiar, small parking lot and cut the engine, Zach opened the door and ran out to the grassy open area and tilted his head up to the brilliant blue sky.

There were at least twenty kite flyers, and their kites soared high, dipping and swooping, long tails like multicolored comets streaking behind. For several minutes, Zach stood silently admiring the dexterity of the people holding the strings.

He and Sam had spent many weekend hours here after the first time Sam had brought him; Sam had taught him the tricks of the strings, how to make the kite sing in the wind while not interfering with the other flyers. After several times watching Sam, Zach bought his own kite, and even if Sam was working a job for Henry, he'd come here alone, determined to gain expertise on his own.

Nothing could prepare him now for the sight of Sam walking toward him with both of their kites in one hand, and a bottle of champagne in the other. His heartbeat quickened, loving the carefree, happy light in Sam's eyes that had replaced the wary sadness from when they'd initially met.

Sam had taken off his tie and rolled up his sleeves, and

Zach's eyes were drawn to the glinting golden hairs on his strong, capable arms. Desire rolled through him like the waves in the bay: gentle, strong, and infinite.

"If you keep looking at me like that we're going to have to go home." Sam bent and kissed him, his lips soft and tasting faintly champagne-sweet. "I want you too, baby, don't doubt it."

Zach clung to him, his mouth opening under Sam's, their tongues tangling. The champagne bottle bumped cold and hard against his back as Sam's arms came around to hug him tight to his hard body. Their kisses deepened, and Zach wished everyone around them would disappear. He pressed himself closer, sinking into Sam.

Sam groaned and broke away panting. "Damn, you need to stop and hold this for later."

"Hmm," said Zach, humming into the curve of Sam's neck. "Let's make later now, and go home." He tipped his head back to stare into Sam's eyes.

"Don't tempt me," said Sam, a pained expression crossing his face. He continued to study Zach's face.

"What?"

"Nothing." Sam let him go and stuck the bottle under his arm. "Let's fly, baby."

Feeling happier than ever, Zach tested for the wind and let his kite go, catching the updraft. He backed up, doling out the string inch by inch until his kite was well above him, higher than he'd ever flown before.

Sheer joy surged through him as the wind picked up and his kite soared, the green and blue tails swirling in the wind. He laughed, twisting his wrists like Sam showed him to dip and swoop the kite. Sam had better be watching; Zach wanted to show him how much he'd improved over the past month.

Farther down the grassy area, several people began to clap and whistle; Zach glanced around but nothing unusual caught his eye. Soon everyone was clapping and pointing up to the sky. Zach looked up, and his heart turned over.

Up in the sky flew a solitary kite—Sam's kite, but altered. Attached at the bottom and top was a banner that fluttered in the wind, but Zach had no problem reading the words he never thought he'd see.

Zach—will you marry me?

He dropped his string and spun around searching for Sam, finding him at the edge of the grassy area. Their gazes locked, and Zach ran to him, heedless of his own kite sailing away.

"Are you serious?"

Sam took him by the shoulders. "I love you."

"I love you too." The words meant something more permanent now. "I never thought I'd find anyone…that I'd be enough."

"You're more than enough. You're everything." Sam kissed him then, gentle and sweet. "So, is it yes?"

"Of course it's yes." Zach threw his arms around Sam, knocking the kite from his hand. Life, love…every day was a gamble. The one thing he'd discovered was sometimes you had to take a chance you never imagined yourself capable of, to win the greatest prize.

Forever.

Zach didn't need to be Sam's everything. Loving Sam and being loved by him in return was the constant—the one thing he knew would always be there for him, like the sun, the moon, and the ocean tide.

"Let's go home." He kissed Sam and took his hand.

"I'm way ahead of you," said Sam, picking up the bottle of champagne. "But we aren't going home, we're going away for a few days."

"We are? Where?"

They walked to pick up his kite, accepting congratulations from the other kite flyers.

"It's a secret. But I'm betting you'll like it."

All during the drive out of the city, Zach peppered Sam with questions, but the stubborn man remained mute. It wasn't until Zach saw the sign for The Garden State Parkway that it all fell into place.

"We're going back? To Atlantic City?" There was no way he could keep the excitement from his voice.

Sam's smile was enough of an answer. What a day this had turned out to be; first his friends getting married and then Sam proposing—the best day of his life. Having sequestered himself for so many years, it was like stepping out from the darkness to a blinding light.

They rode in companionable silence for the trip, listening to the radio and exclaiming over the deer grazing on the side of the road, as only two people from the city could. The sun inched down, spreading out streaks of lavender and periwinkle blue. Twilight was always a magical time of the day, and Zach couldn't wait to get to the ocean.

Zach ran his hand down Sam's thigh. "This is wonderful. You thought of everything."

"Only if you said yes." For a moment, Sam took his hand off the wheel to cover Zach's. "If you said no, I had nothing."

"Not a chance." Zach turned his hand palm up to squeeze Sam's, then released it so Sam could make the turnoff. In the distance, the high rises and hotels came into view and within twenty minutes, they were pulling up in front of the Tropicana.

Leaving the car for the valet, Sam pulled out two suitcases; one his and one Zach's. At the sight of his suitcase, Zach raised a questioning brow.

"I packed for you early this morning while you were still sleeping and put it in the car, along with the kites."

Amazed at Sam's planning and touched at the sentimental streak he hid under the tough exterior, Zach shook his head and followed Sam to the front desk. It took no time for them to be checked into their oceanfront suite. The same elevator from those months earlier zoomed them up to their floor.

"This is wonderful."

Needing to see the lights of the casinos but even more so the ocean, Zach pulled aside the drapes. Down the boardwalk, the hotel lights flashed and glowed in the encroaching darkness.

"Let's change and go to the beach." Sam kissed the top of his head. "Like we did that first night."

"Wait till I tell everyone. They always make fun of me as the sappy, sentimental one." He exchanged his pants for a pair of cargo shorts and his shoes for flip-flops.

"I deny everything," said Sam with a grin as he changed. "Try and prove it."

Hand in hand, they exited their room and rode down in the elevator in silence with an older couple who kept shooting uncomfortable looks at their clasped hands. Once they stepped out on the boardwalk, the scent of the ocean teased him, and Zach forgot all about them, concentrating only on Sam and the magic of the night. He kicked off his shoes and raced down the steps to the sand, leaving a startled Sam behind him.

"Hey, wait for me." Sam pounded behind him, but Zach kept running toward the water. His feet had barely touched the surf before Sam caught hold of his shirttail and yanked him backward. Zach fell into Sam's arms and held on tight.

"What were you gonna do—run in and get knocked over by another wave?" Laughter tinged Sam's voice, but he didn't relinquish his tight grip on Zach.

Sam's eyes glinted in the moonlight, and Zach kissed his neck before he answered. "And if I did, I know you'll always be right there for me. To catch me if I fall, right?"

Sam's hold on him tightened. "You bet I will."

"And I'll be there for you as well. Forever."

Zach took his hand, and they walked along the shoreline, moonlight leading their way.

Want to know how Marcus finally meets his match and falls in love?
Find out in *Second to None*.

THE BREAKFAST CLUB

Beyond the Surface
Betting on Forever
Second to None
What Lie Between Us
Hot Date
A Holiday to Remember
Two Daddies for Christmas

About the Author

Felice Stevens has always been a romantic at heart. She believes that while life is tough, there is always a happy ending around the corner. Her characters have to work for it, because just like life in NYC, nothing comes easy and that includes love.

Felice is the 2020 Lambda Literary Award winning author in best Gay Romance. She lives in New York City and has way too much black in her wardrobe. If she's not writing, you'll probably find her watching Reality TV. You can find her procrastinating on FB in her reader group, Felice's Breakfast Club.

You can find me procrastinating on FB in my reader group:
FELICE'S BREAKFAST CLUB
https://www.facebook.com/groups/FelicesBreakfastClub/

You can find all my books—listed by series—at:
https://felicestevens.com/

To keep up to date on my latest releases and works in process:
SUBSCRIBE TO MY NEWSLETTER
http://bit.ly/2JkIIu7

BOOKBUB
https://www.bookbub.com/profile/felice-stevens

INSTAGRAM
https://www.instagram.com/felicestevens

FACEBOOK
https://www.facebook.com/felice.stevens.1

TWITTER
https://twitter.com/FeliceStevens1

Made in the USA
Las Vegas, NV
13 February 2022

43889467R00164